BEEFCAKE & Cupcakes

JUDI FENNELL

Yum! :)

- Judi

Published by Judi Fennell
Copyright 2012 Judi Fennell
Cover and interior design by www.formatting4U.com
Editing by Helen Hardt

Please contact the author at JudiFennell@JudiFennell.com.

For more information on the author and her works, please see www.JudiFennell.com

This book is also available in electronic formats at online retailers.

10 9 8 7 6 5 4 3 2 1

To my readers

Thank you for allowing me to continue to do this.

And to Pat Shaw. For as solitary as writing can be, there are always people around to help make it not so lonely. People with amazing talent and generosity. I am so lucky to call such a gifted writer and wonderful person my friend.

Bon appétit!

This wasn't her hotel room.

The suit jacket tossed on the chair was Lara's first clue.

The discarded matching pants on the floor in front of it was her second.

The dip in the mattress as someone got off the bed behind her was her third.

Oh my God. What had she done?

Well, it was pretty obvious what she'd done, but, oh God...

Lara clamped her eyes shut as that someone came around the foot of the bed, peeking only when she heard the bathroom door slide open.

Oh my. The guy's bare naked ass looked really good. Probably better out of those pants than in them—too bad she didn't remember what it'd looked like in them.

Too bad she didn't remember him.

The door clicked closed and Lara shot to her feet—to the second shock of the morning.

She was wearing only a t-shirt. And it wasn't hers.

She didn't want to think about whose it was or how she came to be in said t-shirt; she just wanted to grab her dress, shoes, and purse, and get the hell out before her one-and-only one-night stand finished doing whatever it was a one-night stand did the morning after.

She scooped the dress off the dresser—no, she wasn't going to think about how it'd gotten there—tore his shirt up over her head then the dress down over it, and bagged looking for her bra. She just wanted out.

Her shoes were next to the chair—one was under it—and her purse, thank God, was hanging on the hotel room door.

Twenty-five seconds. That's all it took her to escape from the most un-Lara-like thing she'd ever done in her life.

It took thirty-five more seconds for the damn elevator to make its way to the—she squinted at the floor marker above the "Down" arrow—the tenth floor.

Thank God there was no one in the elevator. She didn't need witnesses to her walk of shame.

God, wouldn't Jeff be shocked to see her now? "Sexually boring and uninspiring" was what he'd said to explain the affair—among others—but this walk of shame negated those.

She couldn't believe it. Thirty-years-old with her own up-and-coming bakery, yet one too many shots at her college roommate's bachelorette party had her picking up some random guy for a night of uninhibited monkey sex to soothe her smashed-to-smithereens ego from an ex who didn't deserve the time of day let alone this kind of prove-him-wrong strategy.

It *had* been uninhibited monkey sex, right?

She closed her eyes and tried to conjure up an image, but the last thing she could remember was jitterbugging on the dance floor.

She didn't know how to jitterbug. But, apparently, that hadn't stopped her.

Oh, God, her head. And her stomach. And that cotton mouth thing…

The bell dinged as the elevator arrived at the second floor. She fumbled for her room key and stumbled out into a blessedly empty hallway. Her room was down a few doors, and thankfully she'd decided to forego a roommate on this trip.

Well, a regular roommate.

Who was the guy? She didn't even remember what he looked like, let alone his name.

She groaned as she made it into her hotel room. How bad was it that the only recallable part of him was his bare naked ass and *that* she only remembered because she'd seen it on her way out the door?

She peeled the dress off her body—it'd been on backwards—and headed into the bathroom. Shower, breakfast, and a big glass of orange juice, then she could grab her car and get the hell out of Dodge so she wouldn't have to risk running into her biggest regret anytime soon.

But the question was: what was her regret for? That she'd picked him up in the first place, or that she couldn't remember a damn thing about what had come after?

Gage ran the towel through his hair, then wrapped it around his hips. Didn't want to shock Sleeping Beauty out there with nudity upon opening her gorgeous eyes.

He caught his smile in the mirror. Yeah, it was wolfish, but why shouldn't it be? He'd ended up with the most gorgeous woman at the party, and that included the bride-to-be.

Of course, he'd broken his own rules to do so—no partying with the patrons—but she'd walked in and knocked him sideways.

It'd be funny, really, if it weren't so, well, not. He never went for short, dark, and curvy. Model-thin bombshells were more his type. At least, they had been. But then she'd walked in, her curves making his palms sweat, her curls begging for his fingers to dive in and hold on, and those chocolate brown eyes... They'd screamed *bedroom* so loudly they'd almost drowned out the music, and he'd had a hard time keeping his mind on the show.

Thank God the guys knew their shit. Markus had known it a little too well; he'd been focused on Lara from the first bump-and-grind number.

Luckily, no one had questioned the quick change-up in routines he'd made so that Markus was off stage until the middle of the second act.

By then, the shots that'd been flowing around that table had insured Lara's interest had no longer been solely on Markus.

That's when he'd made his move.

Made his move. Gage groaned. What was he—twenty? He never had to make moves; women flocked to him.

But she'd been wedged in the corner of her booth, surrounded by friends, staring at the stage, and hadn't looked like she was going to get out anytime soon.

He grabbed his toothbrush. He should have moved sooner. Then maybe she wouldn't have done those last two shots. The woman was a lightweight. She'd made it to the hotel elevator and had literally passed out in his arms. It'd put a damper on his evening, but not his libido.

He just hoped she was more awake this morning.

He finished brushing his teeth and poured a glass of water. She was going to need it and it'd give him the excuse to sit beside her.

And hopefully do much more.

He opened the door softly. He wanted to be the one to wake her, not the noise or the light from the bathroom.

Except… she was gone.

He slumped against the doorframe. Served him right. He played to the fantasies of hundreds of women every weekend, but the one whose fantasy he'd personally wanted to grant apparently had no interest in letting him.

Chapter 1

"Get your hands off my cupcakes." Lara tipped the wooden spatula up toward the guy leering at her over her booth at the bridal expo. It might not be a big weapon, but a quick slap could sting, and Mr. Drunken Father of A Bride looked like he could use a slap or two.

Especially when he leered at her. "Baby, I'm not anywhere near your cupcakes, but if you lean a little closer, I'll be happy to oblige."

Lara snorted. That had to be one of the worst pickup lines she'd ever heard.

She flicked the spatula under the two cupcakes he'd squashed. The Romeo and Juliet models. Damn. Those were some of her most intricate designs and always impressed the clientele.

Drunk Dad didn't stop. "How about you and I getting together later on over drinks and discuss your… cupcakes?"

"How about we don't?"

Drunk Dad blinked. "Aw, now that's not nice." He walked to the end of the booth and picked up a spun sugar butterfly. "Like this one, for instance. I bet this tastes really good on my tongue."

She would never look at those butterflies the same way again.

She took it out of his hand.

But that put her close enough for him to grab hold of her. And he did, clamping a sweaty hand around her wrist.

"Come on, baby, it's a party weekend. All this love and sex in the air. Surely you feel it."

"What I feel is you crossing a line, mister." She set the cupcake down and tried to pry his fingers away.

Especially the pinky. If she could bend it back far enough—

He dragged her to him, slobbering a kiss on her lips and a meaty paw on her breast.

She reared back. “Get off me—”

He went flying backward.

“The lady said to leave her alone.”

A guy in tight jeans, a cowboy hat, and a shirt opened to his waist stood there, muscles jacked, his breathing ratcheted up, looking like a hero straight out of a romance novel.

Drunk Dad tried to scramble to his feet. “What the hell was that? I’ll sue your ass—”

“Stow it, dickwad, and pray the lady isn’t going to press charges for assault.”

That sobered the guy up.

But Lara was stuck on the six-pack right there on display beneath her rescuer’s open shirt.

“Up here, sweetheart.” Cowboy dude flicked his fingers by his waist at her.

She looked up.

Oh God, he’d caught her staring. And that full out grin he had going said he knew just what she’d been looking at, *and* that he liked her looking.

She could feel the blush flaming up her cheeks.

He smiled and tipped the brim of his hat, then turned around to help the drunken asshole off the floor.

God, the man had one fine backside. Just like Mr. Bare Naked Ass from the hotel two weeks ago.

She shook her head. She was insane. Mr. B.N.A.’s ass had been naked; this guy’s was covered. No similarity whatsoever. Well, other than the fact that they were both perfectly formed and she wouldn’t mind getting her hands on all four cheeks.

“You got a keeper around here or should I turn you

over to security?" Cowboy wrenched the drunk's arm.

"I'm good. I got a wife."

"Lucky lady." Cowboy waggled his eyebrows at Lara. "How about you go find her and never come back? If I see you here again, I won't go as easy on you as I did this time. Do I make myself clear?"

Drunk Guy ran a hand through his comb-over. "Crystal."

"Good. Now get out of here."

Lara tried to regain her composure as Cowboy sauntered up to her booth. And saunter he did, all hip rolling, boot scuffling sexiness.

"How you doin', Cupcake?"

Oh my. From him, that pick-up line worked. Definitely all in the delivery.

She just wished she were immune. Jeff had done a number on her trust when it came to any guy, but especially dreamy ones.

And this one, with golden blond hair and startling blue eyes, was definitely what dreams were made of.

But no. No more dreaming. No more guys. Focus on her career. That was what she had to count on now, not some guy's fickle libido. "I've heard that one before."

He looked her up and down and Lara felt the heat as if he'd used a blow torch.

"I bet you have. How about the one about finding out if you're good enough to lick?"

She was going to melt right in this spot. "Um, yeah. Heard that one, too." But never like *that*. He was the first guy she actually considered letting find out the answer.

For all of about two seconds. A guy like him would never be interested in her for anything more than a one-nighter—and the one she'd had had convinced her she wasn't cut out for any more.

"Well then, I'll have to think hard to come up with

something new."

She couldn't help it; her eyes flickered to his groin.

Then back to his face when he chuckled.

Okay, just let the convention center floor open up and swallow her now.

No, she was not going to think about anything to do with Cowboy and swallowing.

Then Cowboy stuck out his hand. "Hi. It's Gage. Gage Tomlinson?"

She surreptitiously wiped her sweaty palm—completely Cowboy's, er, Gage's fault, by the way—on her thigh. "Lara. Cavallo. Thank you for taking care of him."

"My pleasure, ma'am."

God, it was sexy when he affected that accent and tipped his hat. Lara was totally getting the cowboy fantasy.

"Would you like a cupcake? I mean—"She really wouldn't mind the floor opening up right now—"as a thank you."

His smile was devastating. So was that dimple in his cheek. "I absolutely would like a cupcake. Maybe two?"

They were talking about sugar and cake Cups & Cakes, right?

"Uh, sure. You can have two. Take your, uh, pick." Any day now… Big ol' crack in the floor. It'd do wonders for her embarrassment.

He took his time, staring at each one of her cupcakes. The ones on the table, that is. An inordinately long amount of time.

Long enough that he attracted the attention of more than a few women. Who all started making suggestions as to which cupcakes he ought to choose.

She'd never had better advertising, but the winks he kept shooting her way whenever someone asked him what kind of cupcakes he liked were way more thrilling.

Sexually boring and *uninspiring*, was she? Hunka

Hunka Cowboy didn't seem to think so.

Lara quickly handed out her take-away brochures and sample bites of the different cakes, gathering a bunch of business cards, while Cowboy worked his magic.

Wonder what other kind of magic he can work?

He caught her staring at him, but aside from a glimmer of a smile, all he did was tip his hat.

It was enough.

"Well, ma'am. I thank you for the offer, but seems to me you're going to need all the cupcakes you have. I'll just wait and see what's left when we're done here. Okay with you?"

She nodded, but if he kept looking at her like that, she wasn't going to have much of anything left: composure, sanity, strength in her legs...

"Okay, then. You let me know when you're free. I'm at booth 263."

She nodded as he turned and walked away.

Man, the guy filled out those jeans like nobody's business.

And she wouldn't mind making it hers.

Chapter 2

Contact made. Well, figuratively. Physically would come next.

He hoped.

Gage took the hat off and ran a hand through his hair. Damn thing was hot in this hall, but it worked on women every time.

"Gone a long time, boss." Murph handed him a stack of business cards.

Gage glanced at them. Amazing how many hand-written phone numbers showed up on the cards women dropped at BeefCake, Inc.'s booth. His email list was going to hit six figures by the end of the weekend.

Hopefully his bank account would follow soon after.

"Good job, guys. If you want to take a break, I'll cover." He shoved the cards into the fishbowl on the booth, then grabbed one of the folding chairs and straddled it, taking a load off. Once those women were finished with Lara's booth, they'd find their way to his. They always did, and while he'd told Lara his booth number because he hoped she would actually come find him, it'd also been good business. He needed all the business he could get.

"You want anything while we're gone?" Tanner undid the bow tie and tossed it onto the table. "Damn thing could choke a horse in this heat."

Gage refrained from the comment that would normally follow that statement. Tanner was their top tip-earner. The guy had more bills in his g-string than the next three highest-earning dancers made combined. Had something to do with a horse all right.

But, hey, it paid the guy's bills and gave Gage a couple extra hundred a month. Every little bit helped.

"Nah, I'm good."

"You don't want a… cupcake?"

Gage smiled and shook his head. He was never going to live that night down. The guys had seen him go ape shit over her, and well, at least they didn't have a clue where she'd spent the night. He wanted to keep it that way.

He also wanted a repeat.

But when they'd seen her booth, the comments had started.

"So? Did you talk to the cupcake lady?" Bry, his business partner, tossed his cop's hat onto the table. The two of them hadn't been in costume—or, rather, out of it—in months, but when it came to drumming up business at trade shows, they were on display just as much as the guys.

"Yeah, I did."

Bry pried the cap off a soda. "And?"

And… nothing. He'd expected… He didn't know what. Something. Some explanation about why she'd run out.

He shrugged, but, it still bothered him. He would've thought he'd get points for not taking advantage of her. "She was working. Not exactly the best time to check her out."

"That never stopped you before." Bry poured some soda down his throat. In the good ol' days it would have been doctored with Jack, but they were businessmen now. Jack was only on the menu after hours.

"Maybe I didn't have as much to lose before."

Bry spit the soda across the booth. "Lose? Her? What the fuck, man? What happened that night?"

Not a damn thing, unfortunately. Not even a kiss.

Gage grabbed one of the guys' beaters and mopped up the mess. They'd spent a fortune on the promo materials; no way was he letting it get ruined. "Not her. This. Our business. I don't have time to sweep some woman off her feet while I'm trying to earn enough to put this place behind me."

"Are you still on that? Seriously, Gage, you might want to rethink it. It does pay the bills."

Not all of them. The ones for his nephew's surgeries, therapy, and medications were looming before him right now in big, gaudy, painfully garish stage lights, the zeroes seeming to multiply exponentially every time he thought about them. Which was a lot.

"Bry, I got into this for the money." At first, it'd been a way to supplement his contracting income when the economy had tanked over a year ago. He and Bry had made some decent bucks stripping back in college. But then, with the surgeries Connor needed and the fact that Gage was the de facto head of the Tomlinson clan, the money had taken on a whole new meaning.

He and Bry had hired more guys and booked more gigs, him with the idea that this was a stop-gap measure. A means to an end. It wasn't as if he loved taking his clothes off for crowds of drunken women at his age—thirty-four wasn't over the hill, necessarily, especially because he kept himself in shape, but around the younger guys… Yeah, he didn't want to dance anymore. Especially after the mess with his last girlfriend, Leslie. Nothing killed a relationship faster than jealousy—even though she'd had no reason to be jealous.

But it made him cautious. He needed the money too badly to give it up and if a woman couldn't handle his job, well then, there was no sense having her in his life. Not until he got things with Connor under control.

But he'd been working the floor that night two weeks ago, keeping the women from throwing themselves onto the stage at the dancers—it happened more than he cared to think about, which was why he usually steered clear of women at the shows—when he'd seen Lara. All bets had been off. He hadn't understood it, but he'd had to talk to her. Dance with her.

So he had. Then one thing had led to another and—

"Did you get the info for Gina's spa's grand opening?" Bry asked.

Gage nodded. "I lined up Tanner and Carlo. It's just an hour gig. Two ought to be enough."

"An hour gig and half a thou. I love those short, sweet shows. Our bread and butter, baby."

Even with the discount they were giving Gina, Bry's cousin, the five hundred minus two bills for the dancers and another one for overhead left him and Bry a hundred each. Not bad for a few phone calls.

He looked at all the business cards in the fishbowl. There were a lot of phone calls to be made in there. If only twenty percent of them panned out, he could be a good part of the way toward his goal by the end of next month. And if the benefit for his nephew came through with what he was hoping it would, well, they'd all be able to breathe a little easier for Connor's next surgery.

Bryan refilled the basket of bow tie key chains with their website emblazoned across the strap. "So you ever going to tell me what's so special about this chick that you broke our iron-clad rule about staying away from paying customers?"

"She wasn't paying."

"Seriously? That's how you justified it?" Bry flung a keychain at him. Winged him right in the solar plexus. Damn plastic was sharp. "She was with the party that was paying. Same difference. I haven't seen you make a move on a chick like that since college. It was like she had a tractor beam on you."

Gage rubbed his abs, trying not to look at Bryan. Yeah, he'd had it bad for her. Still did. Only his bruised ego had prevented him from calling her in the two weeks since their night together. Well, that and the fact that he barely had time to take care of all he needed to take care of without tossing dating into the mix.

But that didn't mean he hadn't thought about it. She'd been pretty darn proud of her and her cousin's bakery, Cavallo's Cups & Cakes, that night.

She'd been so adorable when she'd confessed to supplying the "designer" penis cake for the bachelorette party. If he could've brought himself to eat part of a cake penis, he might have tried it, but there was just something utterly abhorrent about taking that first bite.

He wouldn't have minded taking a bite out of her, though. That's why he'd danced with her.

But, hell, he hadn't even gotten a kiss. He'd held on to some scruples and hadn't made out with her on the dance floor, and then she'd gone bottoms up on him in the elevator so that'd been out of the question.

"Yoo hoo, loverboy." Bry hit him in the cheek with a paper airplane. "Reliving your night of splendor?"

Gage wished, but it hadn't been so splendid. He'd been left hard and aching all night while she snored next to him.

He smiled then and didn't care if Bry thought it was because of a particularly "good" memory. She'd been adorable when she snored.

"So what'd she say when she saw you? Get all flustered and embarrassed or hot and bothered?"

Gage looked up. "Ya know? Neither."

"Whoa. Losing your touch. You used to have them creaming their pants before you even touched them back in the day."

Crude but true. God had given him the face and the gym had given him the body, and he'd enjoyed the fruits of both. Life had been a party back then. Stripping had only added to the pot of available women.

Bry pulled out more of the guys' body shot postcards to replenish the stacks on the booth. So many times their bookings were by special request; it'd been a marketing bonanza to hand out mini portfolios of the dancers. A couple of them were developing their own following, which could only help business.

"Maybe she's gay." Bryan waggled his eyebrows.

Gage choked. "She's not gay." Though, for all he knew, she might be.

The thought was a sobering one. Was she gay? Was that why she'd taken off so quickly the next morning? To save them both that awkwardness?

Was that why she hadn't reacted to him at her booth?

Gage had to admit, even if she were gay, her non-reaction stung. He knew what he looked like; hell, in his business he had to. His looks were a commodity. He couldn't remember the last time someone had been that unresponsive to them or his charm. And he'd tried very hard to be charming back there, all cowboy-polite and alpha male. The drunk guy had given him the perfect opportunity, but Lara had only been interested in trading barbs, not phone numbers.

"Or maybe she just has standards."

Gage flipped his hat at Bryan. "Asshole."

"That's Mr. Asshole to you." Bry stuck the hat on his head and tilted the brim back. "Maybe I'll have better luck with this than you did. Which booth did you say was hers?"

"Eleven twenty-four. Over there." Gage pointed to the far corner of the venue. Away from where Lara was. No way was he sending Bryan after her. The guy got just as many women as Gage did and Gage's ego wasn't up for the competition. Not until he figured out why she hadn't been interested in him.

"Uh huh. That's what I thought." Bry headed in the opposite direction. Right on a collision course with the cupcake lady.

Shit.

And with the guys gone, Gage was stuck manning the booth.

Chapter 3

"Jesse, can you cover for me? I need a break."

The grapefruit juice she'd had for breakfast was demanding attention, but Lara hadn't wanted to do so until she'd talked to every one of those women who'd followed the cowboy over. She ought to hire him to come to every trade show with her. It'd be worth the cost.

Especially if she saved a few pennies by letting him bunk with her...

"Sure, Miss Cavallo."

Lara winced. Nothing like having a teenager make her feel like her grandmother.

"You gonna go check out the hottie?"

Lara choked back… what? A snort? Embarrassment? Big ol' red-hot bunch of yearnin'?

Yeah, that last one.

"No. Mother Nature is demanding a visit."

"Oh."

Funny how the intern could jabber on about hotties, but mention a bathroom break and the kid got as red as, well, that big ol' red-hot bunch of yearnin'.

Still, she did box up two cupcakes; she'd promised him after all. And booth 263 was close to the bathroom…

Oh, who was she kidding? She *wanted* to see him, and the cupcakes were just an excuse.

She almost laughed at herself. Almost. Apparently, the hot monkey sex from two weeks ago had taken the edge off some of her inhibitions.

She could only imagine what others it'd released that night—and she *could* only imagine because she still didn't remember a single thing once she'd left the dance floor with Mr. B.N.A.

Never again. She was never doing shots of Zambuca again. That stuff was lethal.

So what explained this idiocy she was now exhibiting by going to check out the hot guy? Hadn't she sworn off guys?

She had. Really. She'd had enough of guys with her ex-husband. Still, she did owe him for helping her out…

Once she finished up in the bathroom, she took a ridiculous amount of time checking her face in the mirror. Her makeup had melted off in the heat—and she was going with the heat in the convention center, not the heat generated by Mr. Cowboy Gage—and her hair was starting to frizz out of the up-do she normally wore. Normally, she didn't care. Her clientele were brides and their families, and if the occasional groom came along, he only had eyes for his fiancée. No one ever checked her out.

Mr. Cowboy Gage had. God, even his name was sexy.

She ran her fingers under the faucet and tried to stem the frizz with a liberal application of water. Which made her hair look greasy. Sigh.

She grabbed a paper towel and tried to soak up the excess, but that only made it frizz again.

Lara gave up. He wasn't *really* interested in her; he'd been playing a character. Had had most of the women swooning every time he'd opened his mouth with that sexy-as-all-get-out drawl.

But still, she had a debt to pay, so she picked up the box of cupcakes off the ledge by the mirror and set out for his booth.

Booth two fourteen, two twenty-two, two thirty-six… After that, she didn't have to keep looking at numbers because there, at the end, in a booth covered in black velvet with smoking hot pictures of guys and their abs plastered across the back beneath the BeefCake, Inc. banner, was Mr. Cowboy Gage.

With a harem of women hanging on his every word.

The only reason they weren't hanging on him was because the booth separated them. Smart guy, otherwise there'd probably be a stampede. It was a good thing there weren't a lot of grooms in attendance because, with the way the women were fawning all over him, there could end up being a lot of broken engagements.

She ought to go back. Seriously, he didn't need her thanks; most of those women were the ones he'd lured to her booth. He'd known exactly what he was doing when he'd tossed out his booth number.

She turned around to leave.

"Hey, Cupcake!"

She looked up. Gage the cowboy was staring right at her, waving her over. Her face went to flambé almost as fast as her heart rate went into triple time.

But it didn't stop her from heading his way.

"Make way, ladies. Make way," he said as she approached his throng of admirers who parted like the Red Sea at his command.

"Here." She thrust out the box. She was way out of her league with him. Probably had been even before Jeff had raked her self-confidence over the coals. "These are for you. Those cupcakes I promised you. Rocky road and peanut butter swirl."

He grinned, and while his eyes didn't flicker downwards, she just knew that's what he was thinking.

Or maybe that was *wish*ful thinking on her part.

"Thanks. And welcome to BeefCake, Inc."

It certainly was. With a prime specimen now wrapping an arm around her waist and tugging her into the booth.

Lara seriously thought about swooning. Which probably meant she wasn't going to, given that most people *didn't* think before they swooned—or they wouldn't do it—

but right now, her thought processes were quickly disappearing as his fingers did riotous things to her skin and the scent of him—male and sexy, and a little perspiration which could only work on a hot guy—turned her insides upside down and had her thighs quivering.

Oh, God, who knew it was actually possible to have quivering thighs?

"So what do you think?" he asked with that slow drawl he could command at will.

Well, if she had to think, she'd think he was absolutely hands-down the hottest guy she'd ever been hugged by. And that she never wanted to leave his arms. And that she definitely would never forget *him* if she ever was lucky enough to spend the night with him.

"Um, impressive."

And, man, that grin. And those dimples in his cheeks. The guy was pure fantasy come to life.

"I'll take that as a compliment."

As well he should.

"After all, my ego could use a little stroking."

She'd sign up to be first on that list. Oh wait. Ego.

"Especially after you ran out on me."

It took her a few seconds to make sense of his words. And even then, they didn't make sense. "Um, what?"

"Well, yeah. I mean, I'm not exactly used to women running off before a 'good morning.' Etiquette, you know?"

Uh, no. She didn't. "Etiquette?"

He leaned in and her skin shivered when he whispered in her ear. "You know, when I took you back to my room after that party two weeks ago?"

Oh. My. God.

Holy shit.

Un-freaking-believable.

Cowboy Gage was Mr. Bare Naked Ass?

Chapter 4

Interesting that Ms. Lara Cavallo didn't have a snappy comeback. Which meant either he'd pissed her off, she didn't care, or she hadn't expected him to call her on her gross miscarriage of etiquette.

"How much for a lap dance?" One of the women stuck a twenty in the business card fishbowl.

Lara stiffened beside him.

Gage was going to go with pissed off.

He tightened his grip. She wasn't going anywhere until he got some answers.

"I'll give you twice your price." Another woman stuffed a few more bills in the fishbowl.

Then the dollar bills came out.

Gage had to put a stop to it. Fastest way to get thrown out of the expo was to incite a riot. The event organizers had specifically spelled out in his contract there was to be no solicitation. *No solicitation.* As if a group of male dancers—who weren't dancing—were a bunch of gigolos. He'd bet every phone number in that fishbowl that Lara hadn't had to sign a waiver for selling sex by cupcake.

He glanced at her t-shirt. *Her* cupcakes definitely made him think of sex.

He snorted. God, was he really so hung up on himself that he couldn't deal with a woman running out on him? Did he have to prove to himself that he could affect her?

Apparently he did.

He set the box down, then grabbed the fishbowl off the booth with his free hand and locked it between his knees. He wasn't letting go of Lara.

He fished the money out and handed it back to the depositors. "Sorry, ladies, but we're here for advertising only. Not entertainment." And he really didn't need this shoved down Lara's throat the first time he was with her—well, her first *sober* time they were together. Leslie had only been able to put up with the attention he'd gotten for five months.

One woman dragged her twenty across her lips. "Oh, I don't know. Just looking at you is pretty damn entertaining."

If Lara got any stiffer beside him, he'd think she were dead. Her wide, gorgeous dark eyes weren't helping that impression either.

Thankfully, Murph and Tanner showed up just then, catching sight of the throng, and came in through the back of the booth.

"Jeez, boss, we leave you alone for a few minutes and you drag 'em in like the Pied Piper." Tanner picked up his bow tie and clamped it around his neck.

"Guys, can you handle this, please? I need to have a few words with Lara."

"Sure thing. Knock your socks off."

Socks weren't the article of clothing he wanted to knock off.

"Lara?" He held out his free hand toward the opening at the back of the booth. No way was he letting go of her. "Shall we?"

She looked at him with narrow eyes. "Shall we what?"

Ah, the possibilities that question unleashed. He couldn't help smiling. "Well, first I thought we'd start off by discussing that night. Then, hell, I'm open to whatever you want."

She didn't say anything. But she did start walking toward the opening.

He snagged two of the folding chairs from the back of the booth—had to let go of her for that, but thankfully she didn't take off.

"Let's head over there." He nodded toward the back corner of the hall where shipping containers were cordoned off, ready for the event break down. He wanted privacy for this conversation, and given the blush blazing on her cheeks, figured she would, too.

He held back the drape for her then set up the chairs. "Have a seat."

She sat. But she still didn't say anything.

He wasn't getting a good feeling about this. "You okay?"

"Huh?" She shook her head. "I'm not sure."

"Is the show going well for you? I thought you'd get some interest from those women."

"Not the kind you're getting."

Ah, the wit was back. He smiled. "Yeah, well, beefcake does tend to trump cupcakes when it comes to women."

"I guess so."

And there went the wit.

Her blush, however, only deepened. Man, was she a knockout. Dark lashes framed eyes so black he could get lost in their depths, and her black curls were tossed onto her head as if she'd just woken up after a night of passionate lovemaking.

What he wouldn't give to experience that first hand. She'd been gone before he'd seen her that morning. "So why'd you leave?"

Shit. He hadn't meant to just blurt that out, but, yeah, his ego had issues with it.

When she licked her bottom lip, his libido got in on the issues thing.

"I…um." She shrugged. "I wasn't sure what the protocol was. That was the first time I've ever done something like that."

He didn't know how it was possible for her cheeks to get any redder.

"First time? For what? Passing out in a guy's bed?"

"Must you make it sound so crude?"

"Crude? I'm just stating the facts. You passed out. Actually, you passed out in the elevator. It was all I could do to get you into bed."

"So why did you?"

"You wanted me to leave you on the floor?"

"Why didn't you just take me back to my room? That would have been the gentlemanly thing to do."

"Cupcake, I was not having gentlemanly thoughts about you at all that night. And you weren't wanting me to. Not with the way you were dancing up against me. Then you practically threw yourself into my arms the minute we left the club. Plus, I didn't know what room was yours and you were in no shape to tell me."

Lara bit her bottom lip and looked away, blinking as if she had something in her eye.

Or was about to cry.

Shit. "You've never picked a guy up before, have you?"

She shook her head.

No wonder she'd run out and was all sorts of uncomfortable.

"You do know nothing happened between us, right?"

"Really?"

The hope in her voice and the relief in her eyes would have knocked his feet out from under him if he hadn't been sitting down. It stung, dammit. Most of the women who came on to him would be totally bummed if nothing happened between them.

"Of course not. I draw the line at taking advantage of comatose victims."

She blushed again. "I'm not used to drinking that

much."

"So I gathered." He buttoned up his shirt, feeling a little too exposed around her. Innocence and sexy were a potent combination, but given her lack of, uh, enthusiasm, he didn't want to be tempted. Or tempt*ing*, because he wasn't sure he'd survive getting shut down anymore than he already had. "You're going to want to be careful in the future. Not everyone will be as conscientious as I was."

"Thank you for that."

"I'd say it was my pleasure, but, really, it wasn't."

She blushed again.

He could get used to that. Especially if all that hot pink deliciousness spread downwards, too.

Not helping the no-tempting thing...

"So I'm guessing you ran out because you were embarrassed?

She tucked the wayward curl that escaped her bun behind her ear. "Like I said, I've never done that before. I wasn't sure exactly what the protocol was and figured leaving was the better part of valor."

"Coward."

"I beg your pardon?"

"Oh, Cupcake, pardon is not what you want to be begging for."

Her mouth fell open. "I don't know which I'm more offended by. That stupid nickname or your arrogance."

"I'll take either because at least it got you to have a real conversation with me instead of the Miss Manners discussion."

"I'm not sure I want to talk to you."

"Hey, I'm more than willing to find better uses for our mouths."

She stood up. "You really do think you're God's gift to women, don't you?"

He reached for her fingers, entwining them with his.

"Aw, come on. Can't you take a little teasing? Some flirting?"

She tried to yank her fingers back but he wasn't about to let her go.

"Is that what that was? Pardon me if I thought you were auditioning for Biggest Asshole of the Year."

"Nah, Bry's got that sewn up."

"Bry?" She yanked her fingers.

He still didn't let go. "My partner. Bryan Lassiter."

"You're gay?"

"Funny, he said the same thing about you. No, my business partner. BeefCake, Inc., remember?"

"Unfortunately, I'll probably never forget it." She sank back onto the chair. "So you're one of the strippers?"

"No. I own the company. I don't strip."

The once-over she gave him might have had disbelief behind it, but Gage felt her gaze as if she'd stroked him.

"Not anymore, I mean."

"So you used to do... that?"

"Strip? Yeah. I'll give you a private show if you don't believe me." It was just too easy to tease her.

And there went her blush again. "That's okay, I'll pass."

"Sure? Any one of those women back there would die to change places with you."

"Then by all means, go save a life by making one of their fantasies come true. Don't let me stop you." She stood again, picked up the chair, and folded it. "I should get back to my booth. Thanks for being a gentleman that night. I'm sorry if it, uh, inconvenienced you."

Only if she counted blue balls an inconvenience. Him, he considered them a damn shame.

She handed him the chair. "And thanks for your help today. I got a lot of leads. I hope it worked out well for you, too."

He took the chair and leaned it against his. "I'll walk you back."

"That's not necessary—"

"I thought you were all about gentlemanly things? A gentleman walks his lady back to her place."

"But I'm not your lady."

The thing was, no matter how bad of an idea it was to his life plan, he wanted her to be.

Chapter 5

It was all Lara could do to keep her composure as he walked her back to the booth. Granted his buttoned-up shirt helped, but all she could think about was that she'd seen him naked. Okay, just his ass, but it'd been one fine one.

"So how did you come up with cupcakes?"

She glanced at him. Longish dark blond hair brushed his collar and his aquamarine blue eyes sparkled as he looked at her. He was really too pretty for his or anyone's good.

"I've always liked baking. I took some culinary courses and my cousin and I opened Cavallo's Cups & Cakes." She left out The Jeff Years. Not appropriate for most conversations, but especially not with a smoking hot guy who seemed to have some interest in her for God-knew-what reason. "Cupcakes are the newest craze with the bakery crowd. I'm finding most of our business has become cupcakes. Even brides are choosing them instead of the big tiered wedding cake. We can customize them much more easily and at a better price than traditional cakes. And they're fun. People are shying away from the formal social event weddings have been in the past and are opting for a more party atmosphere. Cupcakes lend themselves to that party atmosphere. But we still do cakes. That's never going to stop completely."

"Like bachelorette cakes."

"You saw that, huh?" She'd so hoped to escape this conversation without mention of that cake. She'd been mortified the whole time she'd been baking it. Cara had laughed her ass off when Lara had worked to make the scrotum realistic.

"Who was your model for that?"

"Wouldn't you like to know?" Oh, crap. What was her problem? She didn't want to engage him. Bad enough she'd already come on to him only to fail to follow through—there was a not-so-nice term for women who did that—she should not be flirting with him. That embarrassing night was best left forgotten.

"Hey, I'll volunteer if you need another one," said Way-Too-Mr.-Sexy with a grin that defined *hubba hubba*. "Nothing you haven't already seen."

Actually, it was. She'd only gotten the backside glimpse. But, again, she just wanted to put that whole night behind her. "I think we've got that cake covered, but thanks for the offer."

"Anytime, Cupcake."

"You know, that's a really sexist term."

"I think it's a sweet one. Full of sugar and mouth-watering deliciousness."

Well, when he said it like that…

Crud. Now her knees were starting to melt.

Thankfully, she was within a few feet of her booth. "Well, thanks for the escort. I wish you all the best with your business venture."

He studied her, his blue eyes narrowing as he scratched the opening of his shirt.

And, yes, her eyes were drawn there, regardless of how ill-advised it was. But it wasn't her fault the man's company was aptly named.

"If you need anything, you know how to find me."

"I'll do that."

Not.

Because, yeah, she needed. Wanted too. But she wasn't going anywhere near Mr. Cowboy Sexy Gage. She ought to be immune. Jeff, after all, had been charming and gorgeous, and knew how to sweet-talk a woman. *Any* woman. That'd been the problem.

Which was why she was staying far away from guys. Especially really hot, charming ones.

He touched two fingers to his forehead in a quick salute, spun on the heel of his cowboy boot, and sauntered away with his hip-rolling cowboy style.

Yeah. Stay far, far away.

"Who is *that*?" Jesse asked, the breathlessness in her voice something Lara could totally relate to.

"He owns BeefCake, Inc."

"He *is* beefcake, inc."

So true. Lara forced herself to turn away. Nothing good could come from mooning after a guy like that. A guy women flocked to, drooled over, and if listening to those women back at the booth was any indication, tossed aside the men in their life for, all for the hope of a roll in the proverbial hay.

One she'd missed out on. "So how was the booth while I was gone? Any takers?"

Jesse handed her a stack of orders. "Here are some leads. The one on top seems really promising. She's going with a Disney theme and your Cinderella castle was right up her alley."

"It's the Neuschwanstein Castle. I can't market it that way or I'll owe them my profits."

"Oh, sorry. It looks like Cinderella's castle to me."

That was because her castle was modeled after Mad King Ludwig's Bavarian one, as Lara had already explained, but Jesse had obviously forgotten. Lara couldn't be upset about it; that's what happened with hiring temporary help for trade shows. She and Cara weren't at the hiring-permanent-staff stage yet; they could just afford the overhead for their shop and the payments on the equipment. But if they kept getting referrals like this, maybe they'd be able to in another few months.

"How were the taste tests and sales?" Taste tests were

for giving potential clients a sample of her work and encouraging them to purchase cupcakes on site. She counted on those sales to subsidize her attendance at the expo. It'd worked out well for the other shows they'd done, and with Gage's harem, it should work out even better for this one.

"Sales were great. Those women must have talked to everybody because you're almost out."

Lara breathed a sigh of relief. And of dread. She hated being beholden to anyone, but after what Gage had done for her, she owed him.

Gage brought up his Favorites contact list and pressed Call. "Hey, Gina," he said when she answered. "I need a favor."

"No, Gage, I won't bear your child."

He chuckled. "Damn, woman, you crush me."

"Yeah, well someone has to save my gender from your brand of sexy."

He loved Gina. A hard-ass who'd been around the block too many times to put up with any bullshit. Not that he would feed her any. They'd been friends for forever without a hint of anything else—a good thing or Bry, his friend and her cousin, would have kicked his ass. But it was nice to have that kind of relationship with a woman. Someone he could get the honest truth from and not have to wonder about an agenda behind it.

"Actually, I was hoping you could help out another one of your fair sex."

"How? By setting her up with your dreamy self?"

He could hear her clacking her fingernails against her teeth. She only did that when she was impatient or horny. And since it wasn't the latter where he was concerned, he figured he'd better get to the point. "No. I want you to order some cupcakes from her for your grand opening next weekend."

"I've already got dessert covered, Gage."

"I'd consider it a personal favor."

The clacking stopped. "How hot is she?"

"Huh?"

"You heard me. How hot is she and why doesn't she see your own level of hotness?"

"Gina, you have the wrong idea."

"Uh huh. You forget, I know you, Gage Tomlinson. Other than when it comes to your sister, the only time you ever do something nice for a woman is when you want in her pants."

Ouch. Why was that the impression she had of him? It certainly wasn't true. Sure, he was as horny as the next guy, but he did treat the women in his life with respect. Whether or not they let him in their pants. Lara, included. "Hey, I'm not that bad."

"No, actually, I've heard you're pretty good. 'Spectacular' was the word she used I believe."

"She?" Had Gina talked to Lara?

"Oh no, you're not getting names out of me. Let's just say some of your cast-offs have chosen to share."

"You're comparing notes?" Women. He was seriously going to have to re-examine his M.O. when it came to them if his prowess was a topic of discussion. It always amazed him how much he really didn't know, would never know, about the fairer sex.

"You forget, Gage, I don't have anything *to* compare."

From any other woman he'd think that was a complaint. But not Gina. She preferred her guys bald-headed and ball-less so she could run the show.

"But, hey, thanks for keeping her satisfied. I just wish your women wouldn't feel the need to share."

Yeah, him, too, after this awkward phone call. "Look,

Gina, Lara just opened her own bakery and could really use the business. She helped me out with referrals at this expo and I'd like to return the favor."

"I already ordered food, Gage. And even though you're giving me a great discount on the entertainment, this opening is over budget. There's nothing left to help you play Knight In Shining Armor."

"Geez, woman, your tongue is sharp. *I'm* paying for the cupcakes; I just want you to order them. All you have to do is make sure Lara gets the order and sets them up on site. Oh, and don't mention me."

"Well, duh. If you're going to these lengths to get the job done, you obviously don't want the woman to know she's indebted to you. Are you going to tell her the price when she finds out? Because you know she will; we always do."

That was from Gina's own personal experience. He and Bry had had to do major damage control the one and only time she'd let her heart get involved.

The guy had definitely regretted breaking it. Especially when they'd broken his nose.

"There is no price, okay? I'm just helping out someone who helped me. Will you do it?"

"Of course I will. But you're going to owe me."

"Anything, Geen."

"Ah, Gage, don't tempt me. There's that comparison thing, you know."

He loved Gina and her sarcasm. He could always count on her to keep it real. "No problem, sweetheart. It's not as if I could tempt you anyway."

Gina hung up the phone and sighed. Big and loud and utterly defeated.

Gage really had no clue. She'd been tempted for years. But she wasn't the Plastic Barbie type he went for.

And since he didn't feel anything toward her like what she felt toward him, it was better to be his friend than a broken-hearted ex-lover pining after him for the rest of her life.

But, yeah, she wanted to check out this baker chick.

Chapter 6

Lara didn't see Gage the rest of the expo. She heard about him, though, from every woman who stopped at her booth. Seemed that BeefCake, Inc. was the hit of the show. She couldn't blame the women; if she didn't have to be at the booth, she'd be checking the guys out, too.

Great, she was reduced to ogling.

When had her life gone down the tubes? When had beefcake become her only shot at something remotely resembling romance and sex?

And even that she'd screwed up.

God, she'd passed out on him. In the elevator. Hadn't even been able to make it to his bed.

Jeff would have a coronary if he ever learned about that little incident. His ex almost hooking up with stripper. Or would he prefer the term *exotic dancer*? Either way, it would horrify him. He'd called her Vanilla. Said she'd had no adventurous spirit in the bedroom. Wouldn't he be surprised?

Lara got a giggle out of that. If it weren't so God-awful embarrassing, she just might spread the word around herself.

But thank God none of the girls at the party had figured it out. Not only didn't she want Jeff to get wind of it, she didn't relish the idea of anyone else sharing her shame. It was bad enough that Gage knew.

And, oh God, whoever he'd told. Guys did that, didn't they? Talked about their conquests?

Did anyone even use that term anymore?

Lara quickly broke down the last cardboard box and rearranged the last dozen and a half cupcakes on a disposable tray on the booth. *Think about the cupcakes.*

Think about the show. Not *about what Gage was selling or that show he'd put on.*

Her cell phone rang, saving her from another round of self-inflicted torture.

"Hey, Cara, what's up?"

"Just wanted to let you know that Mrs. Applebaum gave us a fifteen percent tip."

"Hey, great!" Mrs. Applebaum was known to be stingy with tips so the standard fifteen from her was like twenty-five from someone else.

"No, it's not great. The woman *should* tip us that much. I say we raise her price on the next event."

"We can't do that; she'll never come back."

"Oh yes she will. She has the graduation party for Her-Son-The-Doctor coming up and she wants—get this—a re-creation of his college. We can charge her out the wazoo for that and she'll gladly pay it."

"I don't know, Car, it just seems—"

"Do you want that second industrial-sized mixer with all the attachments or not?"

Cara had her there. That one piece of equipment would make all their lives easier.

"Okay, but we can only raise the price five percent."

"Fifteen."

"That's too much."

"And that's why you need to leave the pricing to me. I already quoted her and she agreed."

"Are you serious?"

"I don't joke about business, Lara. That's why you run the creative and I handle the administrative. I want those loans paid off in half the note time. I thought you did, too."

She did. Because then she could stop taking Jeff's alimony.

That was another area where she and Cara disagreed,

but it wasn't any of Cara's business. It also wasn't any of Cavallo's Cups & Cakes's business. Jeff had called her dead weight when they'd signed the divorce papers, a mantra he repeated with every stupid sticky note he attached to each alimony check.

It didn't matter to her that the law said she was entitled to that money. Or, really, that she actually was. She wanted to be done with Jeff even more than he wanted to be done with her. Case in point: she'd dropped his last name the day he'd moved out. And now, under her own name, she was going to prove to him—and herself—that she wasn't dead weight. That she could not only take care of herself, but flourish doing so.

The divorce had ripped her self-esteem to shreds. She'd so willingly quit her job as a restaurant reviewer for the local paper after their wedding, when he'd wanted her to be home, tending to him and the house. "It doesn't look good for a lawyer's wife to have such an inconsequential position," he'd said.

Inconsequential? She'd loved her job. She'd made a difference. Several restaurants had taken off after her reviews.

But in Jeff's Grand Scheme for their future, she was to be the perfect hostess who stayed at home and raised the kids because his career would be the one that set them up for life.

And since she *had* wanted to be home with those future children, and he'd been right about the discrepancies in their income, she'd quit her job, joined the country-club set, studied flower arranging, and learned how to host the best cocktail parties to give him the image he'd wanted.

And then the bastard had dumped her the minute he'd made partner.

So, yes, she'd take his money, but only until the business was paying her a good salary. And if she could convert half the customers who'd signed her email list today, she'd be on her way.

"Lar? You there?"

"Yes."

"So you're on board with this project?"

Lara stacked the display trays and set them in the storage box under the booth. "Of course. I'll do the research tonight when I get back. Pictures and what-not of the school."

"Good. I'll get the contract out to her. Gotta strike while the oven's hot."

"Bad analogy, Car."

"Like I said, you're the creative one. So how'd the show go?"

As she broke down the booth, packing up her decorating supplies, table drapes, and the signage, she told Cara about the mad rush to the booth, but neglected to mention Gage. No need to bring up a sore topic that Cara was not on the need-to-know basis for.

"Great," said Cara. "I'll get started on the calls as soon as you get back. You're going to want to start rebuilding our inventory. Don't forget, we're one of the sponsors for the benefit this weekend."

That was Cara, all business. Lara never thought of her cakes as product. Each one was a customized personal experience for the buyer and Lara was always very aware of that. Pride in her work was her motto; it's what made her cakes stand out and what brought clients back. Like Mrs. Applebaum or the people who'd sampled her work today.

Would they also bring Gage back?

Oh, God. She didn't need to go there. She didn't want him back.

Liar.

No, she wasn't lying. Sure, the attention he'd paid her had been nice, but it wasn't real, and anyway, she'd been completely overwhelmed by her mortification at how they'd met. While hot monkey sex with him might sound good, she just wasn't that person. She wasn't exactly vanilla, but definitely not melted-hot-chocolate-stripper-guy material. Maybe somewhere in between, like red-velvet blush.

"It sounds like it was a successful show. And selling all of the cupcakes gives us a twenty-three percent profit which is up twelve percent from our average." Cara was clicking numbers on the adding machine as fast as she was talking. "What do you think made the difference this time?"

Gage. But there was no way they'd ever be able to afford him—not professionally and definitely not personally.

"I think it was the turnout, Car. There was a lot of buzz about this show and the numbers were there. Aren't you always saying it's a numbers game?"

"Yes. If you get enough opportunities, you'll hit a certain percentage. Shame we can't pinpoint it more. I hate to have to rely on the venue's efforts. We need to brainstorm ways of getting more people interested in our business."

"Okay, Car, but I have to go. It's time to break down." Lara knew what had made the difference, but she wasn't going to share. No need to add exotic dancer to Cara's expense line items.

Chapter 7

Gage opened the screen door to his sister's apartment. "Hey, sis, how's he doing?"

Missy gave him her typical wan smile. "Same."

Which meant Connor was chomping at the bit to get up and run around, but the casts and paralysis prevented him from doing so.

God, he ached for the kid. Would gladly take it on so his nephew wouldn't have to. So his sister wouldn't have to. Bad enough Connor had been hit by a hit-and-run driver and Missy's pitiful medical insurance only went so far. The bills were coming in far faster and much bigger than they'd expected, and it looked like Connor was going to need on-going care. The burden was staggering, and they'd never see a dime from her asshole ex either. The guy had run out before Connor had been born.

"You wanted a kid, not me," had been the cold-hearted reply to her plea for help after the accident.

If the dickhead weren't perpetually unemployed and hanging with a knock-off version of Hell's Angels, Gage would have tracked him down and extracted the payment in physically acceptable terms.

But Missy and Connor didn't need any more drama in their lives. Their daily status quo was more than enough for everyone to handle. Beefcake, Inc. was the best bet for getting them all out of this mess.

"You'll be glad to know we got a ton of referrals over the weekend. I've lined up two gigs already for next weekend on top of the benefit."

Missy smiled again, but it was just as thin. "I am so grateful to you, Gage—"

"Missy, stop." He didn't want her gratitude. Connor

was like his own kid, a fact that'd been rammed down his throat when he'd stood at his hospital bedside pleading with God not to let him die. "I told you to ease your worry, not cause you more grief. Let's enjoy our day, okay?"

This time her smile stretched a little wider. "He's been asking about you."

"When doesn't he?"

"Oh, God. He's got your ego."

"Nothing wrong with that."

She swatted his arm as he headed into Connor's room, and Gage almost collapsed with relief. Ever since the accident three months ago, Missy hadn't been herself. Well, her old self. And with what they'd been through, he couldn't blame her, but slugging him? That was a sign of the younger sister he'd been so irritated with when he'd been a teenager.

What he wouldn't give to have those carefree days back again.

But it was what it was; he was just thankful he had options. That Missy and Connor had options.

He headed into Connor's tiny toy-stuffed bedroom, bypassing the wheelchair all three of them hated. "Hey, buddy, still lounging around, I see."

"Hi, Uncle Gage," said the six-year-old. "You know Mom. One move to the edge of the bed and she's all over me like white on rice."

"White on rice? Where'd you hear that?" The kid was growing up way too fast. It seemed like it was just yesterday that Missy had brought him home from the hospital, alone, scared, without a cent or a diploma to her name. She'd gotten her GED and had started night classes to become a paralegal since then, but Connor's medical care now put that on hold.

"Nicky Pollecco told me. His dad says it all the time."

Nicky's dad said a lot of things all the time, most of

which got him into bar fights.

Gage ground his teeth. That was it; he was putting his foot down. Missy was getting out of this apartment and into the Tomlinson family home with him. He hadn't wanted to take this away from her, some semblance of control in her life, but he'd tell her it was the money, that they could use her rent to pay off Connor's medical bills that much sooner and get her back to school. It wasn't a lie, and sometimes you just had to do what you had to do.

"So what game are we playing today?"

Connor looked at Missy who was hovering in the doorway. "We're good, Mom."

And once more Gage took a shot to the heart. His nephew assuring his mom. The kid ought to be outside climbing trees and riding bikes and beating the crap out of Nicky Pollecco, not consoling his mother by pretending everything was all right.

He started counting the fees he'd earn from the weekend's gigs besides the benefit Gina had put together. That would be a one-off and he couldn't predict what would come from it. No, he needed to keep the money coming in, and to do that, he'd need at least another three gigs a weekend. Two a night. It'd be great to have a standard venue for a Ladies' Night at some of the nearby clubs, but so far, the local clubs weren't biting. An occasional show brought interest, they said, but having a weekly show might dilute the appeal. Not to mention the local Chamber of Commerce was giving him and any locale that had even a smidgen of interest a lot of pushback on decency charges. It was enough to drive him nuts.

"I want to play COD," Connor said when Missy shut the door.

"Call of Duty? I don't think so, kiddo. You're a little young for that."

"But Nicky plays it."

Such the good endorsement. "I don't care. Nicky's not my nephew; you are. You don't need to grow up that fast."

"But what if I don't get to?" He moved his paralyzed arm with his good one, a sight that never failed to move Gage to tears. Tears he choked back. "I want to play COD before anything else happens."

Shit.

Shit. Shit.

Gage's throat shut down. Connor had been obsessed with the fact that he could have been killed. Gage and Missy had, too, but it seemed to define Connor these days. What if he hadn't survived? What if something like this happened again only worse? What if he didn't pull through all the surgeries he needed to repair the damage?

Gage cleared his throat. The psychologist they'd been seeing had said to treat Connor as normally as possible, so while his initial instinct was to give the kid what he wanted, it wouldn't be in his best interests. Plus, Connor really didn't need to see the crap in that video game.

"Hey, Con, you can't think like that. You'll have the rest of your operations and be fine. You don't need those COD images in your brain when you're recuperating."

Connor sighed. "You're going to be a real pain as a dad someday, Uncle Gage."

Wow, the shots to the heart just kept coming. A dad. He couldn't even think about that happening anytime soon. Connor came first, then he'd worry about setting up shop with someone and starting a family.

Lara's face shimmered into view. All hot pink with embarrassment.

He kind of liked the idea that she didn't sleep around. Totally hypocritical, he knew, but, yeah, he liked it. He wondered if she wanted kids.

Whoa. Getting way ahead of himself. And her. She could barely look at him, never mind the fact that she'd practically run out on him at the expo. He'd gone by after they'd broken down BeefCake, Inc.'s booth, but she'd cleared out already.

Couldn't make it any clearer she hadn't wanted to see him. That was why he'd declined the cupcake offer when she'd first suggested it; he'd wanted an excuse to see her again, but she'd negated it by coming to him first.

"You have a funny grin on your face, Uncle G. What's up?"

Kid was too damn perceptive for his own good.

"Just thinking of where I'm going to take you when you're done with all your surgeries."

"Where?" Connor sat up with a gleam in his eye.

Gage's heart melted. God, he loved this kid. "Well, I thought we'd start off with a baseball game. Hotdogs, ice cream, funnel cake, the whole she-bang. Then we can hit up the football stadium. Then, I don't know, you want to go kayaking? Whitewater rafting? Mountain climbing?"

"Can we go back to the amusement park? I want to ride a roller coaster."

Gage's throat closed up again. Connor's accident had happened right when they'd been leaving for the park to do just that. Connor loved roller coasters. "Absolutely. We can ride the coaster over and over and over again. As long as you like."

"Cool." Connor sat back and fiddled with the edge of his sheet. "What about horseback riding? Can we do that?"

"Yeah, sure, if you want." Gage had never been on a horse, but, what the hell. He'd learn with Connor. And maybe he could incorporate some of it into his cowboy persona.

Lara had liked the hat. She'd liked the whole package—he'd seen her watching him stroll up to her table.

Thank God for his looks. He'd always taken them for granted. Sure, they were good for attracting women, but he'd always just gone with the flow on that. But when he'd wanted to attract her interest, he'd been really happy that he kept himself in shape.

"So what are you thinking now?" Connor tapped his chin with his good arm. "What else are we gonna do?"

Gage knew what he wanted to do... "Whatever you want, Con. Let's get through the surgeries and I'll do whatever you want."

"Even playing COD?"

"Ya know what? You get through the surgeries, work really hard at your therapy, and I'll talk to your mom about it." And he would. Hell, facing death for real was a hell of a lot scarier and more traumatic than doing it in some video game. Whatever it took to get the kid through it.

"Okay, then I guess I can wait. Wanna play chess?"

"Since when do you play chess?"

"Since you gave me the iPod touch. I've learned lots of old-fashioned games."

Gage laughed. Old-fashioned. Chess had been around forever. It was the game of kings. Leave it to a kid to reduce it to being old-fashioned.

Gotta love the fresh perspective. Gage was so used to dealing with the stress and angst of Connor's condition that sometimes he forgot to breathe. To appreciate what he had and live in the moment.

That's what he'd been trying to do with Lara. This past weekend and after that bachelorette party. Sure, it'd started out as a pick up, but when she went out on him, it changed. He'd felt something for her. Compassion, not irritation. And then he'd gotten her out of that dress, and yeah, that got him *very* interested. But when he'd put his t-shirt on her, something settled around him. Something comforting. A shared moment just for the two of them, unlike anything he'd shared with any woman before.

Too bad she'd been out of it. But he'd watched her

sleep. The soft little twitches her mouth had made, the way she'd tucked her clasped hands beneath her cheek, the soft little snores...

He'd never watched a woman sleep. Hadn't studied the curve of anyone's cheek or the soft rise and fall of her shoulders. The way her leg had curled up to her chest. How sweetly sexy her bared thigh was...

"Uncle Gage? Are you okay?"

"Yeah. Sure. Why?"

" 'Cause you had a different funny look on your face again."

Lust, kid.

No. Something a bit more than lust. He'd lusted before. But he'd never felt something else with it.

"Okay, Con, where's the chessboard? I'll show you just how fine I am and I'll kick your butt doing it."

"No you won't. I'm really good at strategy now."

Given that Gage would be seeing Lara again this weekend—he'd seen the list of sponsors for the benefit—he wasn't doing too badly on the strategy front either.

Chapter 8

Gage hefted the rest of the two-by-fours into the back of his pickup Monday morning, then strapped them down for the trip out to the gazebo by the fifteenth hole. One thing about working on a golf course: he had to schlep every piece of material from the storage sheds out to the site instead of having it delivered directly there. The owners wanted the gazebo to go up as quickly as possible without letting their members know it was happening. Consequently, he had to show up really early and clear out before eleven a.m. when the afternoon crowd would show up. What normally would've been a week-long project at most was now deep into its second week and would probably need a third.

Normally he wouldn't complain because the interrupted schedule upped his hourly charge, but he hadn't been able to finish any other projects because by the time he got to the Whitmans' kitchen remodel or the Torringtons' basement conversion, he could only put in a few hours. Luckily, the clients were okay with the schedule, but his invoicing depended upon completing the jobs. If it weren't for BeefCake, Inc., he'd have no money coming in to pay the bills. Several of which were due, including part of the balance on Connor's physical therapy.

Yeah, he needed to have that conversation with Missy sooner rather than later.

He drove down the access road to the eighteenth hole and unloaded the supplies at the gazebo. He had the rafters to finish, then the plywood, flashing, and roofing before he could do the final trim and pathway work. Five days tops, but with Gina's party on Friday, he was looking at next week before he could finish.

He set up his saw horses and measured out the next four rafters. He hooked the miter saw to the generator, and was just about to stick his iPod earbuds in when an early golfer rode up in his cart.

Gage held in his derision. Golf carts were good for grandfathers who had trouble walking eighteen holes, but guys in their thirties like this one? He could stand to lose the paunch that was forming.

"You the guy responsible for this?" asked the golfer, waving a gloved hand at the gazebo.

"Technically, the management is, but yes, they hired me to build it."

"You do good work."

Hmm, that was a surprise. This guy had *prick* written all over him from the yellow-and-white argyle vest, tan pants, white shoes and even a glove, to the pinky ring and designer club case that the caddy was carrying as *he* walked the course behind the cart.

God save him from pompous, supercilious assholes.

"I was thinking of having one built by my pool. Would you be interested in giving me a quote?"

God save him from pompous, supercilious assholes who *weren't* looking to hire him.

Gage took a business card from his back pocket. "Yeah, sure. I can do that. When are you looking for it to be done?"

The guy pulled a gold case from his breast pocket beneath the vest—of course he did—and handed his card to Gage. "I'm having a party next month. I'd like it completed by then. The ninth, to be precise. Guests will arrive around four."

Gage checked the address. J.C. McCullough in Fox Run Hills. Swanky. Which meant bucks. As if he couldn't have guessed from the guy's air alone. "I think that's doable. Will you be home later today so I can see the space and work up a quote?"

"Today's not good, but tomorrow works. After six."

Gage ran through his schedule. "Make it seven and I'll see you there."

"Excellent." The guy nodded, then headed toward the hole, holding out a hand to the caddy for his club.

Gage had to laugh as he stuck his earbuds in. Guys like J.C. always made him laugh. Worked their way so high up the corporate ladder with assistants and caddies and maids and drivers that he wondered if they had someone hand them toilet paper, too.

Ah, well, who was he to criticize? The man's money was just as green as anyone else's and his type usually wanted top quality. Bragging rights and all, which was fine with Gage. With the discounts he could get on premium materials, he'd rather work on a high end job any day because the profits were greater.

One more project to up his own coffers for Connor's surgery. It was all about Connor.

"Hey, we got another one." Cara hung up the phone, dancing like it was Christmas morning. Every order was a gift. "Next Friday. The client wants a boardwalk cake with a Ferris wheel full of cupcakes. Our rig still rotates, right?"

Lara pried the lid off the tub of fondant. "Yes, it does. How many people is she expecting?"

"About a hundred. She's having a grand opening for her day spa. A beach party, trucking in sand and what-not. She says she'd like you to stay on site until the cake has been served because she doesn't want to pay the deposit for the machine."

That Ferris wheel had been a big expense, but it was going to be the first piece of equipment that paid for itself. People, for some reason, loved rotating cupcakes. "But my time is worth something, Car."

"I know. That's why I charged her seventy-five percent of the equipment deposit. Cheaper for her and a chance for you to sell our services to her guests while making money doing it."

Lara snapped on a pair of latex gloves so she wouldn't stain her fingers when she added the food coloring to the fondant. "I can't solicit business while I'm working at her event."

"Sure you can. And it's not really soliciting. You'll just be there to answer questions about our services if anyone asks. Same as leaving brochures around, but more interactive. All you have to do is be yourself and I guarantee you, we'll get some referrals."

Lara shook her head. All she'd wanted to do was bake and create. Make people smile. That's why she'd gone into this with Cara who didn't know fondant from buttercream, but knew how to hustle and make sure the bills were paid.

She added the food coloring to the white fondant. Mrs. Keswick's housewarming cake had to match the shutters on her new house. So much so, that Mrs. Keswick had had the builder send one over. Lara was going to do her best to match it. "What time next Friday? I have Marcella Sloan's birthday party in the late afternoon."

"I'll do it. It's just a delivery."

"Not exactly, Cara. There's some on site setup needed."

"So teach me. If I can juggle numbers, I'm sure I can juggle add-ons."

"Come here then and I'll give you a lesson on working with fondant because you're going to have to use it to cover the base of the sunflowers." Six-year-old Marcella was having a garden tea party and her mother wanted the cake to *be* a garden. A life-sized one, with periwinkles and daisies and roses, all things Lara could attach prior to delivery, but the sunflowers were a whole other matter. She'd prepped the PVC holders in the base for the bamboo "stalks," but Cara was going to have to cover them in fondant "grass" on site.

"Give me ten minutes," said her cousin, pulling a pencil from behind her ear. "I have to get a list of ingredients to the woman at the benefit for her to post so people can watch for allergies, and I've got calls in to half a dozen of those business cards you brought back from the expo and want to touch base with them."

Lara didn't need any additional reminders about the expo because she hadn't been able to get Gage out of her head. She'd even gone so far as to check out his website, www.BeefCakeIncorporated.wordpress.com, over the weekend. Yeah, she wasn't proud of herself, but what no one knew wouldn't hurt her.

And there hadn't been many pictures of Gage anyway. Most of the videos and images were of the guys. The About Us page had a shot of him and his partner, but they'd been in business suits, looking all corporate and professional. Such a different image than Mr. B.N.A.

Lara swiped her forehead with her forearm. She should turn up the A/C. It was a constant battle with Cara to keep the costs down while trying to prevent the cakes and frostings from melting.

And now her. She needed to keep thoughts of Gage out of the workroom.

"So did you see the strippers while you were there on Saturday?" Cara stapled a bunch of papers together and impaled them on her invoice spike. "I heard they were the hit of the expo."

"No one got naked." Well, on Saturday…

Cara grinned at her. "Paid attention, did you? You didn't happen to get any of their numbers by any chance, did you?"

She'd gotten *his* number all right… "For what? To

keep us entertained while we work?"

Cara grinned and waggled her eyebrows. "Hey, don't knock it 'til you've tried it."

She *had* tried it—and fallen asleep doing so.

God, if Cara ever found out, she'd never live it down.

"They were the same crew that was at the club for Jenny's bachelorette party, I hear."

"That's not surprising. I doubt this town could sustain many male stripper reviews, so it's not really surprising they're one and the same."

"Hmmm." Cara tapped her lip.

"What?"

"That was quite a lot of words for hot guys. You didn't happen to hang out at their booth, did you?"

Lara wiped her forehead with her forearm again, but this time it wasn't to remove anything out of her eyes. This time it was all about not looking at Cara. They'd practically grown up together; Cara could read her like a book, and the blush on her cheeks was surely a dead giveaway.

"Do you see that stack of business cards?" she asked, hoping to turn the tables on her cousin. "Just when do you think I had time to ogle the participants?"

"Pity. You need to get out more. Look around. Just because Jeff was a dick doesn't mean all men are."

"This from you? The woman who categorizes men by the size of their hands?"

"Hey, at least I know what a man is good for. You seem to have forgotten."

Oh no she hadn't. She'd relived Gage's hotel room incident in Technicolor every minute of the past sixteen days.

"I thought we were focused on making this business a success? Who has time to date?"

"Dating and sex do not have to go hand in hand."

"You know, Car, just because a guy strips for tips

doesn't mean he's available for hire for anything else. Those also don't go hand-in-hand."

Cara tapped her lip again, this time a little smile appearing.

"What?"

Cara's smile got bigger. "Nothing."

It wasn't nothing. Lara could hear the wheels grinding in Cara's head. "Out with it, Car."

"Well you're awfully verbose on a subject that we should have stopped talking about paragraphs ago."

Lara snorted. "Right. Then you would have wondered why I clammed up and made more of *that* than there is. Look, Car, the guys were hot. Of course I looked. Just like we all looked at Jenny's party. It's why the guys were *there*. To get looked at. It's their job. Just like this—"She waved her rolling pin around the workroom—"is our job. So unless you're going to put a line item in the expense list about on-the-job entertainment, I don't know why we need to keep talking about this."

"I heard you left Jenny's party early."

Damn, Cara had always been able to switch subjects at the blink of an eye without blinking at all.

"I told you, I was tired. I'd worked on three parties that day, plus Jenny's cake. I was beat."

"Yeah, but Jenny said she'd called your room and you hadn't answered."

Lara grimaced. "Zambuca. The sleeping potion of choice."

"Damn. I was hoping you'd picked up the guy you'd been dancing with and had a hot night of wild monkey sex."

Lara couldn't stop the bark of laughter. "Yeah, me too, but sorry, I'm just not that adventurous."

None of that statement was a lie. Unfortunately. She *wished* she'd had hot wild monkey sex too, but Gage had assured her that hadn't happened.

She was inclined to believe him. She'd never had hot wild monkey sex before and was fairly certain there would have been some muscle twinges the morning after if they had.

She still couldn't believe he'd been such a gentleman. She wouldn't have blamed him if he'd just left her in the hallway or on a bench somewhere. He could have been nice enough to contact the front desk and they could have found her room for her, or he could've taken her back to the club and left her with her friends. But he'd taken her to his room, and left her alone.

Though he *had* undressed her…

Her cheeks started flaming again. And Cara was looking a little too closely.

"You should've done it, you know. Try something new. Not all guys are like Jeff."

"I don't want to talk about Jeff."

"You never do."

"With good reason."

"Yeah, but if you let him clam you up like this, you're giving him power. You'll never get over him if you don't exorcise him."

She'd like to exorcise him all right. Burning palms, pea soup, a voodoo doll or two… "I'm over Jeff, Cara. Trust me, he no longer has any space in my brain."

"Keep telling yourself that and you might start to believe it. But I've seen you around guys; you don't give any of them the time of day. When Jenny told me you'd actually been dancing with a really hot guy at her party I almost fell over."

"Gee, thanks for the vote of confidence."

"Oh, sweetie, I do have confidence that you can attract them. I'm just not so sure about you recognizing that they're attracted to you. We really need to find you someone who will give you back what Jeff stole from you. Someone who can teach you how to live."

Images of Gage—naked, Cowboy, flirting, sauntering—flashed before her eyes. He could definitely teach her a few things.

She held up the rolled-out fondant. "Can we table this discussion for, oh I don't know, another two years until this place is self-sustaining? I've got three orders to fill today and another eight hundred rose petals to make. Plus your lesson on fondant."

"Fine. Have it your way. Business first."

"You're the one who's always harping on business being first, Cara."

"Since when do you listen to me?" Cara fluttered her hands. "So when is our intern showing up? Those rose petals should keep her busy for a while."

They'd arranged an internship with the local tech school to get the labor they could afford—free—in return for practical experience. And, hopefully, by the time Jesse graduated school, they'd be able to hire her.

Lara looked at the clock. "In about half an hour. So let me finish covering these cakes in fondant so I can get set up before she gets here and then I'll teach you what you need to know."

Cara waggled her eyebrows. "But who's going to teach *you* what you need to know?"

Chapter 9

Gage pulled up the driveway to J.C. McCullough's McMansion. Gabled roof, fieldstone façade, professionally landscaped with a manicured lawn that looked like it could double for a golf course, and, of course, a four-car garage.

Only four? Where did the guy park his golf cart?

He parked the truck behind the arborvitae to shield it from the street view. Most high-end homes had a screen like that just for the contractors they hired.

He grabbed his iPad, clipboard, and tape measure, jammed the Tomlinson Contracting baseball cap on his head, and got out of the truck. He kept a change of clothes in there for client visits after a work day, so the red golf shirt and khaki pants were appropriate attire, and he'd changed out of his work boots to a clean pair, also in the truck for just this purpose. Nothing like trekking construction dirt through someone's house after a day on site to lose a job.

He rang McCullough's doorbell and wasn't surprised to have it opened by an older woman in a black dress with a white apron.

"Hi, I'm Gage Tomlinson. I have an appointment with J.C. McCullough."

"Yes, Mr. McCullough is on the patio. He said the pool gate is open and you're to go on through."

Gage bit his lip. The servants' entrance. He got it.

Yeah, the guy did have *prick* written all over him; Gage hadn't misjudged him.

But, again, a prick's money was just as good as anyone else's.

He found McCullough on a gorgeous stone patio, reading the paper, dining on a rib-eye, with a snifter of something amber beside him. What Gage wouldn't give to be able to afford a place like this. The pool looked like a private pond, complete with a cascading water fall and hot tub, which would do wonders for Connor's physical therapy, and the patio had a built-in cook center with a wood-burning pizza oven. The pool house, complete with bar, was the perfect party hangout. McCullough's party on the ninth was going to be kick-ass.

"Tomlinson." McCullough set down his fork then folded his newspaper. "Thanks for coming. As you can see, there's only one place for a gazebo. Over there." He pointed to the left side of the pool. "I'd like it to seat six to eight if that's possible."

The right amount of money could make anything possible.

Gage pulled his tape measure off his belt, hoping the movement hid the sound of his stomach rumbling. Lunch had been a long time ago and that steak smelled delicious. "Let me get some measurements, then we'll talk."

McCullough nodded, flipped the newspaper open, and tucked back into his dinner.

Gage took the measurements and superimposed them on the pictures he took with his iPad to give McCullough a preliminary idea of what he was proposing. He'd found giving the client a custom rendering helped with expectations.

He took his time, wanting to get the spatial relations correct, but also wanting to give the guy a chance to finish his food because drooling over a client's dinner was also conducive to blowing a job.

When McCullough set down his fork, Gage headed back and took a seat at the table. He laid the tablet with his mock-up in front of McCullough. "How about this? We match the stone from the patio and carry that through the base walls and roof supports. I'll use cinder blocks for the interior, then cover them with the stone. I'm assuming you want the roof to match the pool house, right? Slate is a great product for this sort of feature."

"Of course. I want the best."

No surprise. Gage kept the smile off his face. The guy definitely wanted this for bragging rights, or a keep-up-with-the-Joneses thing—which was just fine with him. The more high-end the design, the bigger the profit. "Slate it is. It'll help with the upkeep, too, since that's minimal. A bigger outlay up front, but it evens out over the long-term."

McCullough took a sip from his snifter. It had to be brandy; a guy like him would drink brandy with his meal. Probably brought out the Port and cigars with dessert. "Money isn't the issue. Time and appearance are. This is my engagement party and I want it to be perfect for my fiancée."

Gage had a funny feeling that the appearance and money-is-no-object things had a lot more to do with the engagement than the gazebo.

God, he was cynical. Why couldn't the guy have a fiancée who loved him for who he was and not for his money?

Because this guy was about as lovable as the wrought iron furniture he was sitting on.

"Okay, I have what I need. I'll work up a quote and email it to you by tomorrow afternoon. Sound good?"

McCullough nodded and opened the newspaper again. "I'll look forward to it."

Prick didn't even shake his hand goodbye.

Chapter 10

"Ready to dazzle them with your cupcakes, cuz?" Cara plugged the Ferris wheel display into the cable strip taped between the booths at the charity benefit in the middle of the community center's football field.

Lara had to resist the urge to look at her *cupcakes*. She could still hear Gage's teasing drawl when he'd called her that at the expo.

She had to resist smiling about it, too. Cara would ask, and well, she didn't really want to share. It'd been a long time since flirting had been fun, and with Gage, it definitely was.

"Lar? You with me, honey?" Cara poked her. "I know the Simpson party last night was a late one, but we need to be on today. It's our biggest exposure yet."

"I'm good. No worries." She got her mind back into the here and now since Gage was over and done. "Hand me the cupcakes with the sports team logos, will you? I'm expecting them to be a big hit today."

Given that the benefit was for a six-year-old boy, she figured sports were a safe bet since, many times, boys would refuse to touch "girly" cupcakes.

Gage wouldn't. He'd be all *over a girl's cupcakes—*

Oh, Lord. Could she get her mind off him already? He was so one-week-ago and other than that one weak moment when she'd looked him up online, she'd really tried hard to forget.

Obviously that wasn't working for her.

By the time she and Cara finished setting up the rest of the booth, there was a line waiting. Food was always a draw at events like these. Lara had made sure to bring double the amount she normally would. Cara had designed new brochures to capture local attention and handed them out at the front end of the booth. Lara then hooked them with samples in the middle, and the newsletter list sat at the end, all alone, begging for email addresses, which almost everyone was gladly filling in.

"I have to run to the ladies' room," Cara said during a lull. "Think you can manage by yourself?"

"No problem. I'm just going to replenish the table. Can you grab me a lemonade on your way back?"

"Sure. See you in a bit."

Lara bent down to open another box of cupcakes. She'd discovered that people were less likely to approach a booth if the set up was sparse, so she always brought more than what she'd thought they'd need. She'd only miscalculated once.

"Hey there, Cupcake."

Make that twice.

Lara looked up. Cowboy Gage was standing at her table. Sans hat, chaps or boots, but it was definitely him. Those aquamarine eyes were one of a kind. And so was his effect on her.

She stopped herself from running a hand through her curls to make sure they were manageable. The humidity made it futile anyway, and there was no reason to call attention to the unruly mess when he was looking *very* well put together in navy shorts, a white button-down, and a smile.

Lord, that smile. The man could heat a third world country with the power it packed.

"Uh, hi. Are you, that is, is your company participating in the benefit?" She would've thought strippers were too risqué for a community event, but maybe the organizers were counting on the draw factor.

"No. BeefCake's not exactly appropriate for this crowd."

True. It was more the Zambuca-bachelorette party crowd—of which she was now a card-carrying member, much to her chagrin.

"I'm here because I'm Connor's uncle."

"Connor Nelson? The boy the benefit's for?" She didn't know why she was surprised; Gage was certainly entitled to have a family. She just hadn't thought of him that way.

Maybe because she'd been thinking of him in other, inappropriate, ones.

"Yes, Connor's my nephew. I'm going around to all the sponsors to say thank you in person for helping him and my sister out. They really need it and greatly appreciate what you're doing. We all do."

His voice had thickened in a way that had nothing to do with flirting, and it made her want to comfort him. She reached for his hand. "I'm happy we can help. I hope this works out for all of you, and that Connor will be okay."

He squeezed her fingers. "He *has* to be."

"If there's anything I can do, all you have to do is ask."

"Thanks. It's been…" He looked away. "It's been rough."

She couldn't imagine what they were going through. Bad enough for the accident and the injuries, but then the added stress of the mounting medical bills; it was no wonder Gage was on edge.

It was also no wonder why she wanted to comfort him. For all his teasing and flirting, there was something very real about Gage. Something that called to her.

No no no. She wasn't going down that road again. She had a business to see to. A broken ego to pull back together. Self-esteem to rebuild. By and for herself; *not* because of a man.

"Hey, want a cupcake?" She held up one of the

"girly" ones. The ones she'd baked, that is. Not the other—

She put a lid on that thought.

But her question did get a smile out of him, just as she'd intended.

"Pink and rhinestones? Is that what you think of me?" he asked, his smile wreaking its own special brand of havoc.

"That's actually tiny rock candy, but it got you to smile, didn't it?"

And *that* got him to chuckle. "Give it to me. I'm sure it's terrific no matter how you decorated it." He peeled the hot pink foil wrapper off and took a bite.

She so should not have watched him do that.

He closed his eyes as his tongue made a quick swipe over his lips and he moaned. All things she'd missed out on that one drunken night.

"Wow, Lara. Your cupcakes are spectacular."

She was not going to mention the Seinfeld episode. She wasn't.

But she was going to think about it.

"Glad, uh, that you like it." She went back to refilling the table. And the Ferris wheel. And heck, she put more brochures out, too. Anything to keep from watching him lick hot pink buttercream off his lips.

She wasn't very successful at that either. Especially when he licked his fingers.

Where was her cousin with that damn lemonade? Lara needed to cool down pronto.

Gage balled up the wrapper and shot it—two points, of course—into the trashcan behind her. "Hey, thanks. For the cupcake and for participating."

"You're welcome. Like I said, I hope it helps."

"I'm sure it will."

"Good."

"Yes."

Okay, now it was awkward. Especially since he had the tiniest bit of buttercream on the corner of his mouth and she really really wanted to be the one to lick it off.

"Cupcakes!" The squeal cut into the awkward moment, thank goodness. So did the hundred or so summer-campers that descended en masse onto her booth.

"I want the Eagles!"

"Lakers!"

"Nah, give me the Cowboys!"

Lara wouldn't mind a certain cowboy…

She got her mind off of Gage and onto the hungry pre-teens who were demanding every team she'd made, which wouldn't be a problem if she could remember which logo went with what team. While she enjoyed sports, this was pushing her knowledge.

Luckily, Gage jumped in to help, grabbing cupcakes left and right to meet the demand. "Who wants the Marlins?" He held up the cupcake like an auctioneer.

Six kids raised their hands.

"I want the Dolphins!" hollered another.

"What's a marlin?" asked another.

"It's a baseball team, dummy. And the Dolphins play football."

A girl shook her head. "Nuh uh. A marlin's a big fish. My dad caught one once."

"And dolphins are mammals," said another girl, this one all decked out in pink and bling. "They're smarter than most people."

Lara had the perfect cupcake for *her*. She handed over the twin to the one she'd given Gage.

He raised his eyebrows at her and smiled.

"Anything's smarter than you," snickered one of the boys, and his cohorts laughed with him when the girl's face fell.

Lara was just about to say something when a gangly

boy pushed through the crowd and confronted the bully. "Hey, Miller, watch it."

"Whadya gonna do about it, Greeley?" Miller crossed his arms with a grin that made Lara's skin crawl.

"This."

She wouldn't have thought Greeley had it in him, but he slugged Miller in the arm.

It was a very bad decision. Miller and his cronies puffed up with pre-pubescent anger that might be lacking in testosterone, but not by much.

It was just about to get ugly when Gage barked out a, "Hold it right there, guys!" and ran out of the booth to put himself between the two kids. "Hey, chill. This is supposed to be a nice, relaxing day. No fighting allowed."

"He started it," said Miller, petulantly.

Gage eyeballed him. "Let's not go there. You were just as guilty. Let's talk about what today is all about instead."

"Some kid got hit by a car." Miller flipped that off as if it were no big deal.

Lara could see the hurt rush into Gage's eyes, but he tamped it down.

Her heart went out to him. Today was personal for him on a very real level.

"That kid is a six-year-old boy named Connor. Do you guys remember what it was like to be six?"

The oh-so-sage ten-year-olds nodded solemnly. Lara had to hide her smile. Gage was really good with them.

"Awww, he's just a baby," said the pink-and-bling girl, now gazing adoringly at her knight in shining shin guards.

How bad was it that Lara was jealous of a ten-year-old with her first crush?

"That's right; Connor *is* someone's baby," said the object of *her* crush, hunkering down to be on their level.

"His mother loves him very much. Just like your parents love you. And she's very sad that he got hurt when someone hit him with his car. He can't walk and can use only one of his arms because of his injuries. So we put together this family day with the help of all of these caring people in the booths to raise money for Connor's medical bills so he can concentrate on getting better instead of worrying that he won't get the proper care. How would you like to be stuck in a wheelchair all the time and not able to move unless someone helps you?"

Miller and his sycophants nodded sagely. "That would suck."

In a word, yes, it would. Lara had to choke back the tears while listening to Gage. He was speaking to them on their level without allowing the emotion she knew he was feeling to cloud his voice.

"It does suck, er stink for Connor. He can't do anything by himself, and he can't go outside to play with his friends. Even eating one of these cupcakes would be hard for him because he can't get it out of the wrapper by himself. So what do you say we treat each other kindly and everyone will get a cupcake without bloodshed, okay?"

The brawlers shuffled their feet. "Yeah, I guess," mumbled Miller.

" 'Kay," said Greeley—whose hand had somehow migrated into bling girl's.

Lara's lips twitched. Ah, young love.

Gage stood up and glanced at her.

No. She wasn't going there.

"Good. That's settled." Gage clasped the boys' shoulders. "Now let's get everyone a cupcake."

After that, the kids behaved themselves, getting into an organized line and each waiting their turn. The harried counselors thanked Gage as they brought up the end of the line.

"That was amazing," said Lara when the group cleared out.

"Yeah, they really wanted cupcakes. You're almost out."

"Not that." Lara grabbed one of the boxes they'd emptied and broke it down to give her hands something to do other than migrate to *his* hand like Greeley's had. "I meant you. How you handled them. You're really good with kids."

He shrugged. "Comes from dealing with adults, I guess. You wouldn't believe how many women I have to pull off the guys. Then there are the jealous boyfriends or husbands. Sometimes it can get hairy. At least with these kids, I didn't have to worry about getting physical."

"Well you really have a way with people." Her included. She could feel her resolve to stay uninvolved when it came to him melting. For as charming as he was in his flirty, cowboy mode, he was even more dangerous to her equilibrium right now. This was the real Gage and he was a potent blend of sexy and sweet.

"I'm used to dealing with a six-year-old who's confined to a wheelchair and scared about never getting out. Trust me, I can handle the emotions these kids were spilling a lot easier than dealing with Connor's."

And there went another chink in her armor.

Gage wiped his hands on a paper towel and scored another two points. "I guess I should be going. There are a lot of other people I need to thank."

"Thank *you* for helping out."

He gave her arm a squeeze. "My pleasure."

Hers, too. "Um, yes, well, thanks for stopping by. It was nice to see you again."

He smiled a cute side-smile, complete with that dimple. "You, too," he said before leaving the booth, taking part of her resolve with him.

But as she watched him walk away, she wanted to groan. *Thanks for stopping by*? *It was nice to see you again*? Forget about today; he was the man she'd been in *bed* with. The one who'd changed her out of her dress into his t-shirt. Who'd been gentlemanly enough to not take advantage of her (but who'd probably been planning to that next morning), and she *thanked him for stopping by*?

No wonder she hadn't had more than two dates with anyone since the divorce if that's how she treated a guy. She didn't deserve any more.

It took everything Gage had to walk away.

Your cupcakes are spectacular.

Good God. He was completely off his game. He'd never say anything so cheesy to a woman if he was thinking clearly, but then, obviously he hadn't been. His emotions were all over the place today which wasn't the time to be around a woman who had that same effect on him.

He'd recognized the line from that sitcom and knew she had, too, and it'd sent his brain off on a tangent it had no business traveling when his nephew was stuck in a wheelchair and facing the possibility of never again being the way he was before.

Thank God those kids had come along; he'd needed the distraction. Lara had looked gorgeous even with her chef's hat on, a tough thing for anyone to pull off. But her hair was a riot of curls he'd wanted to sink his fingers in, and the flush on her cheeks from the heat had made her eyes sparkle, and the smile she'd had for him when she saw him…

He'd like to think there was more there than just a "nice to see you again" thing.

Yet he'd left her with just that. Where was his charm? Could he have been any more awkward?

He was never awkward with women. But he was

coming to realize that Lara wasn't just any woman.

He scraped a hand over his mouth. Shit. Icing. He was batting a thousand in the impress-Lara department. She'd passed out on him, couldn't wait to get out of his booth, left the expo before he could see her again, and now he was walking around with pink icing on his face on top of the "nice to see you again" thing. He ought to just cut his losses and move on.

Except, thanks to his knight-in-shining-armor complex, he'd be seeing her at Gina's gig next weekend.

His phone rang. "Hey Miss, I'll be right there." Connor had arrived. It was important for everyone to see him, but he and Missy had to be careful not to overdo it. For as stir crazy as the kid got, something like this would sap his energy.

Hell, look what it was doing to Gage.

Lara watched Gage leave and for once her thoughts weren't on the splendid backside hidden by his pants.

Well, not much.

He was hurting. It was so at odds with the guy she knew. Not that she knew him. Not really. He was good-looking, could dance, owned an interesting business, and could flirt like Casanova, but she didn't really know him.

She did now. Or, she knew a little bit more about him than she had before. And what she now knew, she liked. A lot.

She bent back down under the booth, both to get more cupcakes to refill the display and to get her eyes off of him. She couldn't *want* to like him. Anything between them wouldn't be practical. She had too much to do, too many hours to put into Cavallo's Cups & Cakes, to even contemplate ditching her no-relationship rule. She wasn't like Cara who could do casual so easily. It was one of the few differences between them, but Lara didn't sleep around—the night with Gage notwithstanding. And that had been an alcohol-induced bid to feel good about herself. Logically, she knew Jeff was the one with the problem, but emotionally? Emotionally, she'd been grasping at validation.

And grasping at Gage, too, apparently, if the flashes of memory that kept showing up at inopportune moments were anything to go by.

"I don't believe it."

This would be one of those inopportune moments. Jeff.

"You actually went ahead with this. What were you thinking, Lara?"

She stood up, this time not about to smooth her curls back. Her ex-husband had always hated her hair when it was wild and free.

"Hello, Jeff." It took everything in her to be civil, but she wouldn't give him the satisfaction of being a weeping, crying mess in front of him. Been there, never doing it again. Bastard.

"I can't believe this is what you've been reduced to. You shouldn't have gone ahead with the divorce, Lara."

"You cheated on me. I didn't have a choice."

"We always have choices, Lara."

"And you made the wrong one when you made a move on her."

"She meant nothing."

"Which makes the fact that you ruined our marriage for it even more pitiful."

It was the same old argument and it could have been any one of a dozen or more women. They'd seen a good-looking, wealthy attorney and hadn't cared that he was married.

Neither had Jeff.

But Lara had. "Is there something you need or did you

just come by to mock me?"

Jeff ran his hand down his abdomen. It was an affectation of his, trying to convey old world charm and sophistication, but she saw through it. Jeff was proud of his abs.

They were nothing compared to Gage's.

Great. Not what or who she needed to be thinking about when dealing with her ex-husband.

"Actually, I came to hire you."

"No way." Cara showed up out of nowhere and practically glued herself to Lara's side. "We're booked that day."

Jeff arched an eyebrow at Cara. They'd never gotten along. "You don't even know what day it is."

"Doesn't matter. For you, we're booked."

Lara loved that her cousin was trying to protect her, but the reality was, they did need jobs, and taking Jeff's money for doing what she'd wanted to do was actually something that made her smile. "When is it, Jeff, and what did you have in mind?"

"Lara—"

She squeezed Cara's hand. "Let's hear him out."

The event was exactly what she'd expect of Jeff. All his lawyerly types over for a fancy buffet on the back terrace. He actually called his patio a terrace. It wasn't the house she'd lived in with him—with his partnership had come a new address. But she'd googled it. Saw the landscaped *terrace* and the pool. A big mausoleum for one man—because, of course, the flavor of that month had never moved in. Lara had heard from a few mutual acquaintances that he'd moved on. Several times. If there was one consolation in the fact that he'd cheated, it was that he hadn't cared about the woman any more than he'd cared about her.

"We'll work up a quote and get it to you this week,

Jeff. Thank you for your business."

"Just make sure it's special, Lara. Like that party we had catered when the Garretts got married. I can't have my own engagement party eclipsed by a past one."

"Engagement?" Shit. He'd done that on purpose, trying to catch her off guard.

It'd worked, dammit, but she wasn't going to give him that satisfaction. She would *not* cry. It would *not* bother her.

And why should it? The poor woman he was marrying should be the one to be pitied. And warned. In that order.

"Yes. I'm getting married again. You didn't think I was going to sit back and wait for you to come to your senses, did you?"

Cara growled. Actually *growled.* "Look, you pompous ass—"

Lara grabbed her cousin's arm. "Car, it's all right." She looked at Jeff. "I guess congratulations are in order. Do I know her?"

"Hardly. You don't travel in the same circles anymore."

She filed the dig away. Jeff was a master of digs. "Well congratulations anyway. Would you like me to talk to her about what she wants before I give you the quote?"

"Right. Like I want to give you the chance to poison her against me."

"We ought to poison *you,*" Cara muttered.

Jeff glared at her.

Lara shook her head. "Knock it off, you two. Jeff, are you certain you don't want me to speak with her and get her input? It's her engagement party, too."

"She'll be fine with what I pick."

Of course he'd think that. Because Lara had been. Nothing had changed for Jeff except the name.

"Fine. Like I said, I'll have a quote to you by

midweek."

"Good. And I expect *you* to be on-site. Not your cousin." He sneered over the last word before he left, not even looking at Cara. Thank God, because *she* looked like she was ready to go for his jugular.

"*What* was that?" Cara rounded on her the minute Jeff was out of earshot. "Are you out of your mind? What do you think you're doing working for him? The guy's scum. Didn't you go through hell learning that?"

"Of course I did, Cara. But this is a great opportunity."

"To get hurt again."

"Not that. Think about it. We need jobs; Jeff has one. And he wants *me* to do it. He thinks he's insulting me by putting me to work, but he doesn't get it. We can charge him double and he'll willingly pay it. So who's the one getting used now?"

It took a couple of seconds, but the light dawned in Cara's eyes. "Why, you devious little thing. I didn't know you had it in you."

"Neither does Jeff. That's what makes it so great. And even better would be if we got more jobs from his so-called friends. That'll horrify him. He hasn't really thought this through. He thinks he's degrading me by having me work for him, but he's not going to like other people seeing me there, not when I used to have his name. He's not going to be able to stand the shame."

"Can you?"

"The thing is, I was on good terms with a lot of his co-workers, and there's nothing shameful in working his party. I'll be fine. I'll be more than fine, actually. I'll be laughing all the way to the bank."

Chapter 11

"I'll have the rib-eye, a baked potato with all the fixings, a side of onion rings and a side of slaw." Lara shut the menu and handed it to the waitress.

Cara's mouth dropped open. "You're seriously not going to eat all of that."

"Yes I am. I'm famished." She'd worked all weekend after the benefit to get ready for this week's deliveries and had skipped lunch to put the finishing touches on the McBrides' anniversary cake they'd dropped off before treating themselves to the special at Donegan's.

"I'll have a house salad."

"Ah, come on, Cara. Weren't you the one telling me to live a little? Be adventurous?"

Cara smacked her hand with the menu before giving it to the waitress. "I doubt anything on Donegan's menu could be considered adventurous."

"Oh, I don't know, those Rocky Mountain oysters aren't for the faint of heart."

"And they're not for me, either, so don't even think about it. But maybe we should get some wine or something." Cara fiddled with her straw in her soda. "Today was a good day, Lara. We had two more orders and a commitment from the senior center for their open house. It's happening. Our name's starting to get out."

Lara took a deep breath and sat back in the booth. Just the news she needed. Seeing Jeff over the weekend had brought up all the crap she'd been through once more. She'd tried not to, but had ended up watching a sappy chick flick Saturday night, trying to figure out how she A) hadn't been able to make her marriage work, B) had been stupid enough to marry him in the first place, C) had given up what she'd given up for someone who hadn't appreciated it, and D) still had to cash his alimony checks.

She'd re-thought his job offer. A lot. It'd been on her mind all weekend. But she wasn't going to cut off her nose to spite her face. The engagement party was a paying job and the bakery was too new to be selective about customers, but someday, she'd love the opportunity to turn him down. Who knew? Maybe she'd get enough business out of his guests that she could.

Ah ,well, she could always dream.

"Hey, Joe, how's it hangin?"

And there would be the guy she'd been dreaming about. Gage had entered the building.

She'd known it even before he'd spoken. It was as if the air changed. Shifted. Her senses became more heightened.

She choked on a snort. Yeah, and little fairies fluttered around her head sprinkling pixie dust and love potion number nine all over the place. God, she had it bad.

"Well helloooo." Cara, of course, *would* hone in on him. "Do you see *that*, Lara?"

Cara would be surprised to know exactly how much of *that* she *had* seen. "Uh, yeah. Nice."

"Honey, that's more than nice. That's some prime real estate."

No, he was prime *beefcake*, but Lara wasn't going to share.

Lara ran her wrist against her cool soda glass. "So what are we doing for the senior center? Cake or cupcakes? Theme?"

"Seriously? You want to talk shop while there's a gorgeous guy over there sitting all alone?"

Lara picked up the soda. "Since when are you on a manhunt? Does Nick know? And besides, this isn't a pick up joint; it's a restaurant. Who's to say he's not meeting someone?"

Oh, God, that thought hadn't even occurred to her until right now. It should have. Gage was, as Cara had so crudely put it, a prime piece of real estate. No way was he going to be single for long. Probably had a dozen women lined up, one for every night of the week and two on weekends.

Of which she'd been one.

She took a big gulp of the soda. And proceeded to choke on a piece of ice.

Cara jumped out of her seat to whack her on the back. "You okay?"

The darn ice was stuck. And it didn't help that half the restaurant was looking at her.

And, of course, *he* was in that half.

Gage was out of his seat and yanking Lara out of hers quicker than it took her to realize she was in trouble.

He wrapped his arms around her, dug his fist into her diaphragm, and jerked upward.

The ice cube flew out of her mouth.

He turned her around in his arms and she got an up-close-and-personal view of the sexiest pair of eyes she'd seen in a long, long time.

"You okay, Lara?"

"I am now." God, he looked good. A hint of five o'clock shadow, his hair mussed, and those lips of his within kissing distance. He wore a golf shirt and khakis, and somehow, that look was just as sexy on him as the cowboy get-up and what he'd worn to the benefit.

And the nudity.

She so didn't need to think about that. Not when Cara was watching them like a hawk.

Actually, she didn't need to think about it period. Not because of Cara, and not because of Gage. But just because.

Cara cleared her throat and held out her hand. "Hi,

I'm Cara Cavallo. Thanks for saving her life."

It took Gage three heartbeats to look at Cara. Lara counted.

"Gage Tomlinson." He nodded at Cara, but he didn't let Lara go. "I'm just glad I was here to help."

So was Lara.

"You want to join us for dinner?" Cara asked.

Lara wanted to kill her. She hadn't been able to drink a soda when he'd been clear across the room at the bar; no way was she going to be able to eat with him at their table.

"That'd be nice. Thanks." Gage unwound one arm from her waist, but kept the other firmly attached. "Okay with you, Lara?"

She nodded. What was she going to do, say no? Cara would never forgive her.

Though from the looks Cara was giving her, she was going to want an explanation of how Gage knew her name.

Which would lead to how Gage knew her.

Which she hoped wouldn't lead to how *well* Gage knew her. As in the biblical sense.

Well, technically, she didn't know him in the biblical sense. She'd seen the glory that was Gage, but only from a distance. A short distance, to be true, but enough to prevent biblical knowledge.

Great, she was babbling in her thoughts. Again.

She scooched into the booth, then scooched some more when Gage sat beside her.

Cara slid onto her side with her wide-eyed "you *will* tell me everything" look.

Lara smiled. Sort of.

"So, Gage." Cara made a big production out of opening her napkin and putting it on her lap. "How do you know Lara?"

Gage didn't take his eyes off her. "We met at the bridal expo."

Lara wanted to kiss him. He really was a gentleman.

Well, she wanted to kiss him for more reasons than that, but it was a start.

"The expo?" Cara tapped her fork tines on the table. "You're getting married?"

One side of Gage's mouth kicked back to a smile. "Not yet, no. I was one of the vendors."

"Really. What were you selling?"

Lara rolled her eyes. *Here it comes…*

Gage's grin went full on. "Bachelorette party services."

That was one way to put it.

Cara got it immediately. "You're one of the strippers?"

That finally got Gage's attention focused on Cara. "The official term is exotic dancers. What the guys take off or don't take off is entirely up to them. And no, I don't dance."

Oh yes he did. He'd offered to give her a private viewing, too.

Lara could feel the heat steal through her bones—though having Gage plastered to her side could have something to do with that also.

She reined in her happy hormones before Cara got any more interested than she already was.

"I bet that place was a bonanza for you if you did as well as we did with referrals. Lara said it was overrun with women," said Cara, back in business mode, thankfully. Cara was passionate in everything she did, whether it was running the business, or being serious about a guy—or cursing one out. If she was focused on the business side of the event, she might forget about grilling Lara later. Unfortunately, after listening to her cut Jeff to verbal shreds all weekend, Lara wasn't counting on it.

"It went well," said Gage, linking his fingers together

on the table.

Strong hands. Capable ones. That could have been all over her if she hadn't had that last Zambuca shot.

"I'm glad we attended. The organizers gave us a hard time at first, but in the end, it was worth the hoops we had to jump through."

"Hard time?"

"Yeah. People hear what we do and immediately think the worst. I actually had to sign a clause that basically said we wouldn't charge for any private services on site."

Cara set her fork down. "You're kidding."

"My thoughts exactly. Talk about objectification. But I get it. A lot. People hear what our guys do and immediately think escort service and all the baggage that goes with that. Most don't realize it's a job the same as being a waiter or a check-out clerk. Most of my guys are students who see dancing as a way to pay for school. I did and came out with very little debt, kept my integrity, and earned money doing something fun. No one should have a problem with it."

Cara raised her hands. "Hey, don't shoot the messenger. I'm all for free enterprise."

And naked dancing guys. Cara was definitely all for them.

The waitress returned to their table with a menu. "Can I get you something to eat, Gage? Their meals are almost up."

"I ordered at the bar, but if it's all right with the ladies, you can bring it here."

"Fine with me," said Cara.

Lara just nodded. She still didn't trust herself to speak. How was she supposed to eat with him mashed up against her? Her hormones were singing and she doubted she'd be able to hold a utensil with any degree of stability.

"Hey, Gage!" Joe, the bartender yelled across the

room. "Phone call."

Gage pulled his cell out of his pocket. "Damn. Battery's dead. Will you ladies excuse me for a second?"

"Sure," said Cara-the-verbal.

Lara-the-not just nodded. Again.

Then took a deep shuddering breath when he slid out of the booth.

Cara fiddled with her fork. "You know, choking to death isn't a way I ever would have thought of to catch a hot guy, but I have to say, the idea's growing on me."

Lara rolled her eyes. "Yeah, right. I risked my life on the off chance he'd know CPR. Get real, Cara."

"Honey, they don't come any realer than Gage. Did you see his muscles?"

Yes. She had. Especially his glutes.

"So why didn't you feel the need to share that you'd met the owner of the beefcake factory when I'd asked you about them?"

"I meet a lot of people at those shows. Do I tell you about every one of them?"

"Do any of them look like him?"

"Well, no, but—"

"I rest my case. So why didn't you?"

Lara tucked her hands under her thighs. "It's not a big deal, Cara. We met, we chatted, we exchanged business cards. It's a professional thing."

"I didn't see his business card in the stack you gave me."

"He's not a potential client."

"Lara, everyone's a potential client. And some are just potentials."

"That's why. That's exactly why I didn't tell you. I knew you'd react like this."

"Can you blame me? I mean, he's gorgeous!"

"So was Jeff."

"Different league. Lar. Completely different league."

And so far out of hers that this discussion was ridiculous.

Luckily, Gage came back to the table just then.

"Everything all right?" asked Cara.

He nodded. "Yeah, mini family crisis averted. No biggie."

"You have a family?" Cara leaned forward.

"Doesn't everyone?"

Now would be the perfect time to clue Cara in about Gage's nephew, but Cara, never one to miss an opportunity, was flashing some ta-ta-age as payback for keeping him a secret. And since Gage was tall enough to have a perfect beeline view right down Cara's ta-ta-age, it would work, except that he was looking at *her*, so excuse her if she wasn't into sharing anything with Cara right now. Especially Gage.

"You okay, Lara? You look like you had a couple of shots of Zambuca."

She glared at him. Not fair.

She put on her sweetest smile and crossed her arms under her breasts.

That got his attention.

"Why, no, Gage, I'm feeling just fine."

"Want me to be the judge of that?" he whispered.

Uh, yeah, she did.

Cara tapped the table to get his attention back on her, a move for which Lara was profoundly grateful. "I meant a family like a wife and kids and stuff?"

Gage jerked his head around. "A wife? Kids? No. Not me. Not now."

Interesting answer. So he didn't have any but might want some down the road? Lara tucked that away for future reference.

The waitress, praise be to God, showed up then with

their food. Cara's little ol' salad looked pretty darn pathetic next to the two steaks, baked potatoes with the fixin's on the side, and two orders of slaw.

"Hey, you got my favorite meal," Gage said, stealing one of her onion rings.

She grabbed one of his back. "No, you ordered *my* favorite meal."

"Well you're both making me kind of sick with all that food. Maybe I should get my own table."

Cara, thankfully, knew when she'd lost. The ta-tas went off display and her tractor beam eyeballs started roaming the room instead of Gage's shirt, and she got up to "get herself a drink at the bar," code-phrase for see-if-you-can-make-this-hook-up-happen-cousin.

Lara shouldn't be inordinately pleased by that, but she was.

"So everything's all right with your family?" she asked after Cara left.

"Yes. Connor needed me to tell his mom that he didn't need her help with, um, some personal needs."

"Can he do that by himself?"

Gage shrugged. "Not my place to second-guess him. He's old enough to want his privacy and, yeah, I get it. My sister tends to hover."

"Can you blame her?"

"Hell, no. I hover, too. It's been… rough."

He'd said that before and Lara had a feeling there was a lot more to it that he wasn't saying.

Gage cleared his throat and drummed his fingers on his table. "He needs two more surgeries and a lot of PT, but we're hoping for a full recovery."

"I hope the benefit raised a lot of money for him."

The smile Gage flashed wasn't exactly full of happiness and light and Lara's heart went out to him. She put her hand on his arm.

He didn't move it away. "The final tally isn't in yet, but more than the money, it was the outpouring of support from everyone. When something like this happens, you tend to want to turn inward and block everything out. But you can't. We need help, even if it's just meals or a few hours for someone to sit with him to give us a break. That was the surprising part of Saturday. I didn't expect it, but my sister now has a list of people she can call when she needs a break and I'm not able to be around. It's tough with two jobs."

"Two?"

He covered her hand with his. "BeefCake is just for after hours, but it takes up as much, if not more than my day job. But my sister needs more money than either of us have coming in for Connor's care."

And right there, Lara fell a little bit in love with him. And she wasn't even going to give herself a hard time over it because if someone *didn't* fall in love with such a selfless guy, there had to be something wrong with them. And no matter what Jeff wanted her to believe, there was definitely nothing wrong with her.

But falling even a little bit in love with him was a huge problem.

"So are you really going to eat all of that?" Gage waved his fork over her plate.

"I wouldn't have ordered if I wasn't going to."

"Seems like an awful lot for a tiny thing like you."

He just *had* to keep giving her reasons to fall in love with him, didn't he?

"Trust me, I can put it away."

"Care to make a wager on that?"

"Seriously? You're going to bet me that I can't eat all of this?"

"Yup."

"You're on." She dug into the potato, ready to get

started. "What are we betting?"

"A lap dance."

She spit out the bite of potato. "A what?"

He wiped the blob up. "You heard me. First one done wins a lap dance from the other."

"I'm sensing a theme with you."

"Can't put one by you, can I?"

No but he could lay one on her.

"So are you in or are you going to chicken out?" He slid a piece of steak into his mouth, and yes, she did see the tongue action that ensued, and yes, it did make her hot.

What the hell would a lap dance do if just watching him eat turned her nerves to mush?

Be adventurous. Cara's words mocked her.

Kind of like Cara was doing from the bar. The woman's eyebrows were going a zillion miles a minute. God only knew what they'd do if Cara could actually hear this conversation.

Fine. He wanted to be all sexy with the lap dance dare? Two could play at that game.

She picked up an onion ring and broke it in half. Then she slid one end between her teeth. "I'm in." And she worked that onion ring into her mouth with her lips inch by tasty inch.

Gage swallowed.

Twice.

She looked down at her potato and oh-so-nonchalantly swirled some cream cheese into it, then licked a forkful off one tiny lick at a time.

Gage shifted in his seat.

"Aren't you hungry?" she asked him, giving her lips a quick lick.

"Uh, yeah. I am."

That was definitely hunger flaring in his eyes, and she'd bet a lap dance it wasn't for food.

Good God, what had come over her? Lara almost choked on her next helping of potato. Who was this woman who'd invaded her body and jump-started her libido into hyper drive?

This wasn't her. Not at all. Inviting carnal thoughts in the middle of Donegan's by virtue of a baked potato? That was as unlike her as taking a dare for a lap dance.

Yet she had.

She swallowed the potato. She'd taken it because she didn't want to look back on this years from now and regret not taking a super hot guy up on his invitation. It didn't mean anything, wouldn't amount to anything, but now, in the moment, it was fun.

Yeah, and that'd probably been her last coherent thought at Jenny's bachelorette party, too, and look at how that'd ended up.

"You slowing down already?" He nudged her elbow.

"Hell no." She shoveled in another forkful of potato.

"All the fixin's, too."

"Well of course. There's no other way to eat a baked potato." She dipped her tines in the butter then licked them off. One at a time.

Gage reached for his beer and took a chug or two.

Lara cut a piece of steak and lovingly wrapped her lips around it. Oh, and oops—she just had to catch that tiny little drop of juice that dribbled out of the corner of her mouth with her tongue.

Gage reached for his beer again.

She nodded at the glass. "I think you ought to eat something."

His beer froze halfway to his mouth. So did her fork. She hadn't meant… She didn't want him to think…

She shoveled a heaping forkful of potato in. Then another. And, hell, why not a third?

She downed half of her soda on top of it.

Seriously, when was the floor going to crack open and swallow her up?

Gage swore his heart had stopped.

Lara was *flirting* with him. Hell, she was doing a lot more than flirting—*eat something*?

No. Hell no. She didn't mean what he wanted her to mean. She couldn't. The woman couldn't keep a blush off her face when he merely *looked* at her. Doing *that*…

He drank another mouthful of beer, took his time swallowing it, then set his glass down. Then he carefully picked up his knife and fork, sliced another piece of steak, and put it in his mouth, concentrating on how good it tasted.

She'd taste so much better.

He shoved an onion ring in.

"So, uh, how long did it take you to make all those cupcakes?" He really didn't care but he needed something to get his mind off the image of her in his shirt and that skimpy little pink thong she'd worn in his bed the first night they'd met.

The image had been seared into his brain with a branding iron.

"Making them doesn't take all that long. We have two commercial ovens. It's the decorating that does. I worked on the sports team ones for three days straight."

"They were a big hit."

"So was Greeley's."

They laughed, remembering the boys.

"So what's your other job?"

Gage cut another piece of steak. "I'm a general contractor by trade. Remodeling, carpentry, that sort of thing. Times are a little tough in that arena right now, so BeefCake, well, every little bit helps."

"It can't help that you've taken on the burden of

paying for your nephew's medical bills."

"Connor's not a burden. Ever."

"I didn't mean—"

He blew out a breath. "Sorry. I'm on edge when it comes to him. My sister is a single mom—his father's a jerk—and I'm all she has."

"It's just the two of you?"

"No, we have another sister. She's a college freshman, thankfully on a scholarship. She was going for teaching, but this thing with Connor… She's changing her major to medicine." He was so darn proud of Jayna. When their parents had been killed in the accident three years ago, she'd channeled her grief into becoming the best student she could be and applied for every college and scholarship she could find. After seeing what Missy hadn't done with her life, she'd decided she wasn't going to follow in her big sister's footsteps.

"So what about you? Just you and Cara? And what's with the rhyming names? Are you twins?" They could be; they looked enough alike and were about the same age. But where Lara's curvy petite-ness clocked him six ways to Sunday, Cara's blatant sexuality didn't.

"No, we're cousins. Born three weeks apart. Our moms thought it'd be fun to do that with our names. They were best friends growing up who married brothers. One big happy family who like to snow-bird it in Florida on the golf course. They'll be migrating north in the next few weeks."

"No siblings?"

She shook her head and scooped some coleslaw between her lips. "That's why we're so close. Not only were we raised like sisters, but we're each the only one either of us will ever have."

A sliver of carrot lingered on her lip.

Gage wanted to suck it off.

"You slowing down?" He didn't care which one of them won the bet; it was a win-win any way he looked at it. And actually, he could have won it by now; this amount of food was nothing to him. But he was enjoying the conversation and how she was so determined to win, and hey, losing wouldn't be any skin off his back… side.

"Slowing down? Me?" She scooped more potato in—damn, the butter slicked her bottom lip. "No way. I'm going to win."

Good. He'd love to resurrect his old moves just for her.

"What happens if we have a tie?" She polished off the last of her slaw.

"We give each other a lap dance."

She dropped her fork. "What is it with you and lap dances?"

"You don't like them?"

"I don't know; I've never had one."

It was his turn to drop his fork. "You're kidding."

"No. It's not exactly something I've put on my bucket list."

"No ex has ever done that for you?"

There was that hot-as-hell blush again. "Hardly. My ex-husband wouldn't have been caught dead doing that. Yet he says *I'm* the one who's vanilla."

Ex-*husband*? Shit. And *vanilla?* "That hot pink thong you had on at the bachelorette party wasn't vanilla."

She turned the same shade as that thong. God, she made it so easy.

"I didn't wear thongs with him. It was my post divorce liberation statement. Seemed the thing to wear to a bachelorette party."

"How long's it been since the divorce?"

"Not long enough."

Shit again. He didn't want to be Rebound Guy. Not

with her.

"Two years."

"How long were you married?" He pegged her at twenty-nine—he pegged all late twenty/early thirty something women at twenty-nine. Made him a hero most of the time. So that'd put her divorce at twenty-seven, a year for the marriage to go bad…

"Three years. I was young and stupid. He was older and shallow. I never saw it until he was up for partner in his law firm and decided a partner should have a willowy blonde mistress to complete the stereotype."

"I'm sorry." That her ex-husband was an ass, not that she was divorced.

"I'm not. I'm over Jeff. I'm focusing on making the bakery a success."

Probably to rub it in the ex's face, but Gage got that. He'd like to rub his fist in the guy's face, though he should probably thank him for putting her back out there so Gage could find her.

She finished the baked potato before he'd even made a dent in his. He shoveled two more small bites into his mouth, taking his time. Every woman was entitled to at least one good lap dance in her life.

He was planning on at least two for her.

"Hey, guys." Cara walked back to the table. "Nick's here, and well, we've got some stuff to clear up, so I'm gonna head out. Is there any chance you could take Lara home, Gage? I don't want to have to rely on Nick after our, um, discussion."

"Car—"

"Absolutely. Not a problem." He lowered his voice so only she would hear. "Perfect time for the bet pay-off."

"That's okay with you, right, Lara?" Cara asked.

He had to give her credit for caring about her cousin, but no way was he letting Lara go tonight.

Lara looked at him, finally some heat in her eyes instead of embarrassment. “You’re sure?”

“I wouldn’t have offered if I wasn’t.”

She picked up her last onion ring. He prayed she didn’t do that shimmy-it-between-her-lips thing again. He’d barely been able to stay upright when she’d done it the first time.

“Yes, it’s fine, Cara.”

“Great.” Cara waved—with a smirk.” Have fun you two.”

Gage wanted to smirk back. Fun was exactly what he was planning to have.

Chapter 12

"So I guess I owe you." Gage opened the passenger door and held out a hand to help her into the cab. He was glad he hadn't splurged on running boards. He was tall enough that he didn't need them, and though Lara could use them, he'd prefer to just wrap his hands around her waist and hoist her inside.

But when she hopped up on her own and her breasts jiggled every bit as impressively as her cousin's had back in the pub, he decided he'd rather watch her get in by herself.

"No, really, Gage, you don't owe me. It was just fun making the bet."

He didn't let go of her hand once she was in the cab. "Paying it off will be a lot more fun. Trust me."

Her eyes widened again and she slicked her tongue over her bottom lip.

God, he wanted to do that.

One little tug on her fingers had her leaning toward him, and hell, Gage couldn't help himself.

Just a nibble…

Her lips were as soft as he'd fantasized, and she tasted of butter and steak and soda. Even the onion rings tasted good in her mouth. And the tight little breath she took… It had his blood steaming through his veins.

Then she touched her tongue to his and it blew the roof off his composure.

Gage snaked his arms around her waist and dragged her across the seat as he positioned himself between her thighs, and the kiss went carnal. He swept his tongue into her mouth and plastered her breasts against his chest and if he could have crawled inside her right there without getting arrested for public indecency he would have.

The only indecent thing about this kiss was that it had to end. Making out in a parking lot was so fifteen years ago and Lara deserved better. A lot better.

He pulled back—not too far because he was still not letting her go—and rested his forehead against hers, their heavy breaths matching each other's rhythm.

"I'm not going to apologize for that." He couldn't because he wasn't sorry.

"Good."

And she managed to surprise him.

He pulled back, this time his eyes were the wide ones. "Really? I thought you'd turn pink again and start stammering."

"I don't stammer."

"Then I haven't done a good enough job of rendering you speechless."

She tugged his hair. "You certainly have a high opinion of yourself, don't you?"

She was teasing, but still… She could take him down a few pegs if he let her. "I'd say a *good* opinion, not high. I know that I affect you; that's not bragging. I can see it in your widened pupils and the flush on your skin, and the way you're breathing."

She followed his gaze as he looked at her chest. Her breasts were damn impressive. Just the right size for his hands—if he could ever get them on them—and they were moving very impressively, causing a correspondingly impressive (at least he liked to think so) bulge in his khakis.

He leaned against her. "You do the same thing to me. What do you say we go deal with the bet and see what happens from there?"

She wanted to; he could see it in her eyes. But he also knew she wouldn't. *Vanilla*, her ex had called her. It was going to take a lot more than a kiss in a parking lot to undo *vanilla.*

He could dare her or he could kiss her into melting that particular flavor out of her psyche, but he wasn't going to. He wanted her to want it. To want him. And not because he was dancing or she was drunk, but because she saw what she liked and went after it.

He'd wait.

"Come on. Let me take you home."

He felt her wide-eyed stare the entire walk around the front of his truck.

Lara was having a hard time processing what had just happened. One moment she'd been a surging sea of hormones, and the next… nothing. Well, okay, her hormones were still doing cartwheels, but he'd stopped.

Stopped.

What the hell was with that? Those khakis weren't exactly chain mail; he wanted her. She'd *felt* how much he'd wanted her. And now he was walking away? Taking her home?

Jesus. Was Jeff right? *Did* she have vanilla written all over her? A big fat sticker on her forehead? Gage was probably so opposite of *vanilla* that she'd scared him off.

He pulled his car key from his pants pocket. "So, where to?"

She took a deep breath. "Your place."

The key fell out of his hand. "What?"

"Your place. After all, you owe me." There. How un-*vanilla* was that?

"You're sure?"

Not a drop of ice cream's chance in hot fudge sauce was she sure about this, but she'd already committed herself. "Would you make me pay up if you'd won?"

The heated look in his eyes was her answer.

"Exactly. Pay up or I'll tell everyone you reneged."

Seriously, who was this woman who'd invaded her normal *vanilla* self and turned it red-hot chili pepper spicy?

Gage jammed the key in the ignition, dragged the gearshift into reverse, and peeled out of the parking lot.

Lara squirmed in her seat, fully copping to nerves. He barely glanced at her. His eyes were glued to the road when ten minutes ago they'd been glued to *her*.

What if he was disappointed? After all, she hadn't been able to keep her husband interested. The man who'd supposedly pledged to make love to her for the rest of his life. Gage had women flinging themselves at him. She'd seen it first-hand. Why on earth would he want her?

"You're over-thinking this."

His cowboy drawl didn't turn her on near as much as his real voice did. Because it was his. Real. And laced with all sorts of skin-shivering tones and inflections, and the way his lips formed the words…

He grabbed her hand and intertwined their fingers.

Yes, he was right. She was over-thinking it. All she had to do was look at where their skin touched and realize it didn't need any thinking. They did it for one another. What that would mean down the road, she didn't know. And right now, she didn't care. All she wanted to examine was what it would mean for them down *this* road.

He turned into an older sub-development. Two left turns later, he was pulling into the driveway of a 1970s split level with newer siding, replacement windows, a two-car garage, and a plastic swing set in the back yard.

"This is your house?"

"My parents'. We inherited when they died."

He'd brought her to his parents' house.

Sure, *they* no longer lived there, but this wasn't some hook-up joint bachelor pad. This was where he'd grown up. Where his family had lived. Reality.

Crud. She most definitely was *vanilla.* She couldn't

insult this house, those family memories, with a lap dance. Especially her first lap dance.

He had her door open before she'd processed that last thought.

Then he held onto her arms with his strong hands and the last thought disappeared in a surge of that red-hot yearnin'.

"I told you to stop over-thinking it."

The yearnin' fizzled. "I can't help it. This… Is your boyhood bedroom still like it was when you lived here? Trophies and posters and baseball gloves?"

He looked away. "It's not like that. I mean, yes, my bedroom's still the same, but I sleep in the master bedroom now."

His parents' room. She raised her eyebrows.

"I've remodeled it. I'm doing the whole house. Bringing it up to date. Undoing the way it was."

But he'd never get rid of the memories and she'd never forget that he'd probably skinned his knee here, or ate his mom's homemade chocolate chip cookies, or made out with his first crush in the basement.

Yes, she really was *that* vanilla.

The front door opened and a little boy sat in a wheelchair in the doorway, waving at them as if the house were on fire. "Gage! You're here!"

"Connor. Hey, buddy." Gage dropped his hands from her arms and tilted her chin up. "Looks like I'll have to give you a rain check on that lap dance."

She didn't know whether to exhale in relief or regret.

Then he grabbed her hand and led her up the ramp to the front door, a modification he'd obviously made for his nephew's injuries.

Regret. Definitely regret.

"Hey, Con. This is my friend, Lara."

"Hi, Lara."

"Hi, Connor."

Gage ruffled Connor's hair. "What are you doing here? Where's your mom?"

"She's in the bedroom, unpacking."

Gage's hand stopped mid-ruffle. "Unpacking?"

A woman who looked enough like Gage to be his sister appeared behind Connor. "Yes, unpacking. You were right. It makes more sense for us to live here. You haven't changed your mind, have you?"

"No. Not at all. I just, that is, I wasn't expecting it to be tonight."

"I can see that." The woman held out her hand and, yes, that smile was all her brother's. "Hi, I'm Missy. I'm Gage's sister."

"Lara. Uh, Gage and I…"

He squeezed her hand. "We had dinner together."

His sister didn't miss the hand squeezing. "Oh."

Lara didn't know who blushed more, she or Missy.

"I was just, uh…" *Coming here so your brother can light my fire.*

"Connor and I, we could go out. For a movie. Or something," said Missy.

Gage bit his lip and Lara could see his smile just itching to get out. "Don't worry about it, Missy. We were just stopping by for me to pick up a few things."

They were? Lara just kept blinking. She'd let him handle this.

"I'm going to fix something for Lara, so I'm just stopping in to pick up my tools."

He had all the tools he needed already on him.

Lara gulped and prayed no one heard it. What the hell had been in her dinner? As far as she knew onion rings and coleslaw were *not* aphrodisiacs.

"Oh. Okay." Missy turned back into the house. "Come on, Connor. You can see Gage tomorrow."

"Can I come with you, Gage? I can hand you your tools."

The adults looked anywhere but at each other.

Gage ruffled his hair again. "Not this time, kiddo. I might not be back 'til after your bedtime."

"Aw, man. It's summer. Can't I stay up late?"

"You heard your uncle, young man. Let's go." Missy grabbed the wheelchair's handles and spun Connor back into the living room. "Have fun, you two."

They would if they could just find a place to be alone.

Chapter 13

Lara's house wasn't that place.

Gage had had all sorts of fun ideas planned for them: first he'd start with some straight up dancing, then he'd get down to the lap part of it, and then, well, maybe there'd be some horizontal dancing.

But when they pulled into the parking lot of her condo complex and saw Cara's car—with a crying Cara in it—Gage kissed the idea of *any* kind of dance goodbye.

He'd rather be kissing Lara.

He put the truck in park and rested his forearms on the steering wheel. "Guess it really is a rain check, huh?"

Lara winced—that, at least, salvaged his ego somewhat. "I have to see what's wrong."

"You don't sound enthused."

"Would you be? I have the choice between a hot guy giving me my own personal show or listening to Cara's heart breaking."

"You think I'm hot, huh?"

She smacked his arm. "You know you are. That's not a newsflash."

He grabbed the back of her neck and pulled her in for a quick kiss. He'd show her how hot he was—for her.

There was nothing quick about it.

Lara sucked in a breath and his tongue went with it, and Gage was gone. He fumbled with her seatbelt and dragged her up against him. Thank God for bench seats.

He wrapped his arm around her legs and drew them across his thigh.

Ah, yeah, there. He needed pressure right there.

She groaned and shifted, and yeah, even better.

He angled her head and thrust his tongue into her

mouth in a motion the rest of his body wanted to make.

Then she cupped his cheek and Gage about blew a gasket. Her fingers lit up his skin like fireworks on the Fourth of July.

He dragged his lips from hers and buried them in the crook of her neck. God, she smelled as good as she tasted, though no onion rings this time. Some sweet fruity scent that made him want to lick every square inch of her.

He shuddered as his cock jerked against her leg. Man, he wanted her. But not in the front seat of a truck in a parking lot where anyone could see, with her cousin twenty feet away, crying her eyes out.

He framed her face with his hands, capturing those sensuous curls between them, and kissed her cheek. The tip of her nose. That top lip that he wanted to bite—

He nibbled it.

Lara sighed. Shuddering-ly so.

He smiled as he kissed her again. A last kiss. A sweet one. One that wouldn't have him hard and aching the rest of the night—

Or might, but in a good way.

"I had a great time tonight," he whispered as their foreheads and noses touched.

Her eyes—dark with passion—blinked at him and it was all Gage could do not to lay her back on the bench and finish what they'd started.

"You did?"

He wanted to kill her ex-husband for putting that doubt there. He was making it his personal mission to wipe it away and maybe wipe up the floor with the ex, should he ever have the dubious pleasure of meeting the prick.

"Yeah, I did. But there's some unfinished business here, you know."

"I know." She wet her lips.

His good intentions about letting her walk out of this

cab without him making love to her were sorely tempted. "You're not going to be the one to renege, are you?"

Another lip-licking.

His fingers curled into her hair.

"No. I won't renege."

"Good. I'll hold you to that." He took a deep breath—and committed that sweet scent to memory—before sitting back. "You better go in. She needs you."

Lara nodded. "Thank you. For…"

He put a finger on her lips. And never wanted to move it. "Nothing to thank me for." He leaned over and opened her door. "Yet."

Chapter 14

Lara wasn't sure how she managed to make it out of Gage's truck and over to Cara's car without dissolving into a puddle of pheromones.

Cara's tear-stained face looked up, startled, only to dissolve into another crying jag.

Lara opened the door. "Come on, Car. Let's go in."

"Why are guys such pricks?" Cara hiccupped as Lara opened the door to her condo.

"You want me to list the reasons alphabetically or just shout them out in random order?" Lara asked as she dropped her keys on the table beside the door and headed into the kitchen for the bottle of zinfandel she'd bought last week but had been too beat to open since. "What'd Nick do?"

"Nothing. That's the problem." Cara flopped on the sofa that'd been the second thing Lara had bought for her new "single" place when the divorce had been final. A bed had been the first—one she'd covered in frilly, flowery sheets and way too many pillows. No more of the monochromatic "grown up" bedroom décor Jeff had insisted on.

"So why are you crying? I thought you guys had a casual relationship." She poured two glasses of wine and brought them into the living room.

Cara sniffled. "So did I."

Lara handed her a box of tissues. "Then what's the problem?"

"He wants me to move in with him."

"You're kidding." Lara plunked down on the sofa next to her.

"I wish." Cara yanked a wad of tissues out of the box.

"Why'd he have to go and mess everything up?"

Lara stroked Cara's curls. "You know, most women wouldn't be upset about this. Most of them would be thrilled."

"I'm not most women."

That she wasn't. Cara was one of a kind. "So what are you going to do?"

"I'm certainly not going to move in with him. I mean, come on, Lar, can you see me doing the domestic goddess thing? Me, who'd rather drive twenty minutes for take-out than boil water? I don't know one end of a broom from the other, and making homemade chicken soup and nursing someone through a cold is worse than an IRS audit in my mind. How could he want to live with that?"

Lara grabbed another wad of tissues as Cara dove into the one she already had.

"What if you start out slow? Just do two days. Forty-eight hours. You go to his place after work, have dinner, hang out, do whatever… You get up the next morning, go to work, then back to his place afterwards. By the time dinner the second day hits you'll know if you want to stay there or go back to your place."

"See? Now that's what I told him, but he's Mr. All-or-Nothing. He can't be happy with stop-gap measures."

"Car, give the guy a break. Most people aren't stop-gap measure sort of folks. He cares about you; he wants you to be around."

"Yeah, but what about what I want?"

"What *do* you want? You wanted happily ever after with Dale—"

"Don't mention that jerk to me if you want to live to see tomorrow."

"Is it possible you're not over him?"

"Seriously, Lara, you might be my cousin, but I am not above taking you out if you keep going with this train of thought. Dale and I are over. Done. Finished. He lost out on the best thing that ever happened to him and I am not about to dig myself back into the hole that it took too damn long to climb out of it, and if you think for one minute that I'd even *consider* a repeat, then you don't know me—"

"Car—"

"—as well as you think you do—"

"Car—"

"—and I am so not going there."

Lara clamped a hand over her cousin's mouth. "Hey. Quiet for a second, will ya?" She took her hand away, just an inch, fully prepared to slam it back in place if Cara even thought about opening it again.

"Good. Now shut up and listen to me for a second." Lara tucked her hand under her thigh. "I don't know if you just heard yourself, but everything you were saying about Dale? You're projecting that onto Nick."

"I am not—"

Lara whipped her hand out. "I mean it; stop talking." She waited until Cara scrunched her face into a scowl before nodding.

Her hand went back under her thigh. "Okay, then. What I heard you saying in that lovely little tirade is that you don't want to be hurt like Dale hurt you ever again, and by giving in to what Nick wants, by opening yourself up to a more serious relationship with him, you're opening yourself up to the possibility that he might do it."

"That's ridiculous, Lar. Nick's not Dale."

Lara crossed her arms, sat back, and smiled.

"Oh, you think you're so smart, don't you?" Cara socked her in the stomach with a pillow.

"Uh, if I were so smart, I would have dodged that punch." Lara shuffled around on her seat so she could protect her midsection from any more wayward pillow attacks. "But seriously, Car, think about it. Nick's done nothing but treat you wonderfully, given you your space, and now he wants to live with you. Where's the problem?"

"The problem is..." Her mouth swished back and forth in a classic four-year-old's temper tantrum grumpy-face look, one Cara had perfected at age two and never outgrown.

"Yes?"

"What if he can't live with me? What if it's *not* okay that I fold the towels in thirds as soon as I'm finished using them? What if he can't stand having a utensil drawer that's arranged by size and usage? What if he leaves the toilet seat up?"

Lara tucked the pillow under her arms and tried really hard not to laugh. If only that had been her and Jeff's problem.

"Honey, those are minor things. I know, I know. You don't see them like that, but you and Dale were compatible that way and it still didn't work out. Maybe this is the Universe's way of telling you to give Nick a chance. Try something different. Go outside your comfort zone."

Or maybe it was the Universe's way of telling *her* that because Gage was *waaay* outside her comfort zone.

Cara got it the same time she did. "Oh, like I should *be adventurous*?"

It was her turn to get socked in the stomach with the pillow.

Which erupted into a giggle-fest of pillow smacking that sent a cloud of used tissues snow-falling onto the rug.

When the giggles subsided, they were on the floor in front of the sofa with the tissues squashed beneath their butts.

"We're a pair, aren't we?" Cara said, slumping against Lara's back.

"We're something, that's for sure. Two women terrified of the one thing everyone else seems to want."

"Love."

"I was going to say commitment."

"Aren't they the same thing?"

"Not in my world. What about yours?"

Cara shrugged. "True. I loved Dale, but that didn't have a damn thing to do with his commitment."

"Jeff, too."

"Pricks."

"Yeah."

"What about Gage?"

"Oh, I'm sure he'll become one eventually, but right now, no, he's not."

Cara sat up and squidged around with her legs curled beneath her. "Why do you think he'll eventually become one? He seems like a nice guy. He certainly seems like he's into you."

Lara picked a pair of tissues off her left thigh and flicked them onto the stack of newspapers on the coffee table. "Because guys like him always do. I mean, I'm okay, but look at him. He can get any woman he wants and then I'll be out the door. Been there, don't want to do it again."

"Ah." Cara scrunched the tissues in the front page of the sports section. "Jeff rearing his ugly head."

"Jeff's head was not ugly. That was part of the problem."

"I wasn't talking about the one on his shoulders."

That got a chuckle out of Lara. "I wish I could say you were right, but that wasn't Jeff's problem either."

"Bullshit. That little head of his got a sucky idea in its tiny little pea-sized brain and decided you weren't good enough for the collective *it* that was Jeff McMonster."

Lara raised an eyebrow. "McMonster? Please tell me you never called me that when I had his last name."

"Of course not. And I only called him that in my mind. Though I think I might have slipped up once. His mom gave me a funny look at that last birthday party you had for him."

The birthday party where she'd wanted to show him her idea for her cake business. She'd slaved over that cake, and dammit, it'd been good. She'd taken pictures of it and it would stand up to the ones she made now. But Jeff had been horrified that his wife had *baked a cake* instead of ordering it from the high-end bakery his firm used.

And she'd stood there, taking his derision because *she* hadn't wanted to make a scene.

"Can you imagine what McMonster would say if he saw you with Gage? Especially if he saw Gage at work."

"BeefCake isn't the only thing Gage does, you know."

Cara snorted, the giggles still coming. "Sorry, Lara, but that just sounds so wrong."

"You know what I mean."

"I do, but you have to admit, it's funny. I mean, couldn't they have come up with an, oh, I don't know, subtler name?"

"You have to admit, it gets your attention."

"So do the guys."

"Therefore, it's the perfect name. I mean, there's no sugar-coating what they do. Might as well go for it."

"Words you might want to consider taking to heart, Lar. The man wants you."

"I could say the same thing to you, Car."

The giggles dried up like spilled milk and a roll of Brawny.

Gage was rather brawny…

Cara ran a hand through her curls and Lara refrained from telling her she looked like Medusa. That'd been their secret terror back in high school. With good reason.

"Okay, I will if you will."

"Gage hasn't asked me to move in with him." And she was *not* mentioning the lap dance thing. TMI, even between cousins.

"Not that." Cara had mastered the Evil Eye from their Italian grandmother on their fathers' side. "Give him a chance. Give you guys a chance to get to that point. And I'll see if I can convince Nick about the forty-eight hour thing. Maybe seventy-two if he's lucky."

Progress. Cara was definitely making progress.

Now, did *she* have the courage to do so as well?

Chapter 15

The Universe decided not to cooperate.

Between Gage's day job and her sudden influx of orders, not to mention his after-hours BeefCake, Inc. activities, there wasn't any time for them to finish what they'd started. By Thursday night—at eleven-oh-seven—Lara had to think that the Universe was trying to tell her something.

"I hate fondant," Cara muttered, trying to open her car with her key upside down.

Lara flipped it over for her. "Fondant is paying your mortgage."

"Hey, I have an idea. Let's make a bunch of fifties and hundreds out of the stuff. Think the tellers at the bank would cash them?"

Lara put her hand on Cara's head and pushed her down into the driver's seat like a cop with a suspect. "I'm not so sure you ought to be driving home."

Cara sank back against the seat. "I'm not. I'm going to Nick's."

"You did it? You convinced him?"

Cara nodded. "I told him relationships were all about compromise. I was willing if he was." She opened one eye. "Plus, it's closer than my place right now."

Lucky Cara. Gage's house was an extra half hour beyond hers, and at eleven o'clock at night, too far to drive. Plus his sister and nephew were staying there.

Yeah, what was with the Universe anyway?

"Drive carefully. Text me when you get there."

"You too, Lar." Cara pulled the door shut, turned on the car, and lowered her window. "Love you."

Lara practically flopped into her driver's seat. "You,

too."

God, she was tired. She didn't think she'd ever been this bone-weary. They were going to have to splurge for the rubber mats by the prep tables that she hadn't wanted to spend profits on yet, but the Crocs she wore didn't cut it on fifteen hour days. Her back was killing her.

She turned on the A/C, rolled up her windows, and cranked the show tunes station to loud, needing something to keep her awake, but the fact that she couldn't sing shouldn't have to keep others awake.

She caught a glimpse of herself in the rear view mirror. Oh, God, her curls had tightened up like corkscrews thanks to the humidity, with green buttercream "highlights" from when Cara had turned the mixer on too high and sent frosting flying all over the place (note to self: check the top of the cabinets tomorrow before sugar-addict mice show up). *She* looked like Medusa. Good thing she wasn't seeing Gage tonight; he'd run screaming in the opposite direction.

Although, since he'd put up with her Zambuca coma, maybe he wouldn't.

How in the world had he been interested in her that night?

She'd never thought to ask Jeff what had attracted him to her back in the beginning. She'd met him at a restaurant she was reviewing. She'd been sitting at the bar, sampling the menu with all the self-confidence of a recent college graduate who'd landed her dream job, and he took the seat beside her. One thing had led to another and he asked for her number. He was nine years older, gorgeous in a blond, country club sort of way, with a law degree and the right amount of charming to get her stomach twirling with butterflies.

She'd figured out later—too late—that her age had been her biggest draw for him. Someone he could mold into his perfect ideal of a partner's wife. Even before the night she'd caught him cheating on her with the blonde, she'd thought he should have been with someone like the bimbo. He'd dated a few model types before her, but he said the Barbie and Ken comments had gotten old over the years. He'd wanted something—someone—different, and a short, dark, curvy Italian was definitely different. The fact that she'd hung on his every word probably only added to the appeal.

For a little while at least. At least, she'd *thought* they had a couple of good years. But then she'd caught him, and well…

He should've gone with the trophy wife in the first place. Blue-blood instead of pasta-sauce. Those types would never want any career other than being his perfect hostess.

She wondered what his fiancée did for a living. Or didn't do. And if she were named Barbie.

Lara pulled into her condo's parking lot as the last note of *Evita's* hit song faded away. She wasn't a big fan of the Madonna version, but at least she knew all the words. Jeff's fiancée's name didn't matter. Nor did the fiancée.

Nor did Jeff.

But Gage, on the other hand… What did he see when he looked at her? Was he into pasta-sauce? He'd been into steak and potatoes, so they had that in common. But was that enough of a foundation for a relationship?

And who was to say he even wanted one? A couple of good nights, yes, he was definitely on board for that, but the long-haul?

Lara climbed up the steps on the walkway to her condo. She was thirty-years-old; she needed to think about the long haul. Guys didn't have to worry about it so much, but her eggs weren't getting any younger, and if the pain in her lower back was any indication, she wasn't going to be up for chasing toddlers around for many more years.

She couldn't waste those years with a guy just out for a good time. Great sex, no commitment, get together when they could… all of that in-the-moment stuff would've been fine in her twenties—except she'd blown those by being married to Mr. Ken Doll—but this was the rest of her life she was thinking about. She needed to stay focused on that and not the fact that Gage was like sugar on a stick and all she wanted to do was lick.

She climbed the two steps to her front porch, opened the screen door—

And saw the flowers.

Not roses. Of course not. Roses would be too common. Too cliché. Too *trophy wife.*

These were lilies. Tiger lilies, day lilies, calla lilies, with irises and chrysanthemums mixed in, running the gamut from red, to orange, and every shade of pink there was—with strands of rhinestones woven through.

Saw these and thought of you.
But you're prettier.
~ G

Okay, maybe there was something to be said for being in the moment.

Chapter 16

"Remember to leave the sunflowers in the cooler until the last minute, Cara, so they don't wilt. This heat is going to be a killer on all the frosting." Lara shoved several rolled-up dish towels under the box of sunflowers on the back seat of Cara's car. She'd had to cut the stalks down to four feet instead of five, and also come up with a last-minute way to attach the actual flower part to them because she needed the van for the beach party delivery and Cara's backseat was significantly shorter than how she'd planned to transport them. "And add another delivery van to our wish list."

"Before or after that second mixer?"

"How about at the same time?"

Cara slid into the driver's seat, knocking her chef's hat off in the process. "I think we'd kill ourselves to do it simultaneously, Lara. Seriously, I'm beat. I don't know how you've been able to keep going."

Sheer determination inspired by Jeff's monthly alimony checks.

"You remember how to connect the stalks—"

"Yes, yes, I remember. Hell, I dreamed about it last night, you have me so worried I'm going to do it wrong. It's not rocket science, Lar. If I can pass the CPA exam, I can certainly screw a few bolts into some bamboo."

"But don't screw them in too tightly or you'll crack it and it'll fall over. And if they fall over—"

"It'll have a domino effect on the rest of the garden. Yes, I know. I get it. I think that's why I was up half the night last night."

"Maybe that had to do with Nick."

Cara yanked the door closed. "That was the first half

of the night. You commandeered the rest of it. Now let me get out of here or I'll never get there on time. Have fun at the beach party."

Lara stepped away from the car so Cara could leave, and swiped her forearm across her forehead. It felt like she was going to the beach. Minus the nice sea breeze. Only the beginning of June and already Mother Nature had decided to let out all the stops, upping the heat factor so it felt more like the middle of August.

Especially when she pulled the van up to the party and saw Gage standing there in shorts, a tank top, a pair of flip flops, with his hair turned blond by long days in the sun. The man looked better to eat than one of her cupcakes.

"Hey, Cupcake."

Forget the fondant; *she* was melting. "What are you doing here?"

"Here, let me help you with that." He picked up the Ferris wheel from the back of the van. "Two of my guys are here to perform. Gina is Bryan's cousin."

"His cousin?" She slid the gurney out, unfolded the legs, set the brakes, then went to work dragging the sheet cake onto it. "You didn't happen to have anything to do with us getting this job, did you?"

He shrugged. "Gina needed dessert, you have dessert. Seemed like a perfect solution."

He just kept hammering at her armor, didn't he?

"Thank you." She worked the words around the lump in her throat—and the tight rein she had on her emotions. Not every good-looking guy was like Jeff. Gage was proving that.

"You're welcome. Where do you want this?" Gage held up the Ferris wheel and his biceps flexed.

And Gage *definitely* wasn't like Jeff.

She wiped a drop of perspiration off her forehead. It was really hot here in the sun. "Gina said she'd have two tables for me."

"Ah, yes. They're next to the massage room addition. Follow me."

Gladly. His nylon shorts hung off his butt with a tempting sway, and every so often they curved over his cheeks very nicely.

Yep, really hot here in the sun.

He emptied the rest of the van for her while she set up the wheel and put the finishing touches on the sheet cake.

"These look great, Lara." He walked behind the table and handed her the box of brochures, leaning in for a quick kiss. "You look great, too."

She grabbed her chef's hat self-consciously. "The heat must be melting your brain. No one looks great in a chef's hat."

"You do." He kissed her again—too quick and not near enough tongue action. Matter of fact, *no* tongue action.

She sighed and reminded herself that that was a good thing. The baker shouldn't be drooling all over her cupcakes. All over Gage? Sure. Cupcakes? Notsomuch.

She fanned her cheeks. "Boy, it sure is hot tonight."

"It is now." He gave her that sideways smile that was guaranteed to heat her blood even more than the sun, and ran a knuckle down her arm. "I've missed you."

She shivered, which was ridiculous in this heat. "Me, too. Thanks for the flowers."

"You already thanked me for them."

"A text doesn't count. I wanted to thank you in person."

"I'll hold you to that, say, until after this shindig?"

She wasn't going to be finished here until after eleven, then had to get the van back, clean the utensils, trays, and the Ferris wheel, and get everything ready for tomorrow. "Okay."

This time he ran the knuckle over the tip of her nose.

"Great. It's a date."

She shivered again.

"Gage!" A woman ran up to the table. A really pretty woman.

"Geen—what's up? Have you met Lara?"

Lara relaxed a little. Gina. Bryan's cousin. If Gage had wanted her, he'd had years to make his move.

"Nice to meet you." Gina's welcome was half-hearted at best. Ah, well, Lara was used to Mrs. Applebaum, so this was nothing. The client was always right. "Gage, we have a problem."

"What is it?"

Gina glanced at Lara. "It's um… Maybe we better talk about this in private."

Lara repeated her *the customer is always right* mantra and waved them away. "Go ahead. We can do the cake cutting whenever you want."

"Great. Thanks." Gina dragged him away, and Lara couldn't really complain. Gage looked as good going as… coming.

Yeah. It was *really* freaking hot out today.

"What's going on, Geen?" Gage hurried to keep up with her.

"Tanner's, um, indisposed."

He arched an eyebrow at her. "And?"

"He's not in any shape to perform."

"What do you mean he can't perform?" Gage was already moving toward the house. Shit. He didn't need this. Tonight was the grand opening of the new day spa he'd built for Gina, and her friends and clients were in BeefCake's key client demographic. He'd been hoping to get some business out of tonight, but that wouldn't happen if this gig went down badly.

He strode through the kitchen, but stopped when he

hit the hallway. "Where is he?"

Gina pointed upstairs. "In the bathroom. It's not pretty."

He'd seen Tanner in his costume numerous times. If Gina said it wasn't pretty, something bad had happened.

"Shit." He took the stairs two at a time.

Tanner was curled up on the bathroom floor, Carlo standing by looking helpless.

"What happened?" Gage knelt over him.

"I don't know. I haven't been feeling all that great lately and when I was getting ready I got a really sharp pain." He clutched his abdomen. "I'm sweating like a stuck pig. I hope it's not my appendix."

So did Gage. It'd put their best earning guy out of commission, and hell, Tanner was *not* a good patient. "Gina, call an ambulance."

"On its way. I'll go wait for them." She ran from the room.

"Just relax, Tan. We'll get you to the hospital and see what's what."

"I'm sorry for letting you down, man."

"Hey, don't sweat it. Just get better."

The front door opened and he heard the EMTs climb the stairs. Gage cleared out of the bathroom to give them room to work.

"I can handle this by myself, boss," said Carlo. "I'll dance twice as long. Give them their money's worth."

Gage shook his head. It figured, right? Normally, Bryan would be here. Gina was, after all, his cousin. He should've been the one to oversee it, but Gage had wanted to get close to Lara, so they'd traded. With Bry running security at the fiftieth birthday party (those middle-aged women tended to be a lot more grabby than he would have ever expected), it was up to Gage to fix this.

There was only one way he could.

"Get me the costume, Carlo. I've got a spare pair of shorts in my truck." He'd started carrying them after the first time he'd had to fill in. Dancing was one thing, sharing jock space with a guy an entirely different one. He'd worn a condom and a sock that first time and after that, had kept his own emergency pair in his truck. It'd saved his ass—and his dick—more than a few times.

He ran out to the truck as Tanner was being loaded into the ambulance and glanced over at Lara's table. She was busy with a group of guests. Hopefully they'd keep her that way through the performance. If he'd known he was going to have to dance, he wouldn't have had Gina hire her. Private lap dances were one thing, but publicly? This was going to be too personal.

Ten minutes later, he had Tanner's costume on and was sweating bullets backstage.

He shook out his arms, rolled his neck. This was ridiculous. He never had stage fright. He'd done this dance dozens of times. Had performed hundreds. Maybe thousands. He'd just have to do what he'd always done. Pick out one woman in the crowd and dance for her.

Lara was in the crowd.

That became an issue when his cock realized it, too.

Shit.

The music started and he smacked Carlo in the arm. "Break a leg."

"You, too."

He'd like to break his *third* one because it was becoming way too interested in the fact that Lara would be watching. When he'd proposed the lap dance bet, it'd been with the idea that it would be just the two of them. A rise in his pants wouldn't have been a problem—it would have been the solution, actually, if one thing had led to another, but now? He was going to have to pick out a grandmother to focus on.

Even that thought didn't shrink him. Great.

His cue came and Gage sucked in a deep breath, focused on pumping up his pecs, and gyrated onto the stage.

Lara looked up when the music started. The back patio had been ringed with BeefCake, Inc.'s black velvet panels hung from PVC frames, with their logo banner across the front. The blown-up pictures of the guys weren't there, but then, what was the point when the audience was getting the real thing?

The two dancers came out and—

One was Gage.

Oh my.

He wore a black vest, a bow tie, and a tight pair of black pants that left nothing to her imagination.

And then he started gyrating—which *really* left nothing to her imagination.

Wow, the guy could *move*. What a shame she'd missed out on those moves by passing out in his bed.

He did a couple of pelvic thrusts and his six pack—no, *eight*-pack—contracted in mouth-watering hotness. His partner was doing it, too, but, well, *he* wasn't doing for her what Gage was.

The crowd loved it. The catcalls started and women worked their way up to the stage.

Their boyfriends worked *their* way to her table. She totally got why.

Gage raised his arms and put them behind his neck, his pecs dancing in time to the heavy downbeat that thudded through her veins down to one spot in particular. He flexed his biceps with the rhythm, first one, then the other, then he spun around and—holy hell—shook his ass in triple time.

Those nylon shorts he'd worn earlier should be

burned because they did absolutely nothing for his assets like those pants did. The black leather molded the tightest glutes she'd seen in a long time—well, since the Morning After in his hotel room.

"Uh, miss?" Some guy snapped his fingers in her face. "You have any red velvet cupcakes? They're my girlfriend's favorite."

Lara shook her head, wrenching her gaze off Gage. Business first.

"Um, yes. I do. They're… Let me see…" Damn, she was all flustered. *Business, Lara.*

Right. Get her head in the game. And out of Gage's pants.

It was really freaking hot this evening.

She handed the guy the cupcake.

"Thanks. Let's see if this works," he muttered before heading into the throng of dancing women.

"What about chocolate?" asked another guy. "With chocolate icing? And in the middle? The more chocolate the better."

Lara handed him her Devil's Delight Special that had all three.

Another guy wanted strawberry shortcake, another cheesecake, all of them carrying the cupcakes back into the gyrating crowd, probably to tempt their girlfriends' attention elsewhere.

Good luck with that. Her cupcakes were good, but nothing was going to compare to the sheer perfection of the male form pelvic-thrusting to the sultry, sexy downbeat of the music up there on that stage. This show was a feast for all the senses and sugar was not the taste those women wanted. Gage and Bryan had certainly known what they were doing when they put their business plan together and—*whew*!—they certainly knew how to work a crowd.

The women were practically screaming. Someone

actually tossed a bra on stage. Gage's partner picked it up and winked at a woman in the front row.

Totally irrationally, a tide of green rose up inside Lara, threatening to choke her.

Actually, Lara would like to choke that woman. She hadn't come on to Gage, but what if he'd been on that side of the stage? He must be so used to stuff like that happening. Hell, look how she'd thrown herself at him at the bachelorette party and he hadn't even had his clothes half off. God only knew what she would have done if he had.

What could Gage possibly see in her? The man was sheer physical perfection—more so than Jeff had ever been and *he'd* left her.

Cara's words reverberated in her mind. *Gage wants you. Be adventurous.*

Easy to say; Gage was a huge risk to her fragile ego.

Luckily, she had a steady stream of jealous, cupcake-searching boyfriends to keep her mind off of him, but every so often she'd glance up and… yeah, that tingling would swirl again low in her belly.

The vest came off. He was twirling it over his head like a lasso when she looked up and her mouth went dry as a bone.

Okay, not a good word choice because it sent her gaze right to his crotch, and oh yeah, there was *nothing* left to her imagination. Even from back here she could tell the man had no issues in that department.

Then he ripped the pants off.

Holy mother of— She reached for the water bottle she kept beneath the table and squirted some down her shirt.

It did nothing to cool her off.

He wore tight little black shorts on those gyrating hips, with way too many bump-and-grinds for her liking—well, no, that wasn't true. She liked; she just didn't want other women to like as well.

And then the dollar bills came out. Of course, in the span of about thirty seconds, Gage was sporting a mint's worth.

She was jealous. She had no right to be, really, but *he'd* kissed *her* when she arrived. Granted, it hadn't been as involved as the one a few days ago, but they did have plans afterwards. Those women needed to keep their fingers and their dollar bills to themselves.

In a perfect world, that would happen, but this was what Gage did for a living. He played to the fantasies of those women. He let them shove their grubby little fingers inside his pants. Maybe some of them would go farther, who knew? Did he often take them up on their offers? After all, he had with her.

Lara sat down on a stool. God, she hadn't thought about it that way. She'd been there that night, more than willing, and he'd taken advantage of it.

Well, no, he hadn't taken advantage of her, just her offer. He'd actually been an incredible gentleman about it, but still. It couldn't have been the first time he'd picked up a woman and taken her to his room—would he want it to be the last?

Lara did *not* share.

She blotted the back of her neck with a dish towel. She was being ridiculous. Cara would smack her if she could hear her. *Be adventurous. He wants you.*

But for how long?

That was the question. She couldn't go through getting dumped again. It hurt too much. Was too demeaning. Debilitating. Love just wasn't worth it—and who was to say love was even on the table? Maybe this was just good ol' fashioned lust. That, for whatever reason, Gage found something interesting in her, but a couple of turns in the sack and it'd be over with.

Then where would she be?

He and his partner were making a killing up there on that stage. He could really dance. And didn't they say that the way a man danced was directly related to the way he—

"Not bad, huh?" Gina walked up to the table.

Lara shot back to her feet. "Um, yes. You've had a great turnout for this event. Thanks, again, for using Cavallo's Cups & Cakes."

"I was talking about Gage." Gina nodded to the stage where Gage was now teasing the crowd by feathering the dollars along the waistband of his shorts.

If he took those off, she'd melt into a big pile of goo right here.

"Um, yeah, nice. He and Bryan have a good business model."

She so wanted to bury her face in the sheet cake when Gina smirked.

"That's the first time I've heard it put quite that way, but okay." Gina picked up a Tasty Temptations cupcake. "So Gage tells me this is a new business for you."

Business. Thank God. That was the perfect thing to get her mind off Gage's abs—and ass and thighs and arms. "It's not new. My cousin and I have been in business for seven months now. We have many satisfied customers and orders are coming in every day." She handed Gina one of the brochures, trying not to stare over her shoulder at Gage's rippling abs, but oh, was it hard not to. "Here are some testimonials and I can get you phone numbers if you'd like to talk to them directly."

Gina took the brochure. "Relax. I hired you on Gage's word, and if you're good enough for him, you're good enough for me." Gina took a bite of the cupcake. "Just make sure you *are* good for him."

She was talking about cupcakes, right?

Lara was pondering her response to that when, all of a

sudden, there was a huge commotion up at the performance as a woman *dove* onto the stage. Like, seriously, *dove*. Launched from her girlfriends' impromptu springboard made of their crossed hands—and they'd tossed her right at Gage.

"Oh hell. Are you *kidding* me?" Gina dropped the cupcake onto the table and took off running.

Lara could only stare as Gage staggered under the impact, but somehow managed to stay on his feet with the woman wrapped around him like blanket. *Kissing* him.

Oh, God. Lara closed her eyes. She couldn't watch it. Sure, he hadn't instigated it, but geez, he didn't need to with women literally throwing themselves at him.

She couldn't go through this again.

The music shut off amid the cheering crowd. Great. Poor Gage was getting assaulted and people were cheering the clinging vine on. Lara opened her eyes and saw Gina and a couple of guys from the crowd trying to pry the woman off him, a scene so similar to when she'd seen the blonde wrapped around Jeff at the Schmitts' barbecue. Jeff had extricated himself and told her it hadn't been his fault—that she'd come on to him—but the damage had been done. His ego had been stroked—probably not the only thing—and he'd started looking around. Started finding things wrong with her. Criticizing, demeaning, demoralizing.

Finally, they pried the leech off of Gage, and wouldn't you know? He looked out over the crowd, across the expanse of the backyard, his gaze seeking her like a heat-guided missile.

The apology she saw there hit her every bit as hard.

She needed to find a nice, non-descript-looking guy. Forget about someone hot and sexy; all women wanted that. She needed to find someone she could trust; someone who'd want to settle down with her for the rest of their lives and be content to not look elsewhere. The passion might not be what she felt with Gage, but at least she'd be able to count on forever.

Chapter 17

Gage took the fastest—and coldest—shower known to mankind after the performance, threw on his tank and shorts, and went off in search of Lara.

He'd seen the look on her face when the woman had ambushed him. If he hadn't been concentrating so hard on not looking at Lara, he would've seen what had been happening right in front of him before it'd gotten to the point it'd gotten to. But he hadn't and the look on Lara's face worried the hell out of him.

Leslie had proven just how big an issue jealousy could become. Not that it should have. When he was with someone, he was with her and her alone. But it would take a very secure woman to put up with his moonlighting career. He knew that. Until he'd seen the stricken look on Lara's face from the stage, he'd hoped she'd be that woman.

She ought to be, dammit, regardless of what that prick of an ex-husband had done or said to her. She was beautiful, she was kind, she was fun, and she was successful at what she did—not to mention, sexy as hell. How could she not be secure?

That's what he wanted to find out. To get to the bottom of. To convince her that what happened tonight was nothing. It had no impact on what they were starting.

But hell—the idea that they were starting something terrified him almost as much as seeing that look on her face again.

He got waylaid by a couple of the single women and did his best to extricate himself without being rude. It was part of the job and he couldn't afford to be unprofessional with all this potential business around. But he had to get to

Lara.

"Gage!" Gina grabbed his arm. "I'm really sorry about that. I don't know what got into Megan and her crew. Sure, they're rowdy, but to do that…." Gina shook her head.

"It is what it is, Geen. Can't say it's never happened before." And it probably would again. If only he didn't need the money that these gigs brought in.

"Lara seems nice." Gina handed him a beer and walked with him toward the cupcake table. "Not your usual type, though."

He took a good long cool guzzle. "Didn't know I had a type."

"Gorgeous, blonde, and bitchy. Last five of your girlfriends treated me like I was the help."

"You're exaggerating."

"If you say so."

"But Lara's gorgeous."

Gina cocked her head. "Not bombshell, though."

"You know, Geen, at some point a guy does grow up. Starts thinking with the head on his shoulders instead of the one in his pants." He took another swig, not wanting to think about *that*.

"I'm sure she'll be thrilled to know she's the logical choice and not the one you want to jump all over."

He choked on the beer. "What's with you tonight? You're not usually so in my face about my love life."

She exhaled. "You're right. I'm sorry. It's just that you surprised me with her. I'd never expected you to want someone like her."

"What do you mean, someone like her?"

"Nice. Down to earth. Real."

"Oh." He looked at her. "Have the others really been that bad?"

"Not bad so much as not anyone I could see you

sticking with. Her? Yeah, I can see you sticking with her." She *clinked* the neck of her bottle with his. "I gotta go cut the cake. Good luck, Gage."

He watched her head over to the other table. *Stick with her*. Gina was getting a little ahead of herself. He couldn't think long term. Not now while Connor and Missy and Jayna needed him. There were too many things to do and never enough time to do them. Look at how he and Lara hadn't been able to connect all week. A few texts—not even a phone call—weren't the basis for a relationship.

Plus, they were both too busy building their businesses. She'd come off a bad marriage, and he… well, he didn't know when he'd be ready for forever. Right now, day-to-day was a challenge. And after tonight's debacle, he was facing yet another one.

"Nice show," said a woman who got in line behind him for the cupcakes.

"Thanks."

"Do you do private parties?"

Gage gave her the slow smile that made them melt, while giving him the time to assess the situation. He'd been propositioned hundreds of times. Had taken a few up on their offers in the past, but, these days, was no longer interested.

"Parties of four are the smallest we do and they require a two-dancer minimum." He and Bry had set up that guideline right off the bat, both of them having had too many encounters that could have gone the wrong way back in their prime.

He watched the dollar signs scroll through the woman's brain. Saw her take out a mental scale and weigh that amount against the possibility she'd come out on the lucky end of that bargain. He'd love to tell her that percentage was zero—no one slept with paying customers on company time, which was why he'd had to wait until the show was over to leave with Lara that first night.

"Do you have a card?"

He pulled one from his shorts pocket. "Sure do. Give us a call tomorrow. We'll put you on the schedule and I can round up a couple of the guys."

"Oh, but you could do it. I mean…" Her blush was a complete affectation. "You did it so well up there."

Yes, just what he thought. There would be no party. Or if there were, she'd try to make it end up being a party of one—er, three.

"Tonight was a special occasion. I don't dance anymore. I own the company."

Her eyebrows went up and she moved a little closer. "Is there any way I can change your mind?"

He dropped the smile. No need to reel her in. She'd either hire him or she wouldn't, but he wasn't selling his soul for a couple hundred bucks. Bad enough he was selling his body.

"Sorry, afraid not. Like I said, tonight was a special occasion."

"It certainly was." She licked her lips.

God save him from women on the prowl.

He got out of line. He didn't really want a cupcake anyway, not when he wanted the cupcake *baker* instead.

If she was still speaking to him.

He slipped behind her table, watching her work the crowd. She was personable with the right amount of professionalism so that you knew each one of her cupcakes had her personal stamp of approval on them. Having tasted them, he could attest to her mastery of her craft.

Having tasted *her*, he could attest to her mastery of *him*.

"If you want a flavor we don't have," she said to two women who had brochures in their hands, "I'll be more than happy to look into providing it for you."

He wasn't going to comment on her flavor. That, he wanted to keep for his knowledge alone.

Lara handed the last of the sea-turtle themed cupcakes to one of the guests. Gage knew she kept more beneath the table in the wheeled insulated box he'd helped unload earlier, so he hiked up his shorts, hunkered down beside her, grabbed a box, and passed it up to her.

"Thanks," she said with that tenuous smile that socked him in the solar plexus.

They needed to talk.

"What else can I do for you?" He meant it in every sense of the words.

She swallowed, a tiny movement, but a revealing one. Yes, he definitely needed to get her alone to clear the air.

"Are there any more sea horses? I didn't make many because, typically, kids are the ones to go for the peppermint stick flavor, not adults. But everyone seems to have worked up an appetite for something sweet."

He had an appetite for something sweet all right. And her name was Lara Cavallo.

He dug through the boxes, but the sea horses were nowhere to be found. "Looks like you're out."

Lara didn't miss a beat; she recommended one of the conch shell cupcakes to the guest instead. Said cotton candy was just as sweet and delicious as peppermint stick.

All he could think of was licking something. Preferably her legs. He was sitting right next to them and it wasn't possible for him to not be aware of them. Smooth and tanned and bare… He just wanted a nibble.

He adjusted his shorts. He'd never have thought cupcakes could be a turn on, but with Lara, they definitely were.

She moved to the other end of the table at that point, so Gage threw himself into making himself useful over here, where he wouldn't be tempted—

Scratch that. He'd *always* be tempted around her.

What was it about her that got to him? Gina was right; he'd never been with someone like Lara. Forget her looks—not that he could—but it was that *real* thing he was focused on. She'd been so sexy that night in the club. Her dark, sultry looks had captured his attention in a sea of fake blondes with too much silicone and spray tans, society's strange perception of a supposed ideal.

Then she'd had a little too much to drink and he'd had the chance to meet the real Lara. *In vino veritas* had never been more true. She was adorable. So proud of her bakery, so up for partying and dancing and being with him. She'd even wanted to make out on the dance floor. He'd been the one with the restraint then, wanting to keep that moment private, both because of the ribbing he'd take from the guys and because he'd wanted to savor it. Savor her.

He still did.

Gina walked up while Gage was pulling out the last two boxes of cupcakes, did her schmoozing thing on the mic, then cut the cake. The entire party descended on the table then, and Gage had zero chance of talking to Lara, as they were too busy with handing out desserts for any personal time.

But he'd make time for it once this was finished.

Chapter 18

Gage helped Lara break down her set up and pack everything onto the gurney for the walk back to her van. He'd offered to push it for her, but she'd been adamant that she could handle it, and having two sisters, he'd learned that when a woman says she can handle it, she can handle it, and he'd better leave her the hell alone to do so.

"Lara, about what happened with the show tonight—"

"Oh, yes. That. How are you? Are you okay? What made her do that? Do you know her?"

She was babbling and he found it adorable. Found *her* adorable. And sexy as hell. When was the last time he'd found a woman adorable *and* sexy at the same time? Maybe Gina was onto something about his blonde bombshell type.

"I'm fine. Her pride is probably more injured than anything else."

"Does that happen a lot? Women throwing themselves at you?" She nibbled on her bottom lip while she avoided eye contact by lifting the cake tins in front of her, perfectly obstructing her field of vision.

What Gage wouldn't give to get her focused on him instead.

"Technically, her friends threw her at me."

She lowered the cake tins and glared at him.

Okay, light-hearted banter was not the way to go. "Uh, no, it doesn't happen a lot, but it *is* an occupational hazard. You should know that regardless of our company's non-fraternization policy, I have my own set of standards, and public lovemaking is not one of them."

Private on the other hand…

She wheeled the gurney against the van and fished in her purse for her keys. "But I thought you said you don't dance anymore."

"Tanner got sick. It might be his appendix. I had to fill in. That's why Bryan or I go to every performance. You never know what's going to happen, and like this case, it was a good thing we had someone else available. People paid for a show; they deserved to get one."

"You certainly gave it to them."

He wasn't sure if that was praise or condemnation. "Did you enjoy it? Well, before Megan got out of control, I mean."

"I'd have to have been dead not to." Lara yanked the double doors open and turned back to the gurney. "Every woman here tonight liked it. You have to know that."

"Yours is the only opinion that matters."

She stopped midway to the gurney for the span of a heartbeat.

Two.

"Lara?"

She took a breath, then reached for the stack of flattened boxes. "I'm sure you'll be swimming with business first thing tomorrow."

That wasn't what he wanted to hear.

"I mean, I saw Maryellen Bledsoe talking to you afterwards. That'll be good for a bachelorette party."

"*She's* getting married?" Put a whole new spin on the woman coming on to him.

"No, her daughter." Lara collapsed the gurney and slid it in the back of the van, then she turned around and brushed off her hands. "Thanks for helping me with everything, Gage. I appreciate it."

"So that's it?"

"I don't know what you mean."

"I think you do." He crossed his arms, very aware of what that did to his chest and his pecs, and the effect on women. He wasn't above using whatever God gave him to get her attention. Cheap shot, maybe, but he was desperate. "I didn't come on to Megan. She and her friends got a little out of control. It happens, but no harm, no foul. It's not as if I'm going to take her up on the offer."

She tugged her chef's hat off. "That's just it, Gage. It's not nothing. Every woman here wanted you."

"Yes."

"Yes? That's what you have to say? You know it?"

"Of course. They're supposed to. That's what the show is all about. Delivering a fantasy. It's what I set out to do."

"But their boyfriends were right here."

"You don't think the guys go to strip clubs? If anything, we've brought some equality to the relationships."

"How can it be equal if they're lusting after someone else? Isn't the whole point of a relationship to be *in* one? Isn't that why people form relationships, to be with that one person? I don't get the looking at other people thing. Why bother to be in a relationship at all if that's what you're going to do?"

So her ex had cheated on her, too. A burning desire to rip the guy apart, limb from limb, roared through him. The prick didn't deserve to live. He certainly hadn't deserved her. What in the world would make the man who'd had *Lara* go for someone else?

But thank God he had, because now Gage had a chance with her.

And just like that, his world shifted.

He *did* want a chance with her. More than just a few texts or a stolen night here and there, he wanted *her*. To be with her. Explore what was happening between them. Yeah, it'd be tough, but it'd be tougher not to have her in his life.

He reached for her hand. He needed to touch her and

he wanted her feel him. "Lara, I can't define other people's relationships. There's a demand for BeefCake, Inc.; we're fulfilling it. But that doesn't mean it's who I am. That it defines me or how I live my life. You know why I'm doing this. That's the bottom line to me. Connor and Missy. I work my ass off to help them, both at the day job and this. It's the best chance we have. Don't make the mistake of thinking it's who I am. It's not. It's a fantasy—for the clients.

"I go out, put on a show, deliver what they want, and then I leave. Go back to my real life. Missy and Connor and the day job. And you." He brought her hand to his lips and kissed it. "I came back to you. Worked at your table, helped you finish up, cleaned up with you, and packed up for you. Not anyone else."

He could see her wanting to believe him. He wanted to make her believe him, and while actions spoke louder than words, in this instance it would just cloud the issue because she'd seen all that blatant sexuality tonight and hadn't been able to deal with it.

Just like Leslie.

He exhaled, praying she wouldn't call it quits before it'd even started.

Or… did he want her to? It'd make his life a hell of a lot easier.

But not better.

It was that thought that spurred him on. "I'd really like to go somewhere and be with you. However you want to define that, I just want to be with you."

She wanted to; he could see it in the flutter of her pulse in her throat. At the way her eyes flitted to his and that utterly sexy way she nibbled her lip.

He skimmed his fingers along her temple and down along her cheek. "Please, sweetheart. I just want to be with you. Even if it's just to talk. I like talking to you. I like being with you. I've missed you this week. I was hoping you'd felt the same way."

That was the problem. She *did* feel the same way. And it scared the shit out of her. For all of Cara's *be adventurous*, she just wasn't sure she was up for the risk. Look at what had happened tonight: Gage hadn't been in the wrong, but she was ready to crucify him because of it. All she'd been able to think about was what he could see in her. When the other shoe would drop and he'd be all over one of those women—or, hell, maybe more—and she'd be stuck nursing a broken heart *again*.

But then Gage slid those delicious fingertips that had already sent shivers racing from her temple down her cheek to parts farther south, twisting and tumbling through her heart and tummy, and slid them down over her jaw, along her throat to her collarbone. Just the faintest touch, but it had her attention and she hoped… she really hoped that this time, with him, it'd be different. That she could trust what he said. Unlike Jeff.

Jeff.

She was doing it again. Allowing her ex-husband to define her life and how she saw the world.

No freaking way. Jeff had lost that right when he'd chosen someone else.

"You want me, Lara. You want to be with me."

Well, duh.

"And I want to be with you."

She swallowed. *Be adventurous.*

She'd always followed Jeff's decisions. Whatever he'd wanted to do in any situation. Her job, their home, her baking business, which side of the bed she could sleep on, what clothes she should wear… She hadn't realized how controlling he'd been and how much she'd allowed herself to be controlled until everything fell apart.

If she truly wanted freedom from Jeff, she needed to

do what *she* wanted to do.

And she wanted Gage. For as long or as short as she could have him, regardless of what had happened on that stage tonight, or that women had come on to him the entire time. If she didn't trust him, if she gave in to the paranoia, she was letting Jeff win again.

Be adventurous.

Gage hadn't moved. He was about five inches from her, his finger right above her heart and not another part of him touching her, letting her make the decision.

"Yes, Gage. You're right. I do want you. Let's go home."

Chapter 19

To Gage's credit, he didn't break any laws getting them back to her place, but she wouldn't have minded if he had. It was one thing to take the leap, but another to have to second-guess it for twenty-five minutes while she'd followed him in the van.

But it came down to the fact that she wanted him. It was as simple as that, because even though that Megan chick had been all over him, *he* hadn't been all over *her*. It was very important for Lara to remember that. Unlike Jeff who'd been an octopus around Plastic Barbie that night she'd discovered the affair, Gage hadn't been the guilty party, and if she wanted any chance of moving beyond Jeff, she had to allow Gage to be who he said he was without her projecting her issues onto him.

He opened the van door when she shut off the ignition and held out a hand to help her down—or maybe it was to tug her against him.

She went willingly.

"I didn't get the chance to do this properly before," he said before he kissed her.

It was so not a proper kiss.

It was hot and hungry and everything she needed. Those women could fantasize all they wanted, she had the real thing in her arms and soon, hopefully, in her bed.

Oh God. The images she saw in her mind as his tongue did deliciously sinful things to hers, igniting every nerve ending to full steam ahead, about sent her over the top.

"Inside," was all she managed to get out.

But it was all she needed to. Gage grabbed her hand, pressed one last hard kiss to her lips, then practically dragged her up the walkway. They fumbled a bit with her key but ended up both shoving the door open and almost falling inside.

Gage slammed the door behind them and yanked her against him. "So I'm guessing you don't want to talk."

He was so freaking sexy. His aquamarine eyes were drilling into hers, his hard body pressed up against her so she could feel every ridge and plane, and yeah, talking was definitely overrated.

She nibbled her lip, trying to keep the smile off her face. "Well, if that's what you want to do—"

He kissed her. Hard.

She needed that. Needed him. Needed this. She wrapped her arms around him and kissed him back.

He groaned and Lara's knees went buttery at the sound.

Thankfully, Gage hefted her in those strong sculpted arms of his and carried her down the hallway to her bedroom, never once breaking the kiss.

Her feet dangling between his legs, Lara didn't care. All she could focus on was the heat and taste and utter sensuality of his kiss. His lips were amazing, his tongue even more so, and the coiled tension she felt in him was intoxicating.

He flipped on the light switch by her bedroom door.

"What?" She wrenched back when he set her on her feet, the light too glaring.

"I want to see you, Lara. No fumbling in the dark. I want to see everything you're feeling. I want to watch you come apart in my arms. I want to see you smile afterwards."

Which would happen too quickly if he kept saying things like that. She put her hand on his mouth. "Careful. Don't rush this. I want to enjoy every second."

He nipped her fingers. "Trust me, sweetheart, you

will."

She did trust him. As surprising as that was, given what he did for a living and how women came on to him, she did trust him.

That ought to worry her—a lot—but his hands were skimming everywhere, racing fire along her veins and across every nerve ending as they slid beneath the hem of her t-shirt to skim her belly, and she couldn't worry. All she could do was feel. And enjoy.

"So soft and smooth," he whispered. "Like satin."

Satin *sheets* maybe. She wished she had some.

They were going on her shopping list tomorrow.

His fingers dipped beneath the waistband of her skirt. "I want to feel you, Lara. All of you. Touch and taste and tempt every inch of you."

"You already are."

"Oh, sweetheart, you haven't seen anything yet." And with that, he undid the zipper on her skirt to let it fall at her feet, then dragged her shirt over her head, leaving her in nothing but the two scraps of peach silk and lace that constituted her underwear.

So, okay, maybe she'd been hoping this would happen tonight.

Gage sucked in a harsh breath. "My God, you're beautiful."

No, she was self-conscious. After all, he was the beautiful one. With the perfect body. That he'd had on display for everyone to enjoy.

Be adventurous.

Right. She wasn't going to let her insecurities ruin tonight. Gage was here with her, wanted her, and she'd be a fool to let anything get in the way.

So instead, she replayed tonight's dance in her head, imaging that it'd been just the two of them there. No crowd, no other women, no Gina, just Gage and her, and he'd been dancing for her alone. That every circle of his hips, every wink and smile, every hand skimming over his skin and come-hither look in his eyes… all of that had been for her.

She grabbed the neckline of his tank top and ripped.

Gage's eyes flared and, ohmyGod, she couldn't believe she'd done that. She'd never ripped a guy's shirt off before.

He smiled that wickedly sexy side-cocked smile and dropped his hands from her body. "Have at it, Lara."

No time to be embarrassed now. Especially when she was turned on by it.

She grabbed the last bit of fabric holding the shirt together at the bottom and tore it apart, then shoved it down his arms and plastered her lips to his chest. He tasted so good. Soap and sweat and Gage and… arousal. Oh, yeah, she recognized that scent. He wanted her.

Not that she doubted it. The ridge beneath his shorts couldn't hide that.

She ran her palm along his length.

"Lara." He groaned her name and his head fell back, giving her perfect access to that strong corded throat and the pulse beating at its base.

She kissed it. Laved it. Loved it. Then she nipped her way down, savoring every flex of his pecs, to find his nipple. It hardened at the first stroke of her tongue, which was only fair since hers were aching to have his hands and mouth on them.

All the pent up longing and frustration of the three lonely years since she'd been with a man, been *wanted* by a man, rose up inside her. She fought it; if she allowed herself to think about it, it'd ruin what she could have with him.

So she didn't think. Instead, she felt. And oh God, did he feel good.

She ran her hands over that hard body, not an ounce

of fat anywhere. She rubbed her palm along the cut lines by his hips, then over and around to that perfect backside she remembered so well.

"Geez, talk about rushing it." Gage growled against the curve of her neck. "Careful, Lara."

She didn't want to be careful. She'd been careful and it'd gotten her nowhere.

She rammed her hands beneath the waistband and shoved his shorts—the guy went commando—down his legs.

This time, she was the one who pulled back and looked. "My God, *you're* beautiful."

"Men aren't beautiful."

"Not true. You are." She ran a finger down the center of his chest, over every ripped "pack" of the eight-pack, down to that thin line of hair below his navel that led…

Oh yeah. He definitely wanted her.

"Lara? You're sure about this, right? We don't have to do this."

Oh yes they did.

She ran her finger down his treasure trail to the base of him.

And then she ran that finger along the length, stopping at the very tip.

It jerked and Lara looked up at him. "I want you, Gage. Make love to me."

After that, they needed no words. They tore back the sheets on her bed and touched and caressed, taunted and teased each other, gasping and smiling as they discovered each other's bodies. Gage liked the spot beneath his left ear kissed; she liked the inside of her elbow. Gage's feet were ticklish; Lara loved to lick his instep.

Gage loved to lick any part of her.

And she let him. Opened herself and her body up to him, to his desire, and that wickedly talented tongue of his as he discovered all her secret places, dragging her from her three-year hibernation with a vengeance.

"You are so beautiful, Lara," he whispered against her breast as his tongue and his teeth sent pleasure spiraling through her. "You have to know that."

She did now. Right this second because he made her feel that way.

She needed this. Needed him. For however long it lasted.

She rolled on top of him and parked her fists beneath her chin, her body thrumming as she straddled him. "I want you inside of me, Gage."

He jerked beneath her. "Oh baby, that's where I want to be."

God, did he.

She grabbed his shorts when he said the condoms were in the pocket, then sat above him like a conquering diminutive Amazon and rolled the condom down his cock, and Gage thought he'd never seen anyone more beautiful. She was so unbelievably sexy he couldn't understand how she didn't know that. How she could even think to be jealous of any other woman.

He grabbed her hips the moment the condom was in place, put pressure for her to lean forward, then lifted her and slid into her tight, wet heat. "God, Lar, you feel so damn good."

"You're right. I do." She sank down, taking him to the hilt, her beautiful breasts swaying in front of him.

It was more temptation than any man could be expected to endure, and he wasn't about to try to.

He took one tight, hard nipple in his mouth, the sound of her groan sending desire pounding through his veins, swelling his cock inside her so freaking quickly he thought it might blow the top off. He had to think of something—anything—to calm down and keep from rolling them over and pounding into her.

Wait. Why was he fighting that idea?

He had no idea. He flipped her onto her back, slid a hand around her leg and beneath her ass—that delectable curve that fit perfectly in his palm—and pulled her against him so she'd take him deeper.

He smiled when she groaned. "Like that?"

"Uh huh." She arched into him, her head bowing back, and Gage latched on to the pulse in her neck that hammered in time with his.

He flexed his hips, withdrawing just a little, but she sank her nails into his ass.

"Don't leave."

"Honey, I have no intention of it." Ever.

Ever?

Gage stopped flexing. No no no. *Ever* wasn't the issue here. It wasn't on the table for consideration. This was for tonight. A few weeks, maybe, but it couldn't be for*ever*.

She wiggled beneath him. "Gage… please…" she gasped, her lips trailing across his chest, her tongue teasing his nipple, and her hands—sweet Jesus—her hands were roaming his back, his ass, every part of him, urging him back down into her.

He went. He couldn't *not*.

She clamped her legs around his waist. "More, Gage."

He wanted to give her more. So much more.

He pulled out. Sank back in when she whimpered. Pulled back and repeated it all over. And again. And again. So many times, so hard and fast, that when the blinding rush of pleasure seized him, Gage had nothing left in him to fight it.

So he didn't. He rode it and took her with him, as it thundered over them, crashing down only to ebb out and build again like waves on the shore, over and over, the rise and the rush, as he poured himself into her.

She moaned beneath him, her head tossed back, her eyes clamped shut, and she ground out his name as she clenched him, milking every shred of pleasure from his body.

"Lara," he mouthed against her breast, the slick sheen of perspiration sweeter than any of her cupcakes. "That's it, baby. Come for me."

"I… It's…"

Good. He wanted her incoherent. He rocked inside her again, smiling when she gasped…

He kissed her neck. Her cheek. Her lips. Slicked his tongue along them, wanting inside.

She took him in, sucking him into that moist wet heat as her sheath did to his cock, and Gage felt another surge rise inside him.

He flexed his hips. Yes. There. She felt so good clamped around him. He had to move. Again.

"Oh, Gage." Her breath came in a shuddering whisper, setting his already stretched-thin nerves on fire.

He moved again.

Her legs slammed around his ass, her ankles locked, and she arched into him then came apart all around him.

Gage lost control, pounding into her. Rearing back against her crossed ankles, plunging into her, the driving need to claim every part of her spurring him on. He needed this, wanted her, had to have her, every bit. Every part. Every last response.

Her cries echoed in the room, her nails scored his back and her heels—dear God, her heels were jamming down onto his ass, pushing him inside her so far he couldn't tell where he ended and she began.

And then it didn't matter as he came, one long glorious, breath-and-vision-stealing moment suspended in time as she took all he had to give and then some, and Gage hurtled over the edge knowing nothing had ever been like this and never would be again.

And that he could never go back …

It took a while for the tremors to subside, and when he opened his eyes to find her beautiful ones right in front of him, all the hazy sensual satisfaction he was feeling mirrored in them, the tremors started again.

"Hey," he whispered.

"Hey yourself."

"You okay?"

"I think that might be a mild term for what I'm feeling, but yes, I'm okay." Her fingers drew lazy circles on the small of his back and her smile was one of pure satisfaction.

He slid from her body and rolled onto his side, taking her with him. "That was more than okay, you know. I'm going to go with amazing."

"Works for me."

And she worked for him. Which ought to scare him, but didn't. Not anymore.

Gage cupped her cheek and tilted her head back. Kissed her. Rubbed her lips with his, soft and sweet, but with the promise of so much more.

Just how much was the question.

He tucked her head beneath his chin and wrapped her up in his arms, sheltering them from those thoughts. Reality would come soon enough with the sun; tonight he just wanted to enjoy Lara.

Chapter 20

Lara floated into the bakery. Last night—and this morning—they'd been… Magical.

He'd made love to her—no, they'd made love to each other. Then they'd woken this morning and done it again. He'd cooked breakfast while she showered since they'd agreed that taking one together would only make them late for work, something neither could afford. They'd eaten together, and then she cleaned up while he showered, all the domesticity of the scene tugging at her heart.

Going to bed with Gage had been great; waking up with him even better—to the point that she couldn't remember why she'd thought it wouldn't be a good idea.

"Either you swallowed a pound of buttercream this morning, or some *other* kind."

Lara winced. Cara had always been blunt, but that was over the top even for her.

"Did you get *any* sleep?"

Lara pulled her apron over her head. With luck it'd get stuck on her topknot and she'd never have to face her cousin's knowing smile.

Cara helped her tug the apron down. "You know I'm going to get it out of you eventually, so you might as well spill now."

"There's nothing to spill."

"Uh huh. Right. You haven't looked like that since, well, ever."

Lara winced. She *hadn't* looked or felt like this with Jeff. Not even in the beginning. "The party was a success and I think we'll get a few more gigs from it."

"No way. You're not copping out with a business discussion. And besides, I already heard about what happened. So, was Gage as hot in bed as he apparently is on stage?"

"Geez, Car, can you give it a rest? Do I ask you to kiss and tell?"

"You don't have to. I tell you everything anyway. So does this mean there was some kissing going on?"

Lara rolled her eyes and grabbed a package of fondant. She needed to beat something.

"Come on, Lar. I don't get why you're being so hush-hush about it."

"Because there's really nothing to tell. Gage danced, Megan got out of control, and everyone loved the cupcakes."

"Well from what I heard about his dancing, I'm surprised you can walk today. That must have gotten you revved up."

"Talking about revved up, what's with this sexual dynamo persona you've suddenly adopted?" She wanted the focus off of her.

Unfortunately, Cara was too annoyingly smart to fall for that. She plunked her butt on the prep table. "You're not changing the subject. Dish."

"He had to fill in when one of the guys got sick."

"And did he *fill in*?"

Lara threw a chunk of fondant at her. "You're annoying."

"Pot meet kettle. Get to the good stuff. Explain his truck outside of your condo this morning."

"Oh." Lara sliced off another hunk of fondant with a little more force than necessary. She should have known Cara would check on her way in. "That."

"Yeah, that. So, what happened?"

"Pretty much what you're imagining."

"And?"

"And what? It was awesome." *He* was awesome.

"Thank you Jesus." Cara crossed herself. "It's about time you got back in the saddle."

"He's not a horse, Car."

"I hope he's hung like one."

Lara didn't even dignify that with an eye roll. But yeah, he was. Not that it was any of Cara's concern.

"So are you going to see him again or was this a one-and-done?"

Lara could feel the embarrassment creeping up her cheeks. "I'm making a birthday cake for his nephew." Over breakfast, Gage had invited her to celebrate with them tomorrow night and she'd volunteered.

"The one whose medical bills he's paying?"

"Yes."

Cara cocked her head and twirled a curl. "Amazing-looking, can dance, takes care of his sister and her son… You know, Lar, the guy seems pretty damn perfect. Why aren't you all over him?"

She had been all over him, actually, but that wasn't what Cara meant. "I'm taking my time, Cara. You should know as well as I do that it might not go beyond the window dressing." Cara had held her more times than either of them wanted to remember when she'd cried over Jeff. The bastard.

"Don't judge everyone by McMonster's standards, cuz. You're giving him too much power."

No, she was taking the power. For far too long she'd given it to Jeff. Now she was responsible for herself and lessons learned were well worth remembering. No more being in anyone's thrall. If this thing with Gage was going to go somewhere, she wanted to make the decisions with him, not just go along for the ride.

Though it had been one hell of a ride… "Like I said, we're taking it slow."

"Okay, whatever." Cara tossed the fondant into the

trash can. "I've got to get to the contracts. Mrs. Applebaum changed the date to a week before."

"Ouch, that's going to be tight."

"Not if we bring in help."

"We can't afford help."

"Actually, we can." Cara smiled. "I told Mrs. Applebaum we had to juggle projects to accommodate her and there would be a fee for it."

"You didn't."

"I did. And she went for it. So offer Jesse the job. We're getting our first employee. It can only get better from here."

Lara hoped that was true in all aspects of her life.

Gage couldn't keep the stupid grin off his face as he carried the finish trim up to the gazebo the next morning. Thank God he worked alone. He wouldn't want to take the ribbing from the guys; Lara was too special for that.

And that was a huge problem. One he was going to have to address at some point, but that point wasn't now. He just wanted to enjoy the afterglow. It'd been too long since he'd felt this way.

Actually, he wasn't sure he'd ever felt this way.

Which was also a huge problem.

His phone rang as he set the trim on the sawhorses. "Hey Missy, what's up?"

"I might ask you the same thing. I was worried when you didn't come home last night. Are you okay?"

Okay was putting it mildly. "Sorry. Yeah, I'm fine." He wasn't used to having to check in with anyone and hadn't texted her that he wouldn't be home.

"Was it Lara?"

He pinched the bridge of his nose, not wanting to share this yet. "I invited her to dinner tomorrow night to celebrate Connor's birthday."

She snorted. "And that took you all night?"

He was *not* discussing his love life with his little sister. "Is there anything else you need, Miss? I have to get up on this roof."

"There are tons of things I need, Gage, but the most important one is you. Be careful, okay. On the roof and elsewhere."

She might be his little sister, but she was still a mom and sounded like one.

He shoved the phone into his back pocket and measured out the first board. A few more pieces of trim and this job would be done. Then he could bill it out, and concentrate on the others, including the gazebo for McCullough.

He was just about ready to cut it when his phone rang again. Bryan. Geez. A night out and the entire world had to know his business.

"Hey, Bry."

"When were you planning to tell me about Tanner? I would've thought between you and Gina that I wouldn't be the last one to know twelve hours later."

Hell. He'd forgotten to make that call, too. He'd checked with the hospital on his way in this morning, though. Tanner had been admitted for appendicitis. "I handled it."

"Yeah, heard that, too. Real well from what I can gather. Megan Livezy has been calling here for the past hour looking for you. Says you owe her an apology."

"*I* owe *her*? Where'd she come up with that?"

"Apparently you touched her inappropriately when you were trying to get her off of you."

"Jesus Christ." He pinched the bridge of his nose again, this time because of a headache. "The woman was wrapped around me like a burrito and *I'm* the one who did inappropriate touching?"

"Yeah, I know. I got the story from a bunch of different people. Now I'm trying to get video of it. We need to prove she was the instigator to keep her quiet. We don't need this kind of publicity."

"Shit." Nothing would bring down their business quicker than rumors spreading about what other *services* they offered…

"Exactly." Bry cleared his throat. "So, Missy called here, looking for you. Said you didn't come home."

"What the hell? Does everyone have to know my business? I was off the clock. My time is my own." He set the saw down lest he cut something he shouldn't.

"I'm asking as your friend, not your business partner. Was it the cupcake lady?"

"Does it matter?"

"Yeah, it matters, Gage. You're into her. And since I know everything that's going on in your life—how many times have you told me your priorities—I can be concerned. I mean, don't get me wrong, if you're into her and having a relationship, great. But if not, I have to wonder what you're doing because she's in the industry. We don't need any bad blood."

"There won't be any, Bry. It's fine. Don't worry."

"I'm worried about you. You're stretched thin these days. And with tonight's gig, well, like I said, you've got a lot on your plate."

Gage leaned against the saw horse. "Are you going Dr. Phil on me?"

Bry snorted. "Yeah, that's me. Dr. Shrink. No, I'm just making sure your head's screwed on straight."

"It is. Don't worry."

"All right then." Gage heard him rifle through some papers. Bry hadn't quite grasped the no-paper age. "Do you want to do the Girls' Weekend Fling party on Friday or should I?"

The thought of spending five hours with a group of ten single girlfriends in their thirties no longer seemed appealing. Especially since he had yet another bachelorette party tonight. "I'll pass on that one. Megan's sleeper-hold was more than enough for the month."

"Gotcha. Okay, well let me know how the leads turn out. Gina said almost everyone filled out a card."

And at least two-thirds of them had had personal messages to him or Carlo on them.

He hung up, working cold calls into his schedule after the Torrington's basement this afternoon before the McCullough gazebo. There were never enough hours in the day.

And now he'd added Lara to the mix, though he wouldn't have any trouble making time for her.

He called her. It'd only been an hour, but hey, a guy was entitled to call the woman he'd spent the night with an hour after breakfast if he wanted to.

"Hey." Her voice was soft and throaty like the last time she'd uttered his name when she came in the early hours of the morning.

"Hey yourself. How's your morning?"

"Busy. As usual. I still have to empty out the van, fondant is refusing to cooperate, and Cara's doing deals left and right. We're going to hire our first employee."

"Hey, that's great. Business is booming."

"Just what we need."

"I hear you." And he did. It was good to hear her voice. He was going to miss her tonight, but they both had events and would get home too late to get together. "So about dinner tomorrow. I can pick you up on my way back from the jobsite, but I'll be pretty dirty. I hope you won't mind if I leave you with Missy while I grab a shower." He'd thought about asking her to take one with him, but with Connor in the house, that wasn't the best idea. Plus, then they'd never get to the party.

"Why? Is Missy some dangerous person I should be afraid of being around? I mean, I did already meet her and after suffering through that drunken father of the bride at the expo, I should be able to handle a sister."

Gage scowled at the reminder. That guy had been inappropriately leering, never mind touching. He should be thankful he hadn't touched. "Missy's harmless compared to that guy."

"Seems to me you made that guy pretty harmless."

He could hear the smile in her voice and it brought one to his face. He wasn't above being a knight in shining armor if that's what she wanted. "We aim to please, ma'am," he said, doing his best cowboy impersonation without the chaps, hat, or boots.

"You certainly do, Gage. You definitely pleased me." And with those provocative words, she hung up.

And left him hanging.

Chapter 21

"That has got to be one of the coolest birthday cakes you've ever made," said Cara the next afternoon, checking out Connor's chessboard.

Gage had told her about Connor's obsessions with chess and his favorite video game, so she'd given up her free afternoon to go online to come up with ideas for the chess pieces that looked like the game's characters. She'd made the chessboard the great hall of a castle and used the game's logo as the color scheme. All sorts of medieval weapons, suits of armor, and thrones ringed the edges, with the court made up of more of the characters.

"Any seven-year-old will love it."

"I hope so."

"Oh he will. The problem is going to be when it's time to cut it. I bet he'll want to play with it instead."

The thought had crossed her mind, but with all the birthday parties they'd done, she had yet to meet a child who could resist cake.

Lara closed the lid on the cake box and took off her chef's hat. "You're sure you're okay with manning the place while I go home to shower before dinner? I should be back in plenty of time before Gage gets here."

"No problem. It's Paperwork Sunday. I'll just work on that and answer any calls that happen to come in. I have to figure out how to set up payroll for our new employee." Jesse had jumped at the chance for a full time summer job. "Go doll yourself up for the man."

That's exactly what Lara intended to do.

Back at her condo, she glanced at the latest text message from Gage just before getting into the shower to wash off the day's efforts.

Can't wait 2 C *U.*

She couldn't either. They'd been texting fiends for the past thirty-six hours with one late night hour long call last night.

Her face—and the rest of her—heated at *that* memory. Who knew phone sex could be so hot?

She fanned herself. She'd never done that before but it came as a natural progression when they were both in their respective beds and the night wrapped around them with their mutual desire.

She used her stash of designer scented soaps and oils she'd bought after leaving her former life—fragrances *she'd* chosen—took extra long care to keep the Medusa curls from springing to life like a bunch of steel wool, then agonized over what to wear.

She was being ridiculous. It was just going to be her, Gage, Missy, Connor, and a few of his friends. Pizza and chips with cake and ice cream for dessert, not a trip to the country club.

And for that she could say she was grateful. She'd never liked the lifestyle Jeff had aspired to. It hadn't been her, but she'd done it for him.

And where had it gotten her?

Looking at herself in the mirror, in a sundress and low-heeled sandals, Lara had to admit that trying to fit into Jeff's world had gotten her where she was now: looking forward to dinner with a wonderful man and his family.

Not a bad a place to be to be at all.

Gage pulled into the bakery parking lot fifteen minutes early. Great. Fifteen more minutes he'd have with Lara.

He went inside. The reception area was small. They could use some touch-up paint in here and maybe a lower counter. He always hated when the receptionist couldn't see over it to greet new arrivals. Not that that was an issue for them at the moment, but with Lara's talent and Cara's determination, it would be eventually.

He headed down the hallway. "Hello?"

"Back here!"

He followed the voice. It turned out to be Lara's cousin in an office to the right of the kitchen area. "Hey, Cara. Is Lara here?"

Cara looked up, her curls springing from her head as if she'd stuck her hand in a light socket. "She should be shortly. She went home to shower."

An image he'd had in his head all damn day…

"Want a tour of the place?" Cara slapped the stack of papers she was holding onto the desk.

"That's okay, you're busy."

She stuck her pencil on top of the papers. "No biggie. I'm sick of looking at this stuff. Contracts are not my forte, not when I have to figure out how to do payroll for the help we've hired, go over inventory for a new client's job, stuff like that." She cocked her head, looking enough like Lara that she was pretty, but missing that special something that made him interested. "You're not really interested in hearing this, are you?"

"Sure I am. Anything Lara's into interests me. Plus I know all about supplies and scheduling. I'm working on three construction jobs myself at the moment."

"In addition to BeefCake?"

He shrugged. "All work and no play makes Gage a dull boy." It was sarcastic joke between him and Bryan because there weren't enough hours in the day for all they had going on to think about play. Maybe in five years.

She walked around her desk. "BeefCake is *playtime* for you? You find grope-y horny, ill-behaved women fun?"

Cara obviously hadn't gotten the sarcasm. "Whoa.

Hold on. You misinterpreted what I meant."

She plunked her hands on her hips and walked toward him, a tiny ball of fury. "Well why don't you explain it to me since you're seeing my cousin? She doesn't need some player using her. She's been through enough hell with her asshole of an ex. I thought you were a decent guy, what with all you're doing for your nephew. I mean, I'm all for Lara going out and getting some, but with the way she's been mooning around this place for the past two days, there'd better be a little more substance to you than just good sex."

"She said that?" Here, he'd been hoping she'd thought it was phenomenal.

Cara rolled her eyes. "*That's* what you focus on? Men. I swear to God I'll never understand you creatures."

"Perhaps if you stop calling us creatures, you might."

"When your kind stops acting like them, I will."

Talk about a chip on the shoulder… "You don't let your size stop you, do you?"

"What does my size have to do with anything?"

Apparently nothing since she had him backed up against a wall.

He held up his hands. "Truce? Give me a chance to explain?"

She crossed her arms and tapped a toe. "Two minutes."

He really shouldn't smile. He tried not to. "I'm working three different construction projects at the moment, am trying to drum up more for when they're finished, I have the sales calls to make on the leads for BeefCake, not to mention helping my partner with scheduling, hiring, training, costuming, and everything else associated with putting on a traveling show, am looking for a venue to have a permanent presence, and oh yeah, have an injured nephew who needs therapy and surgery, with a sister who's doing everything she can to make ends meet. So occasionally I do delve into the realm of sarcasm to deal with the stress. You just happened to overhear that little side trip."

Surprisingly, he'd shut her up.

She sat back on the edge of the desk—actually she leaned against it because she wasn't tall enough to sit on it—and studied him.

"Are we okay now?"

She tapped her lip. "I think so. But if you hurt Lara, you're going to have to answer to me."

That prospect frightened him more than Megan launching herself into his arms the other night.

"I'm not planning to, Cara. I care about her. But the reality of the situation is that there are only so many hours in a day, so I have to be happy with what I can get with her."

"That's why you invited her to dinner tonight."

"One of the reasons. The other is that I wanted her there. She's important to me, and Connor's birthday is important to me. If you want to come, you're more than welcome to."

She tapped her lips again. "That's a thought."

Crap. He hadn't thought she'd take him up on the offer.

She stood up. "So, do you want that tour?"

Luckily, the back door in the kitchen opened. "Car, I'm back!"

Lara was here.

"Sheesh. You don't have to look so relieved," Cara muttered as she brushed past him on her way out of the office.

Gage smiled and shook his head. He couldn't blame Cara; Missy would do the same thing if he left her alone with Lara—

Which he was planning to do when he got home. Maybe it was a good thing for Cara to come. She could prevent an interrogation that really didn't need to happen.

He walked out after her.

"Gage! You're early."

He was very glad he was. Lara looked stunning. Her dress clung in all the right places and her hair was a jumble of soft waves falling around her shoulders like it had when he'd threaded his fingers through it the other night as he'd made love to her.

"I got done sooner than I thought, so I headed over. Wanted to surprise you, but the surprise was on me." He looked at Cara. *That's sarcasm, sweetheart.*

Cara glared at him.

Lara looked between the two of them. "Is everything okay?"

"Yeah. Sure," said Cara. "I'm coming to dinner with you."

"Um, what?"

Gage shrugged. "The more the merrier, right?"

"That's what I always say," said Cara.

"No you don't. You hate crowds." Lara put her hand on her hip. "What's going on, you two?"

"Nothing, Lara. Honest." Gage held out his arms. "Can I get a hug or will I mess up your outfit?" Two sisters had also taught him the importance of asking permission for just that reason.

Lara went into his arms. "The day a man can't hug a woman because of that is the day the world should come to an end."

A woman after his own heart—

Whoa.

"Gage?"

He'd stiffened and she'd felt it. "I, uh, don't want to mess up your hair."

She pulled back and looked up at him. "You two are acting awfully weird. Are you sure there's nothing going on?"

"Everything's fine." He tugged her close. Everything was fine *now*.

"Yeah, Lar, everything's good," said Cara, for once on his side. "Now, shall we grab the cake and get out of here? I, for one, am sick of this place today. I haven't seen daylight in hours."

Gage looked at the outside of the building as he carried the cake out to his truck and stuck it on the bench seat. Cara's office had an outside wall. It was cinderblock, but if there weren't any electrical wires running along it, he could put a window in for her relatively inexpensively. He did have that extra one he'd salvaged from a house when the owners had opted for French doors instead. He could use that. And he had a couple of odd shaped pieces of granite that he could work into a new reception counter too, now that he thought about it. Some scrap lumber he could make a chair rail out of, and he had enough left-over paint to spruce the place up. A day, maybe two, and their reception area would look good as new. And Cara could have some sunlight to keep her in a better mood.

He shook his head as he walked around to the driver's side. Look at him; like he didn't have enough to occupy his time, now he was going to put in volunteer work at the bakery.

Lara opened the door and sat in her cousin's car, her dress sliding up to reveal that expanse of thigh he'd spent considerable time getting well acquainted with the other night.

Yeah, he'd make the time.

Chapter 22

The house was overrun with seven-year-olds, most of them in full-on fantasy garb, with Connor dressed up like a king, lording over them all from his chair, in particular a small blonde troll with dimples and angelic blue eyes who looked at Connor as if he really were a king. Gage smiled. Ah, it started young with the Tomlinson genes.

It did Gage's heart good to see his nephew enjoying himself. The kids often came by, but one-on-one got old after a while, and with Connor house-bound for the most part, this was a welcome afternoon.

Missy threw him a grateful smile when they walked into the kitchen.

"Thank God you're here. They all came early. Apparently Connor spread the word that he wanted a full scale battle before the pizza arrived so here they are. I was wondering why he kept bothering me about what time we'd order. Any chance you can supervise while I get everything ready in here?"

"Let me run up and grab a quick shower, then I'm all yours."

"Cara and I can handle them," said Lara. "You go shower and we'll man the fort."

From the look on Cara's face, Gage would guess she wasn't a fan of that idea. But he kissed Lara's cheek on his way upstairs. "Thanks. I owe you."

"And me," grumped Cara. "You definitely owe me. Big time."

Oh Cara definitely had a good grip of sarcasm.

"Thanks so much for helping out," Missy said when

her brother left the room. The poor girl looked worn out and the party hadn't even started.

"No problem," said Lara. "Anything we need to know before we venture in?"

"Just keep the light sabers away from the flat screen. It's Gage's pride and joy."

"Will do," said Lara, heading into the horde of invading mongrels.

Cara snorted. "Gee. A guy in love with a giant boob tube. Why am I not surprised?"

"Did something happen with Nick?"

Cara rolled her eyes. "Of course not. I don't define my entire existence by my boyfriend, you know."

"Are you trying to tell me something?"

Cara looked at her. "Um, no. I'm sorry. You're right. I was being bitchy. Too much paperwork, I guess."

"Ooh, she said a bad word!" One of the kids tossed back his mask and pointed at Cara. "Fifty cents in the curse word jar!"

Five others picked up the chant. Apparently curse-word jars were a common occurrence among Connor's friends.

Lara led Cara away from them. No need to incite a riot.

"*Un guard*!" yelled a minion as it charged toward a troll, his French in need of an overhaul.

"I'm going to *spewer* you," said another, trying to actually do that.

Lara grabbed the light saber. "Hey, no skewering allowed. Otherwise the cake will fall out of his belly."

"Cake?" Twenty pairs of eyes turned her way and the pandemonium came to a standstill.

Only to start on a different tangent.

"Where's the cake?"

"I want some."

"Can I have an end piece?"

"Is there a rose? I want a rose."

"I don't like chocolate."

"I only like coffee cake."

"Do you have pie?"

Cara was spinning around as if the kids were pulling her like a top. Lara had to laugh. It was amazing how similar she and Cara were in many things, but the thought of a child blew her poor cousin right out of the water. Twenty of them could send her to the loony bin.

Lara held up her hands to quiet the horde down. "Now, now, everyone. There will be cake, but not until after dinner. And to get to dinner, we need to keep the house in one piece. You know how to do that, right? If you want to run around, we're going to have to take this outside to the backyard."

"But Connor can't go in the backyard," said a pretty little blonde troll who'd practically attached herself to Connor's side.

"Sure he can. When his Uncle Gage comes down, he'll carry him outside and put him on his throne. Then you guys can honor him as a proper king."

It was the right thing to say. Connor's chest puffed up, his smile grew twice its size, and the troll patted his hand.

"Come on, everyone! Let's go out and make the backyard fit for a king!" Lara swept her hand toward the sliding glass doors out to the deck, and like a flock of birds, they all swooped out.

"How on earth did you manage that?" Cara shook her head. "Do you have Pied Piper superpowers?

Lara patted Cara's shoulder. "Remember babysitting for the O'Malleys? That was training."

The O'Malleys had had eight children, one born each year. Lara had earned all of her high school spending money babysitting them.

"Yeah, I remember. I was conveniently ill any time you couldn't watch them. They scared me."

"Ah, Cara, they were just kids."

Cara shivered. "They were my worst nightmare. All that noise and chaos." She looked around the living room, now free of the kids, but definitely not the chaos. There were more swords and lost capes than Lara could count. "No thank you."

"*I'll* say thank you." Missy poked her head into the room. "I don't know how you did it, but thank you. I've been trying to get them out of here for the past half hour."

"Can I go out now?" Connor asked, his troll still standing by him.

"As soon as Gage comes down, Connor. Until then, I can stay here with you." Lara looked at Cara. "You want to go supervise outside?"

Cara gaped at her. "Excuse me? What part of *worst nightmare* didn't you understand? How about *you* go out there and I'll stay here and keep Connor company? I'm sure I can manage one child."

Lara hid her smile as she grabbed a bunch of juice boxes and headed out. Sometimes Cara was just too easy to manipulate. "That's fine with me. See you in a bit."

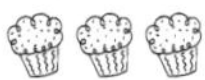

About ten minutes later a clean-shaven, scrumptious-looking Gage walked out the door carrying his nephew in his arms and Lara's heart stuttered.

Not just at the physical perfection that was Gage, though there was that, but the compassion and caring that was so evident as he helped Connor get situated among his friends.

Jeff had wanted children. The prerequisite boy and girl, though how he'd expected them to have his blond looks when she was half their gene pool was beyond her. He'd kept putting off having them "until the time was right." In hindsight, she was glad, but at the time, she'd just followed his lead.

She'd done that way too many times.

She looked at Gage as she was setting up the juice boxes. He'd let her call the shots with what was happening between them. Sure, he'd instigated their night together, but it wasn't anything she hadn't already been thinking. He'd just given voice to it, but then he'd let her make the decision. Whatever she'd decided, he would have abided by.

She was so glad she'd decided what she had. The other night had been perfect. Scarily so. No one could be as perfect as Gage. Yet, he was.

He laughed at something Connor said, the sheer delight on his face making her catch her breath. The outside was definitely very pretty, but it was who he was that came shining through in this unguarded moment. He'd be gorgeous even without that hunky exterior.

She was opening herself up to a lot of potential heartache by letting her guard down around him.

A mini-wizard bumped into the table, knocking down the juice box pyramid she'd made, so she went about re-building it.

"A penny for them." Gage snuck up beside her, dropped a quick kiss on her cheek, and wrapped his arms around her waist. "Or are they worth more than that?"

She shook off the mess of her past and looked over her shoulder. "Nothing we need to think about ever again. So, are you feeling better after your shower?"

"Now that I have you in my arms I do. What do you think the kids would say if I planted one on you right here?'

"Eww, gross! Mr. T is hugging a girl!" One of the elves pointed their way.

"Hey, don't knock it 'til you try it, Nicky. Girls are cool." Just to prove it, Gage kissed her on her cheek again.

A chorus of "ewwww"s arose.

"I don't think they're buying it," she said, laughing as she pulled out of his embrace. Nice as it was, the kids didn't need to see it.

"Wait'll they get older. They'll wish they'd listened to me now."

She smacked his arm playfully. "You're a bad influence."

"I'll argue that point with you. Two nights ago you thought I was a good one."

Two nights ago had been very good.

She felt the blush crawl up her cheeks.

"You're adorable when you blush, do you know that?"

Which only made her blush more.

"Okay, you two are more sickeningly sweet than that cake in there," said Cara as she walked out from the kitchen, only to do a one-eighty. "I'm going inside before I get a tooth ache."

Lara shook her head. "That's just her excuse to get away from the kids. Cara's always had an issue with them."

"What about you? Do you have any issues with them?"

"I love kids. Want a bunch of them someday." Which, hopefully would be sooner rather than later since she wasn't getting any younger. Which meant she had to pour all her energies and effort into the bakery to make sure it was on solid financial footing before she could even consider having children. Of course, she'd also have to find someone to have them with. "What about you? Do you want kids?"

"Definitely. Someday." He looked over at Connor. "Let me go see if he needs anything. Missy said the pizza ought to be here in about fifteen, so he won't have much time out here. I should bring him out more often. I hadn't really thought about it. Thank you."

"My pleasure. He's a sweet kid and my heart goes out to him."

Gage looked over at his nephew. He blinked a couple of times. "He doesn't deserve this. He was just a normal kid, you know? Just having fun one minute and the next, his whole life changed."

"What about the person who hit him? Is there insurance money?"

Gage shrugged. "Not much. And Missy didn't have any because she doesn't have a car. Her renters policy doesn't cover it."

She put her hand on his arm. "At least he has people around him who love him."

He cleared his throat and worked a smile onto his face. "Yes. That he does." He put his hand over hers. "Thank you, Lara. For being here."

"There's no place else I'd rather be." It was true.

"Pizza's here!" Missy yelled out the door, shattering the moment. And the peace. All of a sudden, twenty stomping, cheering kids stormed the deck, threading between her and Gage like a river among rocks.

Gage laughed. "I'll swim downstream to get Connor. You better not fight the current."

She saluted him. "Aye, aye, Captain. See you on shore."

Dinner passed in a flurry of plates, paper airplane napkins, too many noisemakers to think straight, and way too much caffeine and sugared beverages for a throng of beings who had no need of enhancements.

And then they wanted cake.

Lara lit the "torches" on the castle parapet and Gage carried it over to place it before the king.

Sufficient "oohs" and "aahs" followed, and just as Lara had predicted, they all wanted a piece. Connor did save his favorite character she'd made from modeling chocolate, but the rest were up for grabs, even the castle walls that she'd made from crisped rice and marshmallows.

"How long are these heathens staying here?" Cara asked, prying yet another squished glob of marshmallow off her shirt. "They're never going to go to bed tonight."

Missy chuckled. "That's their parents' problems, not mine. Times like these, I'm glad I only have the one."

Once the cake was demolished, er, eaten, and the gifts opened, they herded the kids back outside to work off the sugar rush. Connor was once again on his throne, the kids were playing ghost-in-the-graveyard around him, while the adults lit the chiminea on the deck and kept an eye out that no ghosts got left behind.

"This is nice," said Cara, leaning her head back on the glider. "I can't remember the last time I just kicked back and looked at the stars. Of course, I can barely remember what daylight looks like, too, I've been in my hole of an office so much."

"Speaking of which," Gage sat up and pulled Lara closer to his side with his arm around her shoulders, "I can do that for you. I have an extra window from a job if you're interested."

Cara raised an eyebrow and glared at him without moving her head. "What's it going to cost me?"

"You? Nothing." He nudged Lara. "You on the other hand…"

She squealed when he nuzzled her neck.

"Oy vey." Cara closed her eye but a hint of a smile played on her lips.

"You willing to pay that price?" he whispered when he nibbled on Lara's ear.

She gulped, then nodded.

Good. "And I was thinking I could fix up your reception area. A little paint, a new countertop, and the place will look like a million bucks."

"As long as it doesn't cost that," said Cara, again the mistress of sarcasm.

"The only thing it will cost is time. I've got a basement and a kitchen to finish for two clients, and I'm starting a gazebo in the Fox Run Hills development tomorrow. I'll work your office in as I can."

"Fox Run Hills? Lara, isn't that where—"

"Yes, it is. Let's change the subject."

Interesting how she found her voice for that.

"Isn't that where what?" he asked.

"Nothing. It's nothing."

It wasn't nothing, but he wasn't going to pressure her. She'd tell him when she was ready.

Someone knocked on the front door.

"Looks like the cavalry is here," said Missy, getting to her feet, "rescuing us from all these tiny invaders."

A steady stream of parents came through the door over the next half hour to pick up their tired-out party goers. Gage, Lara, and Cara helped clean up, then it was time for the tired-out adults to leave, too.

Gage walked Lara to Cara's car, but didn't open the door. Instead, he wedged her between it and him with his hands on the roof on either side of her.

"Thanks for coming and for the cake. Connor really liked it."

"I'm glad. It was fun to make. Thanks for inviting me. And for letting Cara come along."

"Somehow the words 'letting Cara' don't seem to go together. Your cousin does what she wants."

Lara nodded. "Yeah, sometimes I wish I could be like her."

"I don't think you need to be anyone but who you are, Lara. I like you just the way you are."

Especially when she nibbled her bottom lip between

her teeth. God, he wanted to do that. But tomorrow was going to be a long day and it was already almost tomorrow.

He took a deep breath. “I’ll miss you tonight.”

That adorable blush spread over her cheeks and he couldn’t resist kissing her. “I’ll miss you, too.”

“So should I be looking for a ride home, or are you two going to get off the car and grab a room?”

Gage took one last nibble of Lara’s lips. “Cara, you are a real piece of work.”

“And don’t you forget it, Gage.” She opened the driver’s side door. “Now let Lara get in the car. We’ve got a big week this week and she needs to be awake enough to deal with it, unlike how she was on Saturday. We’ve got a business to run, remember?”

Gage, more than anyone, understood what she meant. He kissed her once more. “She’s right. I’ll call you. Remember, I still owe you a dance.”

God knew, he wasn’t going to forget.

Chapter 23

Gage drove through the gated entrance to the Fox Run Hills development. Every house was a variant of the same theme, with manicured lawns, wrought iron fencing, pillars at the driveway entrances, Acuras, Beamers, and Mercedes all over the place. So many people keeping up with the Joneses, he could make a killing if J.C. McCullough talked him up.

Regardless of his personal feelings for the guy, he was going to make the best damn gazebo anyone had ever seen in the quickest time possible, so it'd be the talk of not only the guy's engagement party but every neighborhood get-together afterwards.

Did they have neighborhood get-togethers here, or did that only happen at the country club?

He pulled into the driveway, parked his truck and the trailer with the excavator behind the arborvitae again, and pulled his lawn signs out of the truck bed. Sometimes they were the best advertising.

He rang the front doorbell again. Let J.C. tell him to use the servant entrance. If he had the balls.

The maid answered the door again.

The prick *didn't* have the balls. Why was Gage not surprised?

"Mr. McCullough said the back gate is open and you can go on through."

"I'm having cement delivered this afternoon, so if you're going somewhere, you might want to put your car in the street so we don't park you in. Can you pass that along to Mr. McCullough?"

The woman nodded and closed the door, leaving Gage standing there. If there was one thing Connor's ordeal had taught him, it was that when it came down to it, everyone was the same. When you were hurt, you were hurt, so all this noblesse oblige really torqued him. But the guy was paying his bills, so Gage sucked it up and went around back.

The prick was waiting for him, checking his watch as if Gage were punching a time clock.

"I need to be at the office by eight, so if you could get here by seven tomorrow, I'd appreciate it."

Gage made a point of checking his cell phone. Seven-oh-two. It was at least a two minute walk from his car to the front door then around back.

He plunked his tool box on the stone wall surrounding the patio. "Yeah, sure." It wasn't worth the fight.

"Madeleine said there's going to be a cement truck here today?"

Gage nodded and took out his laser tape measure and the ground paint. He'd bring in the Bobcat after he'd outlined his dig site.

"You do have insurance to cover driveway damage, don't you?"

Gage bit back his sarcastic reply as he attached his work belt around his waist. "I do. I can give you a copy if you'd like." He would've thought Mr. Hot Shot Lawyer would have asked about it beforehand, but whatever.

"Great. Leave it with Madeleine before you go." The prick folded his paper and stood up. "I'll be back at six. You'll be gone by then."

It wasn't a question so Gage didn't feel the need to answer.

"Well, then, I'll be off. Try to keep the noise and mess to a minimum, will you? I don't need the neighbors complaining."

Gage gave him a salute—refraining from the one-finger kind—and headed off to the left side of the pool to lay out where he was going to dig the footers, reminding himself that he was here to do a job and he didn't have to like the client.

Good thing, because this guy, he definitely didn't.

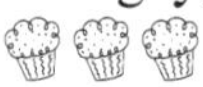

"I give up!" A flurry of papers went flying out of Cara's office door.

Lara picked some of them up and girded herself before entering her cousin's lair. *She* never went in there if she didn't have to. Numbers gave her the hives.

"What's the problem, Car?"

Cara waved a mess of papers at her. "This. These contracts. They're driving me nuts. Wherefores and whences and heretowiths… We need a lawyer just to keep track of all the changes the other lawyer is recommending. It's barely eight o'clock and already I have a migraine." She pinched the bridge of her nose. "I'm a numbers person, not a freakin' English major."

"So just call the attorney and ask him whatever you have questions about."

"And pay him three hundred dollars an hour? Are you out of your mind? I could hire someone part time for a week for that. Maybe even less."

"What about Gage's sister?"

Cara opened one eye. "Come again?"

Lara set the papers on the corner of the desk. She didn't want to disrupt whatever filing system Cara had going. "Gage's sister. Connor's mom? She was going to school to become a paralegal before Connor was injured. We could hire her for a few hours to make sense of things and give us direction on what to ask the attorney. Save us some billable hours maybe. It'd be cheaper than calling the attorney and Gage said she could use a break. It'd be a win-win for all of us."

"Oh. My. God." Cara's arm plunked onto her desk.

"You've got it bad."

"Got what?"

"This thing with Gage. You were into that whole domestic scene last night, admit it."

Lara rolled her eyes. "Cara, I just started dating him."

"Didn't stop you from sleeping with him."

"*You're* lecturing *me*? Seriously?"

"Not lecturing. Just pointing out that you've taken it a lot faster than you normally do."

"Considering I haven't slept with anyone in three years, I think that's pretty much a given."

"But why him?"

Lara crossed her arms. She didn't need this third degree from Cara. Not now when things were still so new. "Weren't you the one who was telling me to be adventurous? Now you're backtracking? Make up your mind, Car."

"I just want to make sure you know your mind. I was all for you jumping in the sack merely to take the edge off. But doing the family thing, hanging out over there, getting to know them—hiring his sister, for Pete's sake… That's going beyond scratching an itch."

Which ironically hadn't gotten scratched last night.

Lara took a deep breath. She'd missed him.

"Next thing you know, you're going to be packing up a picnic lunch and taking it out to his job site."

Now there was an idea… "Considering he's in Jeff's neighborhood, I don't think so."

"Oh yeah. I forgot about that. Wouldn't it be a hoot if he ran into McMonster? Can you see Jeff dealing with all that raw masculinity in his little Stepford world?"

"Wow. You really don't like Jeff. Why didn't you ever tell me?"

Cara made a half-hearted attempt to straighten the mess of papers. "You were so happy with him I figured there had to be something to him that I didn't see. Who was I to rain on your parade? Plus, would you have listened to me?"

Lara shook her head. She wouldn't have. She'd been head-over-heels.

"Exactly. So I decided to suck it up and be here for you if it went bad. Which I thought it would. He wasn't the right guy for you."

She'd found that out the hard way.

"I hate that I'm right."

Lara shrugged and grabbed a couple more sheets of paper off the floor. This was all water under the bridge. "I'd rather not rehash the disaster that was my marriage, if you don't mind. Why don't you think about hiring Missy just to get that mess straightened out? It'll save your sanity, my ears, and a couple of trees who won't have to end up as pulp."

Cara took the papers, giving them the Evil Eye. Lara snatched her hand back; she'd heard too many stories about that Evil Eye—she didn't want to get burned if the papers suddenly erupted in flames.

"Fine. Text me her phone number and I'll give her a call."

Lara went back to the kitchen and grabbed her cell.

Miss you. - G

She hadn't heard the message come through at—she checked the time—six. That's because she'd been sound asleep dreaming about him.

It'd been quite the dream. She might not have physically brought him home last night, but she had in her dreams. And, oh, had he brought *her* home… Over and over again. She'd woken to twisted sheets, a sheen of perspiration on her body, and a throbbing between her legs that she'd had to take care of before getting out of bed.

It was nothing like having Gage there with her, but it was the best she was going to get until their schedules could get in sync.

There were probably had better odds of a meteor hitting the earth.

Miss you, too. Have a great day. –Me

Okay, so it wasn't the most romantic text, but at least he'd know she was thinking of him.

She couldn't *stop* thinking about him. Gage was turning out to be more than she could have ever hoped or imagined for herself after the debacle with Jeff.

Forget the physical; the emotional connection he had to his family was enough for her. The love between his sister and him, the caring and concern for his nephew, the special way he made her feel… Add in the fact that he turned her blood to liquid fire and could turn her on with just a look—hell, even that silly nickname made her feel special—Gage was almost too good to be true.

Chapter 24

Not everyone thought Gage was wonderful.

Lara was sitting at the monthly Chamber of Commerce meeting, listening to Gage address the assembly about a venue for his guys, and all he kept getting was pushback from the other members.

Lewd, disgusting, sexist, pornographic… She couldn't believe the words being tossed around. And the attitudes… She was seriously tempted to stand up and ask everyone exactly which decade—no, which *century*—they were in because it certainly wasn't the twenty-first.

"We would monitor the door the same as any other club. Twenty-one is the legal drinking age, and since we'd serve alcohol, patrons would have to be twenty-one to enter. Legal adults. We're not into corrupting minors." Gage maintained his cool behind the podium, but because she knew him, she could see the effort it was costing him.

She wished she'd arrived early tonight, but she'd had to put the last-minute touches on the Henderson cake before Jesse left to deliver it—which was why she'd been able to make the meeting in the first place. Cara usually did it, but tonight was the only time Missy could get someone to sit with Connor, so Cara was off training her.

If Lara had known Gage was going to be here, she would have gotten up an hour earlier this morning and finished Mrs. Henderson's cake in time.

He looked good up there in his golf shirt and khaki pants. Like a businessman, which was what he was. Not the sleaze they were trying to portray him to be.

"You'll incite riots," said one of the Council members. John Somebody. Who looked utterly jealous that Gage *could* incite a riot.

"We give people a good time and it's closely monitored by security. It's no different than any other club with live performers, whether they're dancers or a band."

"Bands don't typically remove their clothes."

"Oh no? You've never seen a drummer or guitarist whip off his shirt and throw it into the crowd? I have. We, at least, try to keep hold of our clothing. Costumes cost money."

"What about private rooms?" asked an older woman. "I've heard clubs like yours are just fronts for prostitution."

The muscle in Gage's jaw tightened. Lara saw him swallow and his eyes narrowed. "I do *not* run a prostitution ring. Besides being illegal, it's morally reprehensible to me."

"Yet stripping isn't?"

Gage exhaled. Nice and long and loud. "The guys are exotic dancers. What they do or don't take off is up to them, but I guarantee there's never full frontal nudity. That violates decency laws and I'm a law-abiding citizen." He gripped the edge of the podium until his knuckles turned white. "My partner and I run a clean show, full of good entertainment with an eye to public safety. In that regard alone, we should be granted a business license for the Craft Street venue."

Craft Street was two blocks over from her bakery, and a little tingle fluttered in her belly at having him that close since their interaction these past few days had been only texts and phone calls.

The Inquisition went on for another fifteen minutes, with Gage maintaining his professional bearing the entire time.

Funny, but she remembered the one time she'd attended their neighborhood Homeowners' Association meeting with Jeff. He'd wanted to widen their driveway, but the ordinance had said they couldn't without HOA approval. It was sad how quickly Jeff's self-entitled arrogance had turned them all against him, and not only hadn't they been granted the variance, they'd been fined for installing the granite block edging along the driveway, which was also something they should have gotten HOA approval for prior to its installation.

She'd left mortified; Jeff had been indignant with self-righteous anger.

Needless to say, she'd been more than happy to sell the house and move out after the divorce. Now, at least, her neighbors had no issues with her.

The interrogation was over at last, and Lara grabbed her purse, fully expecting to follow Gage out and talk to him, but he surprised her. He took his seat in the front row and stayed for the rest of the meeting. Not that there were any more big issues, just a few measures to pass about how reports were distributed, but Gage made sure his presence was known.

She didn't know how anyone—any *woman*—could fail to know he was in the room.

And not one woman did, apparently, as all of them flocked to him once the meeting was adjourned. Including the old biddy who'd brought up the private rooms.

She'd probably wanted to get him in one.

Lara tamped down the jealousy. It wasn't Gage's fault women were fantasizing about him. Well, not now. On stage? Whole other story. But even then, it was a job. Just a job.

He did the necessary schmoozing, and if she hadn't seen the wink he'd given her when he'd caught sight of her as she'd approached, she would've thought he was sincerely interested in every woman he talked to. He had a way of making each one feel as if she were the only woman in the room, a feeling Lara was all too acquainted with—

What if he didn't mean it any more with her than he

did with those other women?

Her steps and her smile faltered.

Oh God, she was being ridiculous. Of course that wasn't true. He did care about her. She was being paranoid.

Damn Jeff. She used to have self-confidence when it came to guys. When it came to anything.

She'd found that self-confidence when it came to the bakery; why couldn't she find it when it came to Gage?

He shook the last woman's hand and came over to her with a quick peck on her cheek.

"Boy, are you a sight for sore eyes." He took his time drinking her in. "I've missed you." His voice was low, sending shivers all over her skin. "I'm glad you're here."

"I didn't know you were going to be."

"I didn't either until I got a notice in the mail today telling me my application for Craft Street had been denied. I had to come plead my case."

"I think it was very effective."

"I don't know about that. Opinions are hard to change and people do think we're all about the sex trade. It's pretty disheartening."

"Why didn't you mention why you're doing this? For Connor, I mean."

He ran a hand over his mouth. "I thought about it. I did. But this isn't just for Connor. I mean, Con's why *I'm* doing it, but all the guys have their own reasons. This is a viable business. Profitable. The taxes we'd pay should have given us the approval, but the prejudice against it is spiting their budgetary nose, the short-sighted idiots."

"So now what are you going to do?"

"I don't know. If they don't approve Craft Street, they're not going to approve any other location. That place has been standing empty for over a year. I would've thought they'd be thrilled to have an eyesore taken care of. It looks like we're out of luck."

Lara was about to offer a comforting shoulder when she caught sight of the man across the room. "Um, maybe not."

Jeff's boss. For all that Jeff had idolized the man, Mr. Davis had been disgusted at their divorce and had clearly let her know that he would be more than happy to help her out if she ever needed it. Not in any inappropriate way; the man had been married to his childhood sweetheart for over fifty years. He believed in marriage and fidelity and had been ready to fire Jeff on the spot until he'd decided to make him partner so Lara could get more alimony. He'd even directed her to the lawyer she'd hired to represent her. Jeff had cursed under his breath at every meeting they'd had.

Mr. Davis had chuckled about it every time he saw her. "Payback," he'd said. And even with the partnership, Jeff was still the low man on the partner totem pole and Mr. Davis planned to make sure he stayed there.

Oh, yes, Weatherington Davis was a power to be reckoned, and she planned to do just that.

"Excuse me, will you, Gage?"

"Lara, what are—"

She slipped out of his hold. "Trust me. I might be able to help."

She made a beeline for Mr. Davis. His face lit up when he saw her.

"Lara. How good to see you." He reached for her hands and gave her a peck on the cheek. He smelled of lavender soap—his wife's—and cigars—his—with a touch of wood smoke, something completely out of place in the hot summer weather, but that was Mr. Davis.

"Hi, Mr. Davis."

"Now, now, I thought we'd gotten past that. I've told you time and again to call me Weathers. All my friends do."

Jeff didn't. For that reason alone, Lara went for it. "Thank you, Weathers. How have you been? How's Mary? The kids? I heard you have a new grandchild."

"Ah, yes, little Candace. Spitting image of her mother. My oldest, Susan. I don't think you've met Susan."

She'd only been to his house twice for the firm's Christmas party and both times only his youngest son had been there. "No, I haven't, but if that baby looks anything like Mary, she's sure to be a beauty."

Flattering Mr. Davis's, er, Weathers's, wife was a sure fire way to his heart. It'd always warmed Lara's heart to see how much he'd adored his wife.

She wanted someone to adore her like that.

She glanced back at Gage. She'd felt his eyes on her the entire walk over here and the whole time she'd been talking. It was a nice feeling to know he was watching her.

And yes, maybe she put a little extra sashay into her step.

"I'll tell Mary you said that. She always did enjoy your company." Weathers glanced at the two men standing on either side of him. "Well, boys, let's discuss this tomorrow, shall we? I have a feeling Miss Cavallo has something she needs to speak to me about."

The men nodded and walked off.

"Now, my dear, what's on your mind?"

"Why would you think I have something on my mind? I can't see an old friend and come say hello?"

"Lara, I might be old, but I'm not senile. I'm also nowhere near as good-looking as your man over there, so I'm thinking there's something you need to speak to me about that concerns him or you would have brought him with you. And since I did hear his impassioned speech from the podium, I have a fair idea what it is you want to talk to me about."

She smiled and shook her head. "There's a reason

your firm is so successful."

"No thanks to your ex-husband. I don't know how you stayed married to him for as long as you did. I only have to put up with him on an eight hour basis—and not even that—and I want to divorce him."

"I'm hoping you soon can."

"Oh?"

"It's my bakery. Mine and my cousin's. I'm hoping to make it profitable enough that I won't have to take Jeff's alimony anymore. Then you can let him go."

"And lose my gopher? Are you kidding me? And why on earth would you want to stop taking money from the man? You're entitled to it, and God knows he needs to be held accountable for what he did."

"I appreciate that, Weathers. I really do. But I don't like being beholden to him. I hate having to take his money. I want my own."

"So you can rub it in his face."

She cracked a smile. "Something like that."

"Ah, girl, I knew you had spunk in you. Sure, you were downtrodden by what he'd done, but I knew you had it in you to rise from the ashes." He steered her out of earshot of the people who'd been gravitating toward them as they'd talked.

"Now, what can I do for you? You want me to put pressure on the Chamber to give him his business license?"

"I do. It's a good business. Fair, profitable, on the up and up. Gage and his partner have worked really hard to build it and it would help them a lot to have their own space. Put down some roots and grow the company. They'll give back, both in the form of taxes and creating jobs, plus the place is abandoned right now. They're going to fix it up. That's good for urban development, right?"

Weathers regarded her for a few moments, his ice blue stare that had won him many difficult cases, assessing.

Then he smiled. "It does my heart good to see you like this."

"This?"

"In love."

Lara's eyes bugged open. She wasn't in love with Gage. A severe case of like, yes. High in the throes of passion, sure. But love? They'd barely been together enough to fall in love.

And she wasn't *doing* love. Not now. It was too soon since Jeff, and entirely inconvenient.

"I'm not in—"

"Don't try to tell me you're not. I've been in that same state for over fifty-five years, ever since Mary and I were thirteen. I know what being in love looks like."

Lara put her hands on her cheeks, certain they were blazing red right now. "Mr. Davis—"

"Weathers."

"Weathers. Really, it's not what you think."

"Ah. I've embarrassed you. I'm told I've gotten worse with age." He adjusted his collar. "Okay, let's put this talk of love aside. You'd like me to lend my support for your man's business. I agree with you that what he's proposing is a good business decision and the asinine comments made by the board only strengthened my resolve to do so before you even showed up. But I'll take your gratitude any time."

He smiled when he said it and Lara didn't know what she'd done to deserve to have him on her side, but she was very glad she'd done it.

"Thank you so much, Mr., er, Weathers. I really appreciate it and I know Gage will, too."

"Gage is *not* appreciating that you're still here talking to me, so I think we ought to say our goodbyes. Tell him to check his mail. I'm certain that, by next week, he'll find the license he needs."

She gave Weathers a kiss on the cheek, laughing

heartily when he gave her a coy little look, and hurried back to Gage.

"Who was that?"

She explained who Weathers was.

"I don't need anything from your ex-husband's boss. I can do this on my own, Lara."

"Really? Because it didn't look to me that you were doing such a good job, Gage, since they turned you down. And what does it matter how you get the license as long as you get it?"

"Because your ex-husband is involved."

"Only peripherally." She went on to explain Weathers's positioning. "So you see, the only reason Jeff still has his job is because Weathers wants to make sure I have alimony. Well, that and so that they can all boss Jeff around. We both get what we want."

"What about me?"

"What about you? You're getting the business license like you wanted."

His mouth twisted sideways. "I guess."

"Is this any different than you having Gina hire me to cater her party?"

He opened his mouth, but then closed it. Then he swiped a hand over it. "I guess not."

"Gee, don't sound so thrilled."

"No, you're right. Thank you."

"You're welcome. Now how about you take me out to celebrate? I haven't had a chance to eat anything today and I'm starving."

"What, exactly, are you starving for?"

In that instant, with his voice low, and his blue eyes honed in on her mouth, the teasing banter was gone, replaced with another type of teasing.

Lara licked her lips.

Gage groaned. "God, Lara, not here. I won't be able

to walk out and all those people will think they were absolutely right about BeefCake."

She couldn't stop the twitch of her lips. It was good to know she affected him as much as he affected her. "We can't have that, can we? Not when Mr. Davis is going to all the trouble to convince them otherwise."

"Then let's get out of here while I can still walk upright."

She resisted the urge to look down.

Well, almost.

"You are killing me." He grabbed her arm and steered her toward the door, and for the first time since she'd met him, he didn't stop to talk to any of the women who tried to get him to.

And, yes, Lara was feeling just a little bit pleased with herself about that.

Chapter 25

They ended up back at Donegan's, only this time, there were no onion rings, no loaded baked potatoes, and no lap dance bets—because that was pretty much a given.

She ordered the Irish chicken, he ordered a burger, and they scarfed them down in no time flat. Gage had even asked for the bill with the food, so they were ordered, fed, and paid in under thirty minutes.

Twenty minutes after that, they were naked.

"God, Lara, I haven't been able to stop thinking about you. About this." They stood in her living room, their clothing thrown all over the place and he ran his hands over her perfect breasts, taking their weight, his thumbs brushing her nipples until they hardened.

She arched into him. "It feels so good, Gage."

"Yes, you do." He had to taste one. He leaned in and brushed his lips over it gently, smiling when she gasped. He nibbled it then, softly, just his lips, smiling even more when she held his head and pressed herself against him.

"Lick me, Gage." Her breath was harsh, her voice desperate.

He knew the feeling.

Gage did what she asked—what he wanted to do—swirling his tongue around the stiffening peak, then sucked it into his mouth, the taste and the feel of her threatening his sanity. He had to get her to the bed.

He scooped her up in his arms and caught her gasp with another kiss, strode down the hall, and laid her on the bed without breaking the kiss at all.

God, she felt good under him. Soft where a woman should be. Cradling him where he needed the pressure, and the silken slide of her legs against his was pure heaven.

He propped himself up on his elbows and captured her head between his palms, her curls jumbled among his fingers. "I've missed you."

She nipped his chin. "I've missed you, too."

"You are so beautiful, Lara." He nipped her nose, the playfulness new for him, but he wanted every part of her. He wanted her smile and her cute little giggle. He wanted her moans and her shallow, gasping breaths. He wanted his name on her lips as he gave her the best orgasms of her life.

"You make me feel beautiful, Gage."

He shouldn't have to; she should feel beautiful without him. Because she was. Inside and out. How caring she'd been with Connor, with her cousin. And how she gave herself to him unreservedly. That utter generosity and selflessness made her a beautiful person and the gorgeous curls, warm sensuous eyes, that cute turned up nose, and those lips… God, those lips… They were all just window-dressing to the beautiful soul they housed.

"Don't ever let anyone tell you you're not, Lara. There's so much beauty inside of you that it just shines through. Someone would have to be an idiot not to see all of that in you." He'd kill her ex-husband. *Vanilla*—was the guy insane? Lara was so not vanilla. She was decadent chocolate with swirls of strawberry and peppermint, a feast for his palate that he wanted to taste over and over again.

She blinked—twice—against the tears at the corners of her eyes. "Thank you."

Her voice broke at the end and Gage couldn't have that. This wasn't a night for tears. This was a night for smiles and laughs, and oh yes, long drawn out moans of pleasure. Maybe even a scream or two—or seven—of his name. If he could last that long.

He kissed her. Not carnal, not lightly, but enough to show her all he felt about her. Every good deed, every wonderful smile, every aching thought he'd had of her since they'd met.

He'd deal with all that meant for him later.

"You're the most beautiful woman in the world to me, Lara, and I'm going to make sure you know that before morning."

Lara shivered at his words. She wanted to believe him—and maybe, if she let herself, she would. "Just make love to me, Gage. Take me out of myself like you did the other night. *That* was beautiful."

"Your wish is my command," he said with that knock-her-sideways smile just before those beautiful lips descended on hers to sweep her up in a maelstrom of excitement and sensation she could barely believe.

Everywhere Gage touched turned to fire. Her nerve endings shuddered beneath her skin, ripples writhing over her, her tummy aflutter in a response only he'd been able to elicit, and heat stole along her limbs, wending its way into her heart and wrapping around it so tightly she couldn't breathe. She was so far into him this could be a disaster of epic proportions if it didn't work out.

Lara thrust that thought from her mind. At some point she had to let go of the doubt and learn to trust again.

Trust. It was a big issue with her.

Gage nibbled his way along her jaw line and down her throat, taking sweet care with her collarbone, dipping into the hollow at the base, his tongue swirling there, radiating slick, hot desire to every part of her.

"God, baby, you taste amazing," he muttered against her skin and Lara could only nod.

And writhe. She did that rather well when his lips found her nipple.

His fingers played with her other one and the sensations rose in her, fracturing her mind from anything but the glorious friction of his fingers and his tongue and the hard length of him against her thigh.

She ran her hands over his back, every inch an experience of sensual proportions. He had not one ounce of fat, and every muscle clenched and flexed beneath her touch, generating an answering clenching in one very specific area. "I want you, Gage. In me. Now."

He raised his head, those beautiful aquamarine eyes hooded with desire. For her. "You'll have me, Lara. But we're going to take this slow. Make it last. Make it beautiful."

It already was.

Gage kissed his way down her body, delving into her navel, his tongue swirling even more sensations there, each one spiraling out from that center to another one, a little lower and much needier.

She squirmed beneath him, needing pressure—ah, yes, there. God, the length and strength of him…

He cradled her hips with his hands and then, oh, God, then his tongue found her.

"You taste amazing," he whispered against her curls before he took what she so willingly wanted to give him.

He drove her insane with need. His talented tongue and fingers spiked her desire higher, taking her to the precipice, only to fall back and keep her dangling, every part of her quivering with need. She clenched the sheets, she tossed her head, pressed down against his mouth, searching for that ultimate release, but Gage would only tease her with it.

"Please, Gage," she panted, half out of her mind with desire, the other half so firmly focused on what he was doing that it was as if she could see him behind her closed eyelids.

"I'll please you, Lara, but you're going to have to work for it."

Her eyes shot open and she met his teasing gaze. "What?"

He smiled then and it curled her toes.

"Roll over." He picked her leg up and turned her until she was on her stomach and her backside…

"What are you going to do?"

"It's not what *I'm* going to do." He slid off the bed and put his strong hands around her ankles… and dragged her off the bed. "It's what *you're* going to do."

She looked over her shoulder at him as she tried to manage standing. That wasn't working so well; her body was so jacked up her knees were threatening to give out.

"You're going to dance for me."

Her knees did give out and she fell onto the mattress. "What?"

He gripped her around the waist and tugged her upright. "Remember the lap dance?'

"But *you* owe *me*."

"And I'm going to give it to you. But then you're going to give me one."

"Why?"

That damn sexy sideways smile was back. "Why not?"

Oh. Yeah.

"It'll be fun."

Fun, erotic…tomato/tomahto.

"Stay there. I'll be right back."

She didn't move as he left the bedroom. She couldn't.

He was back quickly, with his phone in his hand and a condom on his erection.

The guy was amazing.

He tapped the screen a few times, then music emerged.

"You're kidding," she said, recognizing the lead-in. Robert Palmer's *Simply Irresistible*.

He smiled. "Nope. This has a great beat and the words are perfect. You *are* simply irresistible, Lara."

"You seem to be doing a good job of resisting me, though, since you're all the way over there."

"Oh, don't worry. I'll be all the way over *there* in a few seconds." He set the phone on her dresser. "Now watch."

Like she was able to do anything else. He. Was. Naked.

And aroused.

And dancing.

For her.

"First you get your hips moving." He demonstrated that oh-so-well. "Put a little push into the booty area."

Oh yeah. That worked for her.

"Some shakes." He turned around and her mouth dried up like a desert.

Or was that *dessert*? The man could shake his ass and it was a thing of beauty.

"Now combine all of that with some arm movements." He put his arms behind his head, swiveled around, and his pecs and eight-pack started their own dance contest—which he moved closer.

Over-her-lap closer.

From the back.

Lara trailed a hand down his spine. Electricity sizzled all the way up her arm.

"What do you think?" he asked, looking back over his shoulder as his butt brushed her abdomen and his sac skimmed her legs.

She couldn't think, especially since he was dancing with a full on erection.

He stood back up and held out his hand. "Come join me."

She wanted to join *with* him. Now. Here. Immediately.

She took his hand, though, and shakily got to her feet.

Then Gage spun her around and spanned her waist with his hands, his pelvis still gyrating against her, and oh, God, the feel of him brushing the cleft of her backside threatened to take what little strength she was barely holding onto away.

"Just follow my movements, Lara."

She tried. Really she did. But it was only because his hands were guiding her that she managed to. Her brain was on *fried* as every brush of his skin against hers sent it into overload and all she could see was the wide expanse of the bed in front of her where she wanted to be spread out beneath him, taking that pulsing, throbbing part of him that was doing terribly sinful things to her backside inside of her to completion.

Then Gage cupped her breast and licked the curve of her shoulder.

"Isn't this fun?"

Fun wasn't quite the right word for it.

Lara bit her lip and looked back at him. "I can't take much more."

"Sure you can. I do this for an hour at a time on stage. You can give me a couple of minutes." He released his hold on her then and stepped back.

She wobbled.

Gage caught her. "Uh uh. You can do this. Come on, Lara, show me what you've got."

Embarrassment flooded her. What she had wasn't anywhere near what he did, but…

But he seemed to be into it, so why not? She had nothing to lose but this moment if she didn't.

She didn't want to lose this moment.

Taking a deep breath, Lara rolled her shoulders back and turned around. She could do this.

Gage changed the song. *Addicted to Love*. Was he trying to tell her something?

He sat on the chair by her bed and his smile was utterly charming. And encouraging. "Dance for me, Lara."

The first beat hit and Lara felt it thrum through her. She could dance. In clothing anyway.

Her hips started to move. Apparently she could dance out of it, too.

"That's it, baby. Shimmy for me."

She did, and the feeling of her breasts swinging before him—and the look in his eyes when they did—was utterly freeing. She put her arms behind her head, raising them, and put a little more swivel into her hips.

His eyes flared. "Ah, that's good. So good."

Yeah, it was.

She put out her toe and pivoted off it, her hips picking up every drum beat as she let the music flow through her. She tossed her head back and closed her eyes, feeling the downbeat in her blood, allowing it to course through her, to dictate her movements.

"That's it, Lar." His voice was low and raspy. Like the feeling she had low in her pelvis. "Come closer." This was whispered, but she heard him over the music.

She gyrated her way over to him, her gaze meeting his and not letting go.

His fingers flexed on his thighs. His cock twitched.

Oh yes, she was affecting him.

"Turn around."

She did. Slowly.

"Move back toward me."

She did. Straddling his legs. Open and wet and aching.

Gage groaned when she bent her knees.

She hovered there, over his lap, letting her hips tempt him as she ran her fingers through her hair and over her body. She cupped her breasts, knowing he couldn't see but would know she was touching herself.

It was wicked. It was decadent. It was the most erotic thing she'd ever done and the power of what she could do to him rose inside of her. It gave her the encouragement, the strength to circle her hips a little faster, brush her backside a little lower, tease him all the more.

"You are killing me," he muttered.

"What a way to go," she whispered back with a hint of laughter. God, the empowerment she felt.

"You are the sexiest thing I've ever seen, Lara." His fingers brushed her hips.

She felt like the sexiest thing ever. "Don't touch, Gage. Isn't that what you tell your clients? No touching?"

His laugh was harsh. "You saw how well that works."

She looked back over her shoulder. "So what are you going to do about it?"

His eyes flared again and he clamped his big strong hands on her hips and yanked her against him. "I'm calling an end to this dance and I'm going to impale you on my cock like this and let you ride me through the rest of my playlist."

And, oh, he did just that.

He took her there, in the chair, with his hands on her thighs holding her wide, his fingers playing with her, demanding she reach behind his head so her breasts were high and tight and he could watch them over her shoulder as he pumped inside her in time with the music.

"God, baby, that's it. Ride me."

She did. Bowed her back, flexed her toes on the carpet, and took him inside her, feeling every velvety steel inch along her entire passage and *this* was the most erotic thing she'd ever done.

There were a lot of firsts with Gage and Lara was honestly glad he was the one she was experiencing all of them with.

Their harsh breaths were drowned out by the playlist

that must be what his guys practiced dance moves to because each song had a heavy, throbbing downbeat that reverberated through her blood, spiraling down to that spot where they were joined, raising the heat and need and desire until she was gasping, her head falling back, and she clenched his hair because she needed something—anything—to hold on to.

The wave rose up, a roiling, swirling, blur of aching need, the sensations stealing her breath until, at last, it crested over her in a pulsing, pounding crash, urging her on as she clenched him and milked every sensation when he came, the moment infinite…

Gage was the first one to move. He twitched inside of her, drawing Lara back into every deliciously sated nerve ending in her body.

"You're amazing," he murmured against her neck, his hot breath sending more shivers through her.

"You're pretty amazing yourself. I've never done that before."

"Could have fooled me. You were a natural. All sensuous and alluring and you had me harder than a block of granite. I swear, I thought I was going to explode just watching you."

She couldn't contain a self-satisfied grin.

"Feeling pretty good about yourself, are you?" he teased.

She nodded against his shoulder, feeling the raspy scruff of his beard against her cheek. She wouldn't mind feeling it between her thighs.

Oh, God, she felt herself swell at the thought.

"What are you thinking?" he breathed. He'd felt it too.

She told him.

"That, my dear, can most definitely be arranged."

He managed to separate them and get her onto the bed when her legs refused to cooperate.

Though they did pretty well when he knelt by the bed and draped them over his shoulders, as he proceeded to send her on another round of pleasure.

By the time neither could move, Lara had lost count of how many times she'd come. Lost count of how many different positions they'd tried. But she knew each and every time he'd growled her name as he'd come, clasping her as the shudders wracked him, and Lara was so damn grateful for the gift that was Gage.

He intertwined their fingers as they lay on their stomachs facing each other, their eyes heavy with exhaustion, one of his legs thrown over hers, but there was still the glimmer of desire in his gaze when he looked at her.

"Spend the weekend with me."

Emotion shimmered through her. She'd like nothing better. "I'd love to, but I can't. It's our busiest weekend after the winter holiday season. I'm booked."

"Okay, so let me spend it with you. I'll knock off early on the third and can help you with your parties."

"You really want to spend your holiday working?"

"If it's with you, it won't be work."

It was the right thing to say. "Are you sure?"

He ran his fingertip down her nose and over her lips. Lara resisted the urge to suck it into her mouth.

For all of about two seconds. Seriously, why *couldn't* she suck it?

He groaned at the first touch of her tongue and pulled his finger out. "God, woman, you're going to wear me out."

"Good. Turnabout is fair play."

His smile was way too cocky, but she couldn't really complain. He'd earned it.

"Look, I'd love to take you up on the offer, but we both have to get up in the morning. I suddenly have even more of a rush on the gazebo I'm building, so I need my sleep."

"Party pooper." Though, really, she was just as pooped, but it was fun to tease him.

He rolled over and tucked her against his side, her head resting on his chest, and he kissed the top of her head. "Yeah, that's me. A real killjoy."

She smiled and snuggled up to him. Gage was definitely a *joy*.

Chapter 26

The rest of Lara's week, however, wasn't so joyous. The wedding on Saturday was iffy on the weather, which meant she had to have a contingency plan for the wedding cake and nine groomsmen's cakes, the most intricate order she'd had to date. The wedding cake itself was seven tiers tall, most of which had to be assembled on-site, and the humidity was making that a challenge as the buttercream beneath the fondant started to complain.

Thank God Gage came with her. He rigged up a tent outside that the wedding planner had forgotten, then held the tiers as Lara set them in place in the country club's kitchen so the cake could be wheeled out in time for the reception. Cara would normally have helped her, but she'd taken an order from a last-minute panicked new client whose previous bakery couldn't deliver. Luckily, there'd been an extra cake in the fridge so Cara was off delivering that. Jesse was holding down the bakery, putting more "firecrackers" together for the cake the township had ordered for their Fourth of July celebration the next day.

Lara had three more tiers to assemble when the bride walked past for the start of the ceremony. Gage looked luscious in the tux jacket he'd slipped into. Lara wondered if the pants he was wearing were the rip-away kind.

She wouldn't mind finding out first-hand.

"What are you smiling about? The bride's in tears," Gage stage-whispered to her.

God, he smelled good. Even with the heat and exertion, that special scent that was all his wrapped around her like he had last night.

"Weddings make me smile."

"Sweetheart, that is *not* a happy smile. That's an I've-got-a-secret-I-want-you-to-uncover smile, and you're tempting me to do just that." He nipped her ear.

"Stop. We're working."

"You'd do well to remember that instead of tempting me with your sexy self."

She rolled her eyes. She was in her chef coat and hat. About as asexual as she could get.

He kept up his banter and those heated looks as they worked to finish the cake in time for the reception.

The looks only got worse while they waited for the cake cutting part. "Come on, let's go find a coat closet."

"You're incorrigible."

"No, I'm horny. And so are you."

She rolled her eyes.

"*I* know how to get you to roll your eyes." He waggled his eyebrows.

She tried not to laugh, but yeah, that move he'd done last night with his tongue had not only had her rolling her eyes, but seeing stars, too.

"Gage, stop."

"That's not what you said last night."

How he'd even understood what she'd said last night was beyond her; she'd been incoherent. "You know, at some point, I'm actually going to need a full night's sleep." Texting and sexting was keeping her up far too late.

"That's what retirement's for."

He had an answer for everything. And Lara was coming to think of him *as* the answer to everything.

He made her smile. He made her feel beautiful. He made her feel special and cared for. He made her feel alive in a way she hadn't since long before her divorce.

The cake cutting ceremony went off without a hitch (of buttercream), the bride proclaimed it the best cake ever, and Lara and Gage got out of there in time to help Jesse finish up the last five dozen fire crackers before midnight.

"Well, Cinderella," said Gage, dragging her chef's hat off those adorable curls he'd thoroughly enjoyed burying his fingers in last night as she'd gone down on him and taken him to paradise, "it's the bewitching hour. Do you turn into a pumpkin if we don't have you home and in bed by then?"

"I feel like more like a squash." She plopped onto the bench seat in his truck.

She didn't look like one.

She looked beautiful.

Gage stared at her for a few more seconds, enjoying the way her eyelashes rested on her cheeks, curving slightly at the end. Her makeup had worn off hours ago, and to him, that natural beauty only made her prettier. Lara was so honest with her feelings, with who she was. He couldn't count the number of times he'd looked into her eyes and known she was there, with him, in the moment, and was so damn glad to be there with *him*.

That was the thing with dancing; sure, it got him a lot of women. And, sure, he'd been glad about that. But almost everyone had been into him for the experience. Because he was sexy and his body was cut. Because he knew how to use it. It'd been all about the physical pleasure, and hey, there was nothing wrong with that, but he hadn't ever connected to anyone the way he had with Lara. Not even Leslie though she'd come closest to being The One. But Lara was with him because of *him*, not because of what he looked like, and that made the sex that much more amazing. More sensuous, more pleasurable.

It also made it making love. So different from sex.

He took her home, and for the first time since they'd been together, he just held her. Tucked her against him, stroked his hand through her curls, kissed her gently on the lips, and held her as she fell asleep.

It was the most beautiful thing in his world.

Chapter 27

"Gazebo's looking pretty good."

The prick stood on the *terrace* with a mug of coffee in his hands, his hair slicked back from his shower, argyle vest over a button-down, razor-edged pleats on his linen pants, and even spats, or whatever those funny shoes people wore to play golf were called, while Gage sweated his ass off on the trusses.

He'd left Lara sleeping at five a.m. to get here and finish the framing. The copper flashing was coming on Monday, which had been enough time when he'd ordered it, but that'd been before he started spending time with Lara. A lot of time.

Too much time to keep going at this pace. He knew that, but he didn't want to change things. Already, though, Missy had told him Connor missed him. And he missed Connor, too. The lawn at his house needed to be mowed, he'd promised to put a shower bar in the bathroom before Connor's next surgery, and Missy needed the top shelf in the closet lowered so she could reach it.

But he was going to spend today with Lara, no matter what. Real life could roar back in on Monday.

"You're not cutting corners, are you, to get it finished quickly? I don't want it falling down at the party."

Gage yanked the nails out of his mouth. Normally he wouldn't justify that asinine comment with an answer, but this guy brought it out in him. Then again, most people wouldn't have the balls—or stupidity—to even ask that question. "I don't skimp on my work. My reputation's on the line."

"Glad to hear it. So many times contractors come here, see what I've built, and think I owe them. It's my hard work and expertise that earned me what I have. I want the best and I pay for it."

That was because the guy was the worst. Too bad he didn't realize that what he was picking up from those other contractors was disdain. Just because a guy had a fancy title, a hot car, and five thousand square feet more than one man needed didn't make him any better than the guy who worked with his hands for a living. In J.C. McCullough, it made him *less* of a man.

But Gage kept his mouth shut. A few more days then he'd collect the balance of what he was owed and be done with this prick.

"I was surprised to see you today. I thought you'd take the holiday weekend off."

Gage hammered another nail into the truss, pretending it was this guy's super-inflated ego. "Too much to do. Plus I'm spending the afternoon with my girlfriend at the park."

Girlfriend. The word had a nice ring to it. He hadn't had a girlfriend in a really long time.

"Ah, yes, the annual community picnic. I went once with my ex-wife. It was… pleasant."

This guy had been married before? He'd found not one but *two* women willing to deal with his pomposity? Though the other one had gotten smart and was now an ex.

Gage hammered another couple of nails in, then moved on to the next truss. He didn't know what it was about J.C. McCullough that got to him so badly, but he couldn't wait to finish this job.

But he'd meant what he'd said. It was his name, his reputation, on this gazebo. Regardless of how he felt about the client personally, he was all over making sure this structure was sound and solid. Because that's who he was.

"I was wondering how long you plan to leave that sign on my lawn? Our HOA doesn't permit signage or solicitation and I've been getting some complaints."

The complaints were in the guy's head. Gage knew exactly what the HOA guidelines were; he always checked before posting. Contractors were permitted signage through the completion of the project. Gage had every intention of taking the sign down when he drove his truck off the lot for the last time.

"It'll be down on Wednesday."

"That's cutting it close to the party."

"It'll be finished. I've built in time for any last-minute items and clean-up. Nothing to worry about."

"Oh I'm not worried. That was the date you gave me to be finished. I'll hold you to it or dock your pay accordingly." He took a sip of his coffee, then waved the mug in a half-hearted salute, turned on the heel (and there was a bit of a heel on that pretentious-ass shoe, too), and strode back through the over-sized French doors into the mausoleum he called home.

Gage wanted to shove the cup up the guy's nose. He knew exactly what J.C. had meant; the asshole didn't have to rub his nose in it. But man, would Gage love to rub his fist in the guy's face when he finished early.

Unfortunately, he wasn't going to. Not enough time. He would finish by Wednesday, though, so let the asshole sweat it out, worrying if Gage was going to leave his backyard a mess for the party or not. He might think money talked, but it'd be worth it to take a hit just to see the guy blow a gasket.

Except Gage wouldn't do that either. Besides needing the money and his reputation being on the line, he felt sorry for the woman who was going to be marrying this guy. Though maybe she was just like him.

He wondered what the first wife had been like. Since she'd been smart enough to leave J.C., she sounded like someone he'd like to know—well, if he weren't with Lara.

But he was. He definitely was.

Chapter 28

"I thought you said loverboy was going to show up to help?" Cara hauled the box of twirly lollipop firecrackers—complete with sparklers at the ends—onto their table at the park.

"He will be. He has a job, too, you know." Lara tried to keep her temper under control as she set out the red cupcakes with the strawberry licorice stripes on top. Cara had been getting testier by the day since mid-week, but would deny it every time Lara tried to talk to her about it.

Cara muttered something beneath her breath about where she'd like to light the firecrackers she was putting on the cake.

Lara let it go. She was in too good of a mood to let Cara's bad one get her down.

Gage had left a note on the pillow when he'd left this morning. *Can't wait to see you later.*

So thoughtful. So caring. So wonderful. She'd been floating ever since.

"Ugh. Are you going to be waltzing around here like a cat with a bowl of cream all day?"

She opened the box of cupcakes sprinkled with powdered sugar. "Car, what's going on? I thought you and Nick were doing okay?"

"Nick is—" She jammed a lollipop stick too far into the cake and cracked the fondant. "Shit. Sorry."

Lara pulled the stick out and nudged Cara out of the way so she could repair the damage as best as possible. "Why don't you take a breather?"

"That's exactly what I said to Nick. I told him it was too much. We were in each other's space too much and do you know what he said? Do you *know what he said*?"

Lara resisted the urge to unclog her ear from that shrill squeal. "What?"

"He said that if I need a breather from him, it'll have to be permanent. That he didn't want to be with someone who didn't want to be with him a hundred percent of the time. I mean, come on. A hundred percent? I don't even want to be with *myself* a hundred percent of the time; why would I want to be with anyone else that much?"

"You might want to ask yourself why you feel that way about yourself and then maybe you'll be able to give Nick the answer he wants."

"Oh, God, not you, too."

"Yes, me. I'd love to be with Gage that much. If I could figure out a way to spend all my time with him and still keep money coming in, sure, why not? I mean, don't you have fun with Nick? Don't you like him? Don't you want him?"

"Well, yeah, sure, but…"

"But what? What's stopping you?"

Cara opened her mouth to say something, but didn't. She clamped it closed, spun around, and stalked off toward the van.

Great. Lara couldn't go after her or half the box of firecrackers would disappear in the hands—and mouths—of the kids checking out her table. When today was over, she and Car needed to have a serious heart-to-heart.

Speaking of heart… Gage was jogging toward her and, wow. He looked as good jogging as he did dancing. And she had first-hand knowledge of both.

"Hey, sorry I couldn't get here sooner." He swept her up into a back-over-the-arm sort of breath-stealing kiss.

"You can be late all the time if that's the way you apologize," she said, holding on tight to his biceps. Not because she was scared he'd drop her—she wasn't—but just because his biceps felt amazing.

"Shall I pay in advance for the next time then?" He planted another kiss on her, every bit as fabulous as the first one.

"Ewww!"

Leave it to kids to ruin the moment.

Not that it was ruined, actually. Gage ended the kiss, but kept his arm around her as they faced the sugar-craving horde.

"Hey, gang," he said, all chummy and friendly, as if his heart weren't racing.

Lara put her hand on it just to make sure it was because hers was going a zillion miles a minute. It was only fair his was, too.

It was.

"Are we allowed to have the cupcakes now, mister?"

"You'll have to ask Ms. Cavallo since they're her cupcakes."

She bit her lip. Gage had chosen his wording for a reason; he'd thoroughly sampled and enjoyed *her* cupcakes several times over the last few days.

"Can we, Ms. Cavallo?" asked six kids at once.

"Let me get the rest of them out first. What would a Fourth of July celebration be without the Stars & Stripes?" She pointed to the empty square on the cupcake flag. "I only have the stripes on the table."

Gage brought out a box from beneath the table. "Is this them?"

"Yup." She removed a couple of blue-frosted cupcakes that she'd sprinkled with white nonpareils for the "stars."

It took the kids a lot less time to dismantle the flag than it had for her to set it up.

"Geez, who would have thought kids were like a swarm of locusts when it came to sugar?" Gage shook his head as he helped her re-stock the flag.

"Connor's birthday party wasn't enough evidence of the power of a sweet tooth?"

"Mmm, you're right. How could I forget? Connor hasn't stopped talking about how great his party was. Or how great his cake was. Do you know he still has that figurine you made? Missy finally had to put it in the fridge because it was starting to melt."

"I'm surprised he hadn't eaten it yet."

"Are you kidding? He wanted to sleep with the thing. Missy had a hard time talking him out of that one."

Lara smiled. It made her feel good to hear how happy her work had made someone.

"Looking pretty pleased with yourself."

"It's nice to hear. I put a lot of thought and effort into my work. And sure, I know people are going to eat it. I know it's not a great masterpiece, but for those few hours that it hasn't been touched, it *is* a masterpiece. A memory people will remember the rest of their lives if I do my job right. I'm so glad Connor enjoyed it."

"You know? I never thought about it like that. What you do. You're right. You give people a memory. Those kids earlier, for example. They had so much fun deciding if they wanted the licorice or the powered sugar or the crunchy candy things."

"Nonpareils."

"Easy for you to say. To me, they're crunchy things." He kissed her nose. "And to the kids, too. But I bet whenever they see those things from now on, they'll remember today. You do give people memories."

He nuzzled her neck. "And the ones you've given me these last few weeks… I'll treasure them forever."

Forever. Gage had said *forever*. Granted, he hadn't said it in relation to her; just that he'd remember what they'd done, how they'd been, together, but the fact that he could think *forever* should tell her something, right?

What did she want it to tell her? Was she ready to think about *forever*? What about focusing all her energy on the business? What about becoming self-sufficient before she went back into a relationship?

"You've got that look on your face again."

"What look?"

"The one that says you're carrying the weight of the world on your shoulders. Can't you just accept a compliment and move on?"

"Of course I can." And she could. It was a compliment on her work. That, she could accept. It was when he started in on how beautiful she was, how sexy, that she couldn't accept it.

But why the hell not? Gage wasn't blowing smoke up her skirt; he wanted her. He found her attractive. If all he'd wanted was to sleep with her, would he be here now, helping her? Would he have gotten up extra early this morning to go to work just so he could come back here and help her?

Jeff hadn't done that *ever.* Not when they'd been going on vacation and she'd had to pack for the both of them. Not when they'd had dinner parties and she'd been in the kitchen at oh-dark-thirty making the food before they'd been able to afford caterers. Certainly not when she'd been decorating their house and had gone from showroom to showroom for weeks on end to find just the furniture he'd specified. He'd expected what he'd expected and it hadn't mattered how she made it happen, but she *would* make it happen. He hadn't lifted a finger other than to write the damn check—the affirmation he needed to make himself feel good at being able to afford "the best."

Maybe that was because, deep down, he knew he wasn't the best.

Gage, on the other hand, was, and it wasn't fair to either man to compare them. Because Gage would always come out on top.

Like he'd been that last time…

"Okay, now that look I definitely get." Gage smiled that sexy come-hither smile that set her blood to boil and pulled her close.

"Geez, guys," said Cara. "This is a family event. You might want to cool it."

Gage raised his head but didn't let go. "Hi, Cara."

"Gage."

"Wow. Only one word? No dripping sarcastic comment to go with it?"

"Nope. Seems like you have that area all sewn up."

Lara pulled out of Gage's arms. Much as she wanted to stay there, Cara was right. *And* she was on the job. The township had paid her to be here; this wasn't a trade show where she was on her own dime drumming up business.

Cara held up one of the promotional bags everyone got upon entering the park. "They didn't put our brochures in the bags like they were supposed to. That's what happens when you let teenagers work for free."

"Do you have them with you?" Gage asked. "I'll hand them out."

"What, just walk up to people and hand them out?"

"Sure, why not? And since I'm not an owner, people will be more likely to believe me when I say there are no better *cupcakes* in the tri-state area."

Of course he winked at her when he said that, and Lara had to look away so Cara wouldn't see the blush that blazed its way up her chest into her face. Though why she worried about that after Cara had caught them kissing, she couldn't say.

Cara handed over a stack of brochures without a word. Not even *thank you*, but Lara took care of that when Gage pulled her against him for a quick kiss.

"See you in a little while," he said as he left.

"Is there anything he doesn't do well?" Cara asked with—if Lara wasn't mistaken—a little bit of wistfulness in her voice.

"Not yet."

"Seriously, Lar, the guy's a prince. He must have an evil stepmother or something. Warts? Halitosis? A tiny—"

"Gage is wonderful, Car. Let's leave it at that." She was *not* sharing *that* information with her cousin.

The cupcakes were a big hit, but Lara had a hard time staving off the lollipop-wanters. The event organizers wanted the cake intact for the beginning of the fireworks, which included all the lollipop sparklers she and Cara were going to light up.

Gage's marketing efforts were paying off as well, as more people started to filter by their booth with the brochures in hand. Cara was in her business acumen glory taking names and numbers and even a few orders. She held up her little white square charge doohickey she'd just gotten for her cell phone to process orders with a big grin on her face.

"That mixer is ours!" she said, gleefully.

Lara was just thankful there was a smile on her cousin's face.

And then there was a big one on *hers*. Gage was jogging back her way.

"All out of brochures, but I thought you could use this." He held up a hotdog wrapped in a napkin.

"Hey, thanks. I'm famished," she said before giving him a kiss for it.

Gage took two. And that was okay with Lara.

"Seriously? A hotdog? That gets you two all mushy? Ugh." Cara's good mood disappeared as she flounced into the folding director's chair they'd brought along for down time. This was the first time it'd gotten used all afternoon.

Gage disengaged himself from Lara's arms with a

smile. "I got you one, too, Car." He held out the peace offering.

Cara eyed it as if he'd injected it with arsenic. "Why?" She reached for it.

Gage pulled his hand away. "The correct response is, 'Thank you, Gage.'"

She scowled up at him. "Thank you, Gage."

He gave her the hotdog. "See? That wasn't so hard, was it? I don't bite."

Not unless she asked him nicely... Lara blushed. Gage, of course, noticed and winked at her.

"Hope you like onions and relish on it," Gage said to Cara.

She stared at it as she unwrapped it. "I… I do. How'd you know?"

Gage shrugged. "Seems the guy handing these out knows it, too."

Cara was about to bite into it, but stopped. "Guy?"

"Yeah. Fireman? Built. Square jaw. Had seventeen women drooling around him since he's in pants, suspenders, and not much else. I might have to sign him up to dance for BeefCake."

Cara dropped the hotdog on the table. "I'll be back."

Lara pinched Gage's arm. "That's Nick. Her boyfriend."

"I kinda gathered that when I mentioned I was getting the hotdogs for the women at the bakery. He was all over wanting to know who I was. Jealous type?"

Lara shook her head. "He's probably more annoyed. Cara's not making his life easy."

"Neither are you, Lar. I've smashed my thumb more times in the past week on a job than I have for the past two years 'cause you've got me all distracted."

"Oh, so it's my fault you can't keep your mind on the job?"

"It's certainly not anyone else's."

That was good to hear. She hadn't really thought so, but still, nice to hear him say it. Jeff never had.

"So how'd you know what I like on my hotdog?" Ketchup with just a tad of mustard.

"Good guess?"

She arched an eyebrow at him. "Really? You just happened to luck out and not put the spicy mustard on?"

"I figured you were spicy enough. You don't need any help." He nuzzled her neck and Lara was all for exploring the spiciness of their situation, but a public event was not the place. She might be into trying out new things with Gage, but that wasn't one of them.

"Can I take a rain check until later tonight?"

"Doesn't look like rain."

"Since when has that ever stopped you?"

"Good point." He took one last lingering kiss then backed off. Just enough to be P.C. But he still held her hand.

Lara smiled.

"You're smiling again."

"You make me smile."

"Good, because you make me smile, too."

Which he proceeded to do with devastating results to her equilibrium. Thankfully, someone approached her table just then.

"Hey, Gage. Why am I not surprised to see you here?"

"Hey, Bry." Gage released Lara's hand. "Lara Cavallo, Bryan Lassiter, my partner at BeefCake, Inc."

"So this is the famed cupcake lady I've been hearing about." He shook her hand.

Lara looked at Gage. "He's been hearing *what* about me?"

Gage held up his hands. "Hey, I don't kiss and tell. He knew I was interested in you. That's all."

"So that means there's more?" Bryan leaned a hip against the table and crossed his arms. His big muscular arms. Just like the rest of him. Yes, she could see him as a dancer. "Do tell."

"None of your business, Bry. Have I missed a gig yet?"

"Nope, but hey, I can totally see why you could." He smiled at Lara. "Don't mind Gage, he's just a big tease. Now me, on the other hand…"

It'd been so long since anyone had flirted with her—before Gage had come along—that Lara couldn't help enjoying it if only for a minute. Vanilla, huh?

"Hey, man, back off." Gage didn't sound like he was joking.

It'd been since *never* that anyone had fought over her.

"Wow, chill, will ya, Gage? I'm only kidding." Bryan had his hands up and he'd stepped back from the table. "I was just stopping by to say hi and try one of these famous cupcakes. The guys were saying we ought to order a batch for our next gig. Give the women sweets *and* sex. It'll be a marketing bonanza."

Gage shoved one of the blue cupcakes at him. "Here. Try this. It's amazing."

The thrill Lara got from his endorsement was different from the thrill he gave her when he kissed her—or looked at her—but just as nice.

Bryan made a big production of groaning while he ate the cupcake—even did a tantalizing tongue-slide across his lips that had Gage bristling, but Lara wasn't affected. She was more affected by Gage's jealousy than anything Bryan could do because no matter how good-looking he was, he wasn't Gage.

"Yes, Lara," said Bryan, licking the last of the buttercream off his lips—though he missed one of the "stars"—"you definitely have awesome cupcakes."

He very pointedly kept his eyes above her collarbone. Or it could be that she was just sensitive to any kind of innuendo, but she didn't miss the way Gage stiffened beside her.

"You might want to think about what I said, Gage." Bryan balled the cupcake holder up and also made two points shooting it into the trashcan beside the booth. "Getting cupcakes for our booth might not be such a bad idea."

Gage knew a cupcake he'd like to have in their booth.

Bry was pissing him off. Oh, the guy had no real interest in Lara; he'd never do that to Gage. But he just couldn't help tweaking Gage's protective urges by flirting. Harmless, Gage knew, but still. This was Lara. *His* Lara.

The world shifted at that. She was his. *His*. And he wanted to keep her.

He gave Bry a mock salute as his partner headed off, but his mind was stuck on Lara.

Somehow she'd crept into his heart. This wasn't infatuation or plain lust. He'd called it the other night; they'd made love.

Holy shit. He was in love with her.

"You okay, Gage? He was just teasing, you know." Lara put a hand on his arm and Gage could only stare at it.

He loved her.

He was in love with Lara.

He didn't have time for love. For a relationship. Hadn't these past few weeks proven that? He hadn't seen Connor in a while, had no time to fix anything at his house, was keeping Missy waiting, and had bugged out early from a job to be with Lara. It went against everything he'd been telling himself he wanted. Then there was the whole jealousy issue he'd dealt with with Leslie…

He loved Lara.

Now what the hell was he going to do about it?

Chapter 29

The fireworks lit up the night sky but they couldn't hold a candle to what Gage did for her when he kissed her.

They'd lit the cake, divvied out the slices to the crowd, then taken their seats on a blanket on the hill overlooking the football field where the township was setting off the fireworks, the night cocooning them in its warm embrace. And even though they were smashed in with most of the town, the blanket Gage had spread out for them became their own little slice of heaven.

Anywhere was heaven when she was in Gage's arms.

Lara smiled at the clichéd phrase, but there was a reason it was a cliché. Because it perfectly described everything she was feeling. He had his arm around her shoulders, her head tucked against his, causing her heart to pound with the same intensity as it did with the resounding *boom* of the fireworks as they "ooh"ed and "aah"ed with the crowd.

"Mommipop." A toddler wandered onto their blanket, holding out one of the twisty lollipops from the cake Lara had made. The little girl held it out, the colorful sugar ringing her fist at the base of the stick.

"Yes, that's a lollipop," said Lara, looking around for the parents. "Do you like lollipops?"

The little girl nodded. "Tuptake."

"You like cupcakes, too?" Her fans were starting young, but Lara wasn't thrilled that she'd instilled this kind of loyalty to have a toddler wandering off from her parents. "Where's your mommy?" Lara asked.

The toddler turned around and pointed at a woman half a dozen blankets over who had jumped up and was looking around frantically.

Lara hopped to her feet and scooped the little girl up, not caring that she was now wearing enough sugar on her forearm to attract the park's entire mosquito population. "Here she is!" she called as she ran up to the woman.

The woman spun around. "Oh, thank God!" She tore the little girl out of Lara's arms. "Thank you so much. She was just here one minute and the next—"

Lara patted the little girl's head. "You must have been so scared. She came over to me to show me her lollipop."

"Her lollipop?" The woman looked at her daughter then at Lara. "Oh, you're the cupcake lady. She hasn't stopped talking about you. Thank you so much for bringing her back. She's never wandered off before. I guess the lure of more cupcakes was too much for her."

"Well I'm all out of cupcakes tonight, but if you want to bring her by Cavallo's Cups & Cakes, I'll have another one for her."

The woman kissed her daughter's cheek as she bounced her gently in her arms. "I don't know that I want to reward her bad behavior, but I actually was going to call you for an order. Her birthday is coming up, and well, I guess I know what she wants."

Lara smiled and patted both the mom and daughter's arms. "Sure, no problem. I'll make a special batch just for her. What's her name?"

"Wendy."

"I'll call them Wandering Wendys. How does lemon-lime sound for a flavor?"

"You're really going to design a cupcake just for her?"

"Sure. No one else in town will have Wandering Wendy-flavored cupcakes. What better way to reward my loyal clients than by naming a cupcake after them?"

The idea just came to her, but Lara realized a good one when she came up with it. Cara would love this.

"Oh, thank you so much," said Wendy's mom. "We'll take two dozen for next Saturday. She's having a mermaid-themed birthday party."

"Perfect. We'll have them ready for you in the morning." She pulled out her cell phone and took Wendy's mom's number for a follow-up call when she got back in the bakery on Monday.

"Everything all right?" Gage asked when she returned to their blanket.

"It is." She told him about her idea with Wendy's cupcake. "Remember Bryan mentioned ordering my cupcakes for your shows? I could design a specific one for each guy and name it after him. What do you think?"

"After the guys?" Gage scrunched his face. "As long as it's not something like Gage's Guns, I'm okay with that."

She socked him in one of those "guns." "Hey, this is my business we're talking about. I'll come up with something catchy, but classy."

"Yes, because we all know strippers are all about class."

There was a note in his voice… "Are you ashamed of what you do?"

Gage looked at her. "Are *you* ashamed of what I do?"

"Me? Why does it matter what I think? It's your business."

"Because I know the problems it can cause." He looked at her, his blue eyes darkening. "Some of my old girlfriends… they couldn't handle it. It got to be a big elephant in the room. Jealousy. They got to the point where they didn't like other women fantasizing about me. They started to see me as other women did, and when it came to intimacy, well, hell." He scrubbed a hand over his face, then tucked one of her corkscrew curls behind her ear. "I don't want that to happen with us. I don't want you to see me as that guy up on stage. I don't want to *be* that guy for you. I want to be me. Gage. General contractor by day who has a night job to bring in extra cash. I never intended for it to define me, and when I left it all those years ago, that was it. It was over. But now I'm back in it—occasionally having to dance—and you're in my life. And after what your ex put you through… I don't want it to be an issue."

She nibbled on her bottom lip. "I can't say that I like other women wanting you, but it comes with the territory."

She hadn't answered the question—or rather, she had, but not in a way he wanted to hear.

That was his answer.

The grand finale of fireworks exploded around them, taking Gage's good mood with it. What was he doing? He had no business sitting in this field with her, pretending what they had was normal. Sustainable. Forget about what, exactly, it was that he did, they both worked ridiculous hours and that wasn't about to change in the near future. Connor had at least another eighteen months of surgeries and therapy, and probably a hell of a lot longer for the bills, which meant BeefCake, Inc. was part of who he was for at least that long.

He'd allowed himself to be distracted by Lara. Excited by the possibility. But Connor had suffered and Missy needed him. His damn thumb hurt from hitting it, and the gazebo could have been done that much sooner if he hadn't cut out to be with her.

It wasn't love. It couldn't be. Not the kind that would last, especially if it adversely affected the rest of his life. And because he'd lost his focus, something he'd promised himself and Connor as the little guy had fought for his life after the accident he'd never do, it'd be best to end it now and leave them both heart-whole.

Well, leave *her* heart-whole. His was a whole other matter.

Chapter 30

The next morning, Lara brushed the cloud of flour off her face that'd exploded all over her when she'd dropped the bag on the prep table.

Figured. Her mind had wandered because she'd barely slept last night. Gage had been too quiet on the walk back to their cars. Not that she been a chatterbox either; that discussion about his job had made her think.

She *didn't* like women fantasizing about him as he got undressed in front of them. He couldn't fault her for that. If the tables were turned, he'd feel the same way.

At least, she'd like to *think* he'd feel the same way, but she didn't know him well enough—and didn't know how he felt about her enough—to know if he would. Which was part of the problem

It came down to whether or not she could trust him. Trust was a big issue after what Jeff had done.

But Gage isn't Jeff.

She knew that. Logically, she did. Emotionally was a whole other story.

Was she even ready for emotional?

Last night, she thought maybe she had been before the conversation had gotten weird. She'd sat between his knees with his arms linked in front of her, nuzzling into the kisses he placed on her neck and ear in the darkness between the fireworks, enjoying their perfect day. The perfect date. Everything had been wonderful—so wonderful, she'd let herself imagine *what if.*

Her tummy fluttered like it had last night. What if she and Gage were together? What if this wasn't a passing fling? What if this was the start to forever for them?

And then he'd brought up his job and the questions

had started. The uneasiness. The insecurity. Just like the end of her marriage.

She'd argued with herself all night—the entire, long, lonely night that she'd lain in her bed without him, wondering what they were doing.

He had two jobs. A nephew who needed him. She had the bakery. She'd been deluding herself that a relationship could work—just like she'd done during her marriage. Something she'd promised herself she'd never do again.

Right. She threw back her shoulders and brushed the flour into a trash can. She was independent. Strong. Confident. Made her own decisions. Didn't let her emotions dictate her actions. She'd just relegate Gage to the "good time" portion of her life and let it go at that. He'd been there when she'd needed someone to help her take that first step—and if his first steps had been to music, ah well, at least she'd learned how to lap dance.

Her heart stuttered at the memory, but she pushed it aside. She couldn't allow herself to imagine things that weren't there. And she couldn't ignore the issues that were. Gage might be a great guy, a great lover, but the fact of the matter was, it was too soon. Too much. He couldn't promise her what she needed and it wasn't fair to ask him to. Worse, it was setting them both up for failure. She'd lived that nightmare once already.

Coward.

She could hear Cara's voice in her head, but had to tune it out. Maybe she was a coward, but with what she'd been through and Gage's odd behavior last night, she had to protect herself.

She cut off another chunk of fondant and was about to start rolling it out when a "Hello?" echoed from the reception area.

Crud. She wiped her hands on a dish towel and headed out there. She didn't need walk-in clients today.

"Hello, dear."

She especially didn't need Mrs. Applebaum in all her condescending graciousness. No one could do condescending like this woman. Even Jeff.

"Mrs. Applebaum." She stuck her hands in her coat pockets. "What can I do for you?"

"Is Cara here?"

"No. It's her day off."

"Ah, good." Mrs. Applebaum clutched her purse closer. "I wanted to speak with you."

"Is this about your son's graduation party?"

"It is." Mrs. Applebaum looked around at the empty reception area. "Is there someplace we could sit to discuss it?"

Lara grimaced. They hadn't gotten to setting up the seating area yet. Too bad Gage hadn't had the chance to touch up the paint and fix the counter—

No. She couldn't count on Gage. She wouldn't allow herself to. "I'll be right back."

She ran into Cara's office and dragged out the wheeled office chair and the wooden side one a previous tenant had left behind. It was the best she could do in a pinch.

And pinched was what Mrs. Applebaum's face became when she saw what Lara had brought her.

"Sorry about the accommodations. Our, um, reception furniture hasn't arrived yet." It wasn't a lie; they just hadn't ordered it.

Of course the woman took a tissue from her purse and wiped the office chair down before she sat in it.

"Now, dear, as to Phillip's party." She pursed her lips. "I'm afraid I won't be paying what your cousin quoted me. I'm sure you realize it's highway robbery. You can't tell me that the cost of *cake mix* tripled between my last party and my Phillip's event. That's simply unconscionable."

Lara gritted her teeth. She'd told Cara the price was too high. That Mrs. Applebaum would never go for it.

But… Mrs. Applebaum *had* gone for it. Lara had seen the signed contract. Had cashed the deposit check that covered their cost outlay, *and* she'd done a fair amount of juggling with the schedule to be able to accommodate the woman.

She squared her shoulders. *Confident. Strong. Make her own decisions. Rely on herself.*

"Actually, Mrs. Applebaum, it's a fair offer. We had to hire extra help, rearrange our other clients' schedules, and order more supplies at a higher cost." *And you signed the contract.* Lara wasn't going to go there unless it was necessary—and she really hoped it wouldn't be. She hated these kinds of discussions, but she had to back Cara up.

"I'm going to have to request my money back, dear."

Oh, hell. It *was* going to be necessary.

Lara inhaled and straightened her backbone again. "But Mrs. Applebaum, what are you going to do for your son's party?"

"Oh, that needn't concern you. I'll find another baker."

"They'll charge you the same amount. It's a last minute job, and quite involved at that."

"Nonsense. It's just a cake."

A three-dimensional architectural rendering was *not* "just a cake." But Lara couldn't say that because she was supposed to keep up the illusion that creating her cakes was seamless. If the clients knew too much about the process, how much was involved with the construction, it'd destroy the mystique, and their reputation was built on that mystique.

"I understand you're upset. What can we do to rectify this situation?"

"You'll have to lower the price."

Lara shook her head. “I’m sorry, but I can’t do that. We’ve incurred costs that we’d have to eat, and per our contract, there are no refunds at this stage.”

Mrs. Applebaum gaped at her. “You can’t be serious.”

“I regret this as much as you, but I am serious. It’s in the contract you signed.”

“Well.” She harrumphed. “I never.”

“But perhaps we can do something else for you. You ordered the cake in the shape of his college. Perhaps I could include an individual cake for you and your husband. A re-creation of his degree, perhaps? After all, you were the ones who guided him through his career, right? Paid for his schooling? It’s only fair that you should have a special memory on this occasion, too.”

She had enough batter and fondant to make a plain, rectangular cake with a couple of “scroll” ends, and it wouldn’t take her more than an hour or so, so her only cost would be her time. But if it kept Mrs. Applebaum happy and prevented her from canceling her order, it’d be worth it.

Mrs. Applebaum chewed on her lip as her fingers worked the clasp on her purse. “A cake of our very own… Yes, I do believe my husband would appreciate the acknowledgment of all we’ve sacrificed for Phillip.”

No, *Mrs.* Applebaum would appreciate the acknowledgment, which was why Lara had suggested it.

“Great. So we’re good then?”

“Yes, well, I guess that will be okay.”

“Wonderful.” Lara stood up. “I’m glad we could come to an agreement. I’ll see you Sunday at noon with both cakes.”

Mrs. Applebaum patted her hair as she stood. “Excellent, dear. I’m looking forward to it. And I know Frank will be thrilled.”

Frank. Uh huh. Mr. Applebaum was one of those

beleaguered husbands whose wife ran over him and he'd resigned himself to the tire marks.

Having dealt with Mrs. Applebaum successfully, Laura could say that, for the first time since her marriage, she wasn't feeling that same thing.

Gage scrubbed a hand through his hair as he walked into his kitchen.

"You're here?" Missy turned around from the stove with a pan in her hand. "You haven't been here for breakfast in a while. Is the world coming to an end?"

It felt like it.

Gage swiped the hand over his face. He needed a shave. "Can't a guy spend a night in his own bed without it making the news?"

"Any other guy, sure, but you…?" Missy scooped the French toast out of the pan and put it on a plate. "Did something happen with Lara?"

Other than the fact that he'd realized what he felt for her? And what he couldn't have? "No. We've just been going full throttle and both of us have a lot to do."

"I hear a 'but' coming."

He shook his head. He wasn't going to discuss this with his sister. "No buts."

Missy wasn't buying it. What was it with women? They had a kid and immediately got the Mother's Third Eye, the one in the back of their head that allowed them to see all?

"Okay, if you say so." She set the plate on the table. "If you want French toast you're going to have to make it yourself. I have to get Connor."

"How about *I* get Connor, and you make the toast?"

Missy patted his shoulder. "God, you're easy. Sure, I'll make you breakfast."

Gage headed back to Con's room. Easy? No, he

wasn't easy. He wanted what he couldn't have and was a mass of contradictions and responsibilities, none of which he wanted to deal with, but all of which he would.

Gage sighed as he stood outside Connor's doorway. His nephew was one responsibility he'd never complain about. At least he *could* take care of him. If that car that'd hit him had been going any faster…

Gage shook it off. It was a thought he'd had way too often over the past few months and it never failed to reinforce all he was doing for his sister and her son. Sacrificing his love life was miniscule in comparison.

"Hey, Con, ready for breakfast?" He pasted a smile on and put on the upbeat face he always wore around his nephew.

"Gage!" Connor's face lit up like the fireworks last night.

Fireworks. Oh, crud. Where had Connor watched them? *He'd* been so caught up in Lara that he hadn't even thought about what Connor would be doing. What kind of uncle was he?

"How are you, bud?"

"Good now. Look what I can do." He lifted his left hand in his right. "Watch." His index finger twitched. "See that? It moved. It's gonna get better."

Gage swallowed the tears that rushed into his throat. God, that one tiny twitch and it gave them all hope. "Has your mom seen it?"

"Nah, I wanted to show you first, so you can start planning that trip to the amusement park."

"I got it covered, Con." Hell yeah, he did. Orlando, with its many big-name theme parks. Somehow he'd swing it, but Connor deserved the trip of a lifetime.

"How long do you think until the rest of my hand moves?"

Gage's heart broke a little bit more. "Well, if you

keep working at your therapy, probably pretty soon. Look how far you've come with this." Four months, three days and twenty-two hours.

"I think it's 'cause of all the video games I've been playing. You need both hands for those and this hand was feeling left out."

It'd been heartbreaking to see Connor try to get the controls to work with his bad hand. Even sadder to see him give up in disgust. Maybe Gage should just get him the COD game he wanted and worry about what the images would do to Connor's brain after his fingers started working.

Gage shook his head. Bad idea. Connor was making progress. There was no reason to think he wouldn't make more.

"So did you watch the fireworks with Lara last night?"

Gage did a double take. The kid was a little too astute for seven. "Yeah, I did. She had to work the community picnic." Which he should have taken Connor to.

"Mom asked if I wanted to go, but it would've been too hot in the chair with the casts." He looked at his left hand and twitched the finger again. "She's pretty cool, you know."

"Your mom? Yeah, she is. She loves you a lot."

"Not her. Lara. The cupcake lady."

Everyone with Lara's cupcakes… "Yeah, she's a good baker."

"You gonna marry her?"

Good thing he was leaning against the door frame. "Marry her?"

"You like her, don't you?"

Gage shoved his hands into his pockets. "Yeah, but what's with the twenty questions?"

"I only asked three. And you're not answering one of

them."

"Who are you and what have you done with my video-game loving nephew?"

Connor crossed his good arm over the paralyzed one. "I think you should marry her."

"And why is that?"

"She's pretty."

True.

"She's fun."

True.

"She has great cupcakes."

Absolutely true.

"And you're in a better mood when she's around."

Something thudded in Gage's gut. He was in a better mood? Connor was picking up on his *moods*?

If so, he'd know he was in a shitty one right now.

He pulled his hands out of his pockets. He wasn't going to let the issue of Lara color his time with Connor. He saw him too little as it was. "We'll see, Con. Right now, I have to get you to the kitchen for your mom's awesome French toast."

Connor arched an eyebrow at him. A chip off his uncle's block.

"I'll think about it, Con, okay? I can't make any promises, but I will think about it."

As if it weren't the main topic in his brain already.

Chapter 31

"Any chance you're going to see Gage today?" Cara stuck her head out of her office to shout at Lara in the kitchen a few days later.

"I doubt it, why?"

"I wanted to get these files to Missy. She's going to take a look at them for me."

"I thought she was just working on the contracts?"

Cara shrugged. "I told you; I'm an accountant, not a legal secretary. I did my best, but it can't hurt to have her look over them."

"You're giving her busywork."

"I don't know what you're talking about."

"Yes you do. You're giving Missy busy work, stuff we don't really need done, but she doesn't know that. You're giving her the chance to earn money without making her feel as if she's taking charity."

Cara thrust out her chin. "You're delusional."

"Cara Marie Cavallo, I've known you your entire life. Don't think you can pull one over on me. You're doing a good deed and you didn't want anyone to know."

"You can't tell her. She has her pride. If she knew—"

"Your secret is safe with me, Robin Hood."

"I'm not stealing from anyone."

"But you're giving to her and that's really nice of you."

"She could use the money, but more importantly, it's making her feel needed. Necessary."

"You don't have to convince me, Car. As long as you say we can afford it, I'm all for it. It's really nice of you."

Cara mumbled something.

"What? I couldn't hear that."

There was some more mumbling. "Well, Gage did get me a hotdog."

If Lara could laugh, she would. But she hadn't felt like laughing since the weekend. "You're right, Car. A hotdog does merit mercy work."

"So… you guys looked like you were having fun at the park." Great. Cara was trying to turn the tables on her.

"I was working." She didn't want to discuss Gage with Cara. She didn't even want to *think* about Gage. He hadn't called. Not one word from him in the four days since then.

Was his dancing really that much of a big deal that her discomfort with it put him off being with her? Was her insecurity?

"Oh please. Tonsil hockey is not work. Unless he was paying you for it?"

Lara threw a piece of fondant at her. "Your point?"

"My point is that I'm happy for you. You deserve to be happy and he makes you happy."

But why did a guy have to make her happy? Why wasn't she happy on her own?

Actually, she had been before Gage. She and Cara working together at the bakery, being in her very own condo with things she'd picked out… She'd even thought about getting a kitten, something Jeff would never have agreed to. All of those things made her happy.

Oh, not in the twirl-around-on-her-toes-singing-happy-songs kind of happy like being with Gage, but she'd been happy. Gage had just made her happi*er*.

That was a big difference, being happy versus happier. Her life had centered around Jeff; it didn't around Gage. That was healthy, right? That allowed her to be herself, be who she wanted, *do* what she wanted. And if she wanted him to share with her, that was up to her, too.

If he'd only call her again—

Or she could call him. Nothing better for being in charge of her life and making her own decisions than calling up the guy she couldn't stop thinking about and dragging him back into her life. Other women went through what she had with Jeff. Some had it a lot worse. It was time to stop letting Jeff define her post-divorce life, too, and if she wanted Gage in it, she owed it to herself to try. "You don't mind having him around?"

Cara raised her eyebrows. "Seriously? You light up like a Christmas tree, he does all the heavy lifting and hand-to-hand selling, *and* he brings us hotdogs. Why would I mind?"

"Seriously, Car, am I crazy to think about him like this?"

"Like what?"

"Like—"

The breath whooshed out of her as the realization hit her. "Like… I think I might have fallen in love with him."

Just saying the words aloud had her stomach twisting and turning and flipping upside down as if she were riding a rollercoaster. A really fun, sexy rollercoaster that she didn't ever want to get off of.

"If you *think* you do, Lar, you do. You're not one of those wishy-washy types. When you love someone, you do it wholeheartedly. That's why Jeff was able to do such a number on you. Why his betrayal hurt so much. You were the only one who hadn't seen it coming."

That didn't make her feel any better. If anything, it only reinforced her insecurity. "What if Gage is the same way and I can't see it again?"

Cara got off her stool and walked over to her to hug her. "Gage is nothing like Jeff. Ever. And deep down, you know that. He's shown you in ways Jeff never did. But *you* have to know it, Lar. You can't go on my word. You have to be secure in what you feel for him and the trust you have in him for anything between you to work. If you don't, you're always going to doubt him and his feelings, and nothing will ruin a relationship faster than doubting your partner."

Cara was right. It all came down to trust: in what she felt for him, in what he felt for her, and in what she felt for herself.

She liked herself. She was proud of herself. She'd taken her life back: in her business, in her home, heck, even with Mrs. Applebaum. Love was the next step. She deserved to find love again. To *be* loved, and if she was going to move forward with her life, she had to take the chance.

Gage was worth it.

She hugged Cara back. "You're right, Cara. I do love him."

"Well no kidding." Cara kissed her cheek. "And he loves you if I'm not mistaken."

"You think so?"

"I'm not the one you need to ask."

"I can't ask him *that*."

"I'd say, 'why not,' but he's not the one you need to ask either." Cara tapped Lara's nose. "Do you think he loves you is a question, dear cuz, that you need to ask yourself because if you don't feel it, it doesn't matter what he says."

Gage stared at the piece of paper in his hand. Lara's lawyer buddy had come through. BeefCake, Inc. had a permanent home.

What a relief. He could finally have some semblance of a life. He wouldn't have to make calls to book gigs for twenty hours every week anymore. He wouldn't have to travel twice that long *to* those gigs—well, once the place was operational. Until then, he'd be pulling double duty since he was the general contractor for getting the building into shape. But at least they'd be able to count on a steady stream of income.

And maybe he and Lara could work something out.

He took another swig from his water bottle and folded the license, making a mental note to call Bryan when he got in the truck. It'd be a long phone call and he wanted to clean up J.C. McCullough's back yard and get the hell off the property since he'd finished the gazebo. He'd been working fifteen hour days ever since the weekend to finish this project, determined to have the income rolling in *and* keep his mind off Lara.

Not that it'd worked.

But his lawn had gotten mowed and the shelf moved in the closet. Last night, he'd stopped letting Connor win their chess matches. Since they'd played so many games, the kid was on his way to becoming a master and no longer needed the confidence boost.

But at night, when he'd lain in bed, he hadn't been able to forget her. Had picked up his cell phone more times than he could count, his fingers hovering over her number, only to put it down without making that call because she deserved more from him. They all did. Hell, *he* did.

But there was only so much of him to go around, and it wasn't fair to ask her to put up with that. She should feel loved and cherished and wanted, and while he did feel all those things, flowers and phone calls could only convey that message for so long. It'd be different if he were serving his country or away on business, but in town? No excuse.

You're making excuses.

Was he? God knew, he'd tried to figure out a way to make it work, but until he'd gotten the benefit numbers last night, he'd been coming up empty, what with the medical bills piling up and the supplies he needed for the next construction job. Not to mention his house needed a new heating system. And then there was the trip to Orlando that he knew was totally frivolous given everything else he needed money for, but Connor was only a kid once and he deserved *something* good to come his way.

But now, with the benefit tally more than he'd dared hope for, and the steady income this license represented, he could look forward to more time on his hands once he got the place in shape. And with the income from the this job and the other two he now had time to finish, and Missy pulling in extra cash doing Cara's paperwork—man, he owed Cara big time for that—he wouldn't have to sweat bullets anymore over every medical bill that came through the door. Things were finally starting to turn the corner for good.

Lara was so good.

"So, that's it? You're finished?" The prick was back on his patio, again with the amber liquid in a tumbler, and a ridiculous pair of loafers on his feet that had probably cost more than Connor's last MRI.

It was really hard not to hate the guy, so Gage hadn't bothered trying not to.

Sour grapes.

Possibly. But regardless of his own financial situation,

this guy rubbed him the wrong way for more reasons than just money.

Gage dropped the hammer into the tool box and picked up the packing material from the weather vane and shoved it into the box it'd shipped in. "Yep, that's it. Lighting's connected, too. You're all set for the party."

J.C. rocked back on his heels and studied the gazebo.

Gage dared him to find one thing wrong with it.

"Nice work. Send me your invoice and I'll have my accountant mail you a check."

"Actually—"Gage pulled the invoice he'd printed out last night off of his clipboard—"here it is. If you wouldn't mind writing a check now, I can close the books on it."

It wasn't his normal M.O., but he'd changed the terms in the contract for this job because he'd wanted to have the least amount of interaction with Mr. J.C. McCullough.

The prick raised an eyebrow at him. "You don't think I have that amount in my checking account, do you? It wouldn't be prudent to leave that much where anyone could hack into it. I have to move some money around."

"You can post date the check. I'll cash it tomorrow."

"Oh it won't be available until at least next week."

After the party. Gage gritted his teeth. The guy had known when the gazebo would be finished—had insisted on it. And he'd made such a big production about everything his "hard work and expertise" had earned him, surely the balance wouldn't break his bank account.

"Look, J.C." He enjoyed the way the guy winced when he called him by his first name. "I did the job you hired me to do. And you signed the contract that specifically spells out when I'm to be paid. I'd like my check." Or he'd undo the wiring—at the very least—but didn't say so. He tried not to issue ultimatums, but this guy was on his bad side anyway, so he might break that rule if the guy didn't cave.

But cave he did. "Fine. But you can't cash it until late tomorrow. Friday would be better."

Gage would be at the bank at 3:59 tomorrow afternoon.

He gathered the trash, his tool box, and the miter saw, and put them in his truck while he waited for J.C. to write the check.

"Don't forget the lawn signs," Prick said when he handed it to him on the driveway.

Message received: the help was no longer allowed on the property.

"I'll get them on my way down the drive." Gage pocketed the check and held out his hand. He might hate the guy, but business was business. "Nice doing business with you."

Prick considered his hand, but in the end, shook it. Gage knew he would; the guy was the kind to stick to convention which was why Gage figured he'd pay up if confronted. Bullies usually did when challenged.

Gage wondered if the ex-wife had figured out the same thing.

Chapter 33

"You know McMonster has called here six times in the last two hours to make sure you're going to be on time? We lose power for six hours from last night's storm, yet the damn phones still work. Care to explain the fairness in *that* to me?" Cara dropped the pink phone message slips on the prep table and shoved a pencil behind her ear. "Please let me tell him we can't do the party. Please."

Lara looked up from the rose she was making. Number three hundred and seventy-five. Only twenty-five more to go. "No, Car, you can't tell Jeff that. This is a job. It will help pay bills. Remember that and you'll be able to handle it a lot easier."

"I just don't get it. I really don't. Of course, I don't get anything anymore. Nick, you, Gage—he hasn't called has he?"

Every time Cara asked that question, it jabbed the fact that he hadn't a little more into her heart—and needled her with the reminder that she'd decided to call him regardless and hadn't. She'd been planning to, but then Cara had dropped that little "you have to ask yourself that question" comment and she'd been second-guessing herself ever since. And rightfully so since he hadn't called her either.

Seemed that taking charge of her life and risking her heart for Gage were a lot harder to do than standing up to Mrs. Applebaum.

"The answer hasn't changed since the last time you asked me, Cara. Now, can we focus on what we need to get done? We need to leave in under an hour and still have to get the van loaded."

"You want me to do that, don't you?"

"Not yet. But if you keep interrupting Jesse and me all

the time, we're going to be hard-pressed to make it on time."

Cara held up her hands. "Fine. I get it. I'll go out and move some tree limbs or something. Seems like all I did this morning, too."

A storm had rolled in overnight and taken out traffic lights, downed wires, torn limbs off trees, and created general havoc for the rush hour. Rumor had it there'd been a tornado that'd bounced around town and done some damage, too. Jeff's house had sustained some of it, so it was no wonder he was nervous about the party going well.

Lara really wanted to tell his fiancée that it was an omen. She should run. Quickly. And not look back.

She couldn't believe he'd found someone else willing to put up with his crap. No, not someone *else.* Lara hadn't put up with all of it. She just wished she'd gotten smarter sooner.

Was wanting to be with Gage any smarter?

She mis-piped the rose and had to start again. Apparently, it wasn't smart if she couldn't keep her mind on her job.

She wiped Gage out of her mind as she wiped the rose off the pastry nail and started over. If only real life were as easy.

"I should never have given you that check." J.C. McCullough paced around the bottom of the gazebo and actually handed Gage the slate shingles to replace the ones that'd been torn off from the storm.

Luckily, there was almost a quarter of a pallet left over from the job, and the shed where Gage had stored them hadn't been damaged, but if McCullough kept up the chatter, Gage wasn't sure he'd want to finish the roof in time for the party.

"I *knew* you'd finished too quickly. If you'd taken

your time and nailed these down properly, they'd still be in place."

Gage took the nails out of his mouth. "I did a damn good job, but nothing is going to withstand tornado-strength winds."

"You don't know there was a tornado. You're just saying that to cover your ineptitude."

Gage dug up a nail out of the rafter. The thing looked like a corkscrew. "It was a tornado." He tossed it down at McCullough's feet.

The prick picked it up. "Now you're tossing tetanus around? I called the bank and put a stop on the check."

Gage didn't bother calling his bluff to tell him that the check had been cashed at four yesterday like he'd planned.

"Hey, I'm out here, aren't I?" He'd had it with the guy's attitude. The hell with referral business; it'd feel so good to tell the asshole off. "I came over right after you called and have been working my ass off the whole time." In the drizzling rain, gathering shingles from the yard—and the pool—and sorting them into usable and unusable piles. Sadly, the unusable pile had been bigger.

"How much longer is this going to take? The caterers will be here soon and the band needs to set up here."

Gage looked at what he had left to do. "You can have the band start setting up any time. Unless you're planning to put them on the roof?" There went his sarcasm.

Prick got it. And didn't appreciate it. That was okay with Gage; he didn't appreciate the prick.

McCullough handed up the last of the tiles in his hand. "Can you handle the rest of it on your own? The caterers just arrived."

"Yeah. Sure. Go." *Please*. But he didn't add that. Now that he'd gotten rid of J.C. McCullough, he could find his rhythm and the job would go a lot faster.

Except that one of the catering staff walked through

the pool gate and Gage lost his rhythm completely.

Lara.

He was about to say something—what, he had no idea because the awkwardness of their last goodbye had been compounded by the fact that he hadn't called her since—when Prick came out of the side entrance, walked up to her, and… *kissed her on the cheek.*

Gage almost slid off the slate. Surely, Lara was going to slap him. Any minute now, she would. She wasn't going to allow that asshole that kind of liberty.

But she did allow it. Or at least, she didn't do anything to correct the overly-familiar gesture—

Wait a minute.

They looked a little *too* familiar. And that comment Cara had made about this neighborhood being where something happened/lived …

The Prick patted her on the butt.

Gage was ready to jump off the roof at that, but Lara finally slapped the asswipe.

Gage let go of the death grip he had on the tile, thankfully before he'd drawn blood, but not before he'd realized something.

Lara was the ex-wife. She had to be. It all made sense—as much sense as Lara marrying the Prick in the first place could.

What on earth was she doing here?

Gage mentally regrouped and got back to work, finishing the roof quicker than he would've thought possible. Interesting to see what he could do when motivated.

He stopped.

It *was* interesting to see what he could do when motivated. And what could be more motivating than being with the woman he loved?

He was an idiot to not give it a try—as much of an

arrogant, pompous ass as Prick over there for making the decision for both of them.

He needed to talk to her. See if she felt the same way. See if she wanted to give it a shot.

He climbed down the ladder, glancing up to see where she'd gone. She, Cara, and Jesse were wheeling in folding tables and insulated cupcake carts.

He gathered up a couple more shards of slate off the grass and dropped them into his tool belt as he walked over. "Hey, ladies. You want some help?"

"God, yes." Cara didn't even stop to think; she just leaned toward him with a large cardboard box. "These suckers are heavy. If you can hang onto them, I'll set up the table."

Gage glanced inside. Two white dove sculptures. Prick was going for sickeningly sweet. "What flavor is this, cotton candy?"

Lara looked at him with a secretive little smile. "Vanilla."

Gage chuckled. How freaking perfect. "Was that a special request or did he leave it up to your discretion?"

"What do you think?"

God, he'd missed her. With her eyes sparkling with mischief, it was all Gage could do not to set the stupid doves down right there and sweep her into his arms.

"Hey, Gage, you can set them down here." Cara motioned him over to the table along the outer wall of the terrace.

"We need to talk, Lara," he said before heading over.

"I can't now, Gage. I have a job to do."

"I know. I meant later. After. If you want." God, he was stammering like a schoolboy—and he'd never stammered even then.

"I want."

By God, so did he.

Jeff was picking apart every little detail until Lara wanted to shove the doves in his face.

They were "facing the wrong way?" Hello? The doves were wrapped around each other, their wings gracefully curved, looking longingly into each other's eyes. This was an engagement party; *shouldn't* they be looking at each other that way?

Then there weren't enough white rose and sugar-pearl cupcakes on display in a heart shape around them. Then he thought the white wasn't white enough, the silver foil wraps weren't dressy enough, and when he insisted on tasting a cupcake he complained that the strawberry in the center—that he'd asked for—was annoying.

"Seriously, Lara, you're going to have to step it up if you want to have a chance of making it in this business. I could arrange a consultation for you with the master chef at Koba if you'd like. He's a personal friend of mine."

Jeff obviously forgot that she knew he was lying through his teeth trying to impress her. The master chef at Koba couldn't *stand* Jeff. Her ex had sent so many meals back to the kitchen to be "cooked more" that Lara hadn't been comfortable eating there since.

"Thanks, Jeff, but I'm fine."

"That's the problem, Lara. It was always the problem. You were fine with the status quo. You never had any vision. If you'd applied yourself, you could have become the chair of the ladies' group at the club. You could have had them eating out of your hand by your words, not your baked goods."

Lara counted to ten. Twice.

He'd never change. He was the same condescending

jerk he'd always been. Always thinking he knew best, and putting the blame on her for his disappointment.

She, however, had changed.

"You know what, Jeff? You don't get to talk to me like that anymore. I am here strictly as the supplier of your desserts, not your ex-wife. If you aren't happy with Cavallo's Cups & Cakes, then don't order from us again. I made what you asked for to the best of my ability—an ability you were fully aware of when you hired me—so any dissatisfaction is on you."

Jeff recovered from the shock too quickly. That damn smarmy smile spread across his face. How could she have ever thought he was good-looking? Gage in his scrubby, scruffy best was better looking than Jeff could ever hope to be.

Speak of the devil…

She'd seen him the moment she'd arrived, up on that roof, his t-shirt plastered to that amazing chest, his jeans hugging his butt, and the doo-rag keeping the hair out of his eyes a really sexy look on him, and she'd felt that familiar tug low in her belly. If he hadn't come up to her to ask her to talk, she would've gone to him.

"Did you hear a word I said?" Jeff put his hands on his hips.

"I'm sorry, what?"

"Is this how you treat all of your clients? Do you just collect their money, do whatever the hell you want with their order, then completely ignore them when they're talking to you? You're never going to make it in this business, Lara. You're going to come crawling back to me and it'll be too late. I'll be married to Alexandra and you'll have nothing. If you think I'm going to give you any more money, you're out of your mind. I can't believe you have the gall—"

Gage's arm shot out from behind her to grab Jeff's

shirt collar. "Apologize to the lady."

Lara hadn't even heard him approach. She'd been too focused on trying to respond to Jeff's vitriol.

"I said, apologize to the lady." He moved around Lara and got in Jeff's face.

Jeff sneered. "I'll sue you for this."

"I'd like to see you try."

"I'm an attorney."

Lara put her hand on Gage's arm. "Gage, let go. It's all right."

"It's not all right. No one should talk to anyone the way he was talking to you." He shook his fist enough to remind Jeff where his fist was.

Lara squeezed his arm. "Please. Let go. Let's get through tonight and then we'll talk."

"Yes, why don't you listen to her, Tomlinson? I thought I paid you off. Shouldn't you be going?"

"I would except she hired me to help her tonight."

"She did what?"

Prick's neck turned purple as he stared, wide-eyed, at Lara—who was biting her lip.

Gage recognized that move. She was trying hard not to smile.

"Um, yes. I did. Gage does all the heavy lifting for us."

"What heavy lifting? You make *cupcakes* for God's sake."

Seems the guy had forgotten that lifting Lara's *cupcakes* required finesse—

Shit. Gage did *not* want to go there, imagining dickwad and her— "I'll just head out to the van and get what's left, Lara."

"Thanks, Gage. The cake's there and so is the gurney."

"I'll bring it right in." He didn't want to leave her

alone with the asshole, but had to trust that she could take care of herself. At least she wouldn't punch the guy which is what he was itching to do.

Then, in the driveway, his night got worse.

A beautiful blonde got out of a Jag that had just pulled in.

"Gage?"

Shit. Alexandra Prescott. Of *course* she'd be marrying Prick.

"Alexandra." She'd been to more of his shows than had been coincidental, especially in the beginning when he and Bry had been the talent, and she'd made it more than clear that she wouldn't have minded a private dance lesson.

He'd declined, thank God, but that didn't mean Alexandra had forgotten both her desire and her indignity when he'd turned her down.

"What are you doing here?" she asked, putting way more sway into her walk than was natural. Of course, nothing about Alexandra was natural, which made her the perfect wife for Prick.

"I'm helping out one of the caterers."

"You? Cooking?" She eyed him with an appetite that had nothing to do with food.

"No, just the heavy lifting." Wrong thing to say; her gaze went right to his arms.

Tonight was going to be all sorts of uncomfortable.

She followed him to the van and leaned against the open door provocatively. Alexandra was like a long lick of butter: soft and delicious but so not good for you. He'd never been tempted before; he certainly wasn't now.

He made quick work of setting up the gurney, slid the cake onto it, and rolled it to the backyard without breaking stride, Alexandra following.

"Darling!" Prick plastered a thousand-watt smile to his too-uniformly-tan-to-be-real face and sauntered toward

Alexandra. It was like looking at a pair of animatronic Barbie and Ken dolls.

"Jefferson." She leaned a powdered cheek toward him.

Which the guy air-kissed.

Now it was Gage's turn to bite his lip.

He had to bite it harder when Lara rolled her eyes.

He released a breath he hadn't been aware he'd been holding. She wasn't still into the prick. Not that he'd really thought she might be, but still, looking at this house, all J.C.—*Jefferson*—had, he couldn't help but think that maybe…

"Lara." Prick turned smarmy. Smarmi*er*. "Allow me to introduce you to my fiancée, Alexandra Prescott. Alexandra, this is Lara. My ex."

Alexandra had lady-of-the-manor down pat. Always had, but it burned Gage up that she turned that frozen ice princess look onto Lara.

"I understand you're a baker."

She might as well have said *leper*.

Lara, however, straightened her spine and pasted a genuine smile on her face. "That's right. Cavallo's Cups & Cakes. My cousin and I started it almost a year ago. We're doing the Applebaum graduation party this weekend."

"Priscilla and Frank's son?" Alexandra raised an eyebrow.

"Yes, Phillip."

"O… oh."

Hmm, Gage wouldn't have believed it if he hadn't seen it. Apparently this Applebaum gig was a big enough deal to impress even the Ice Princess.

"You didn't mention the Applebaums, Lara." Prick looked put out.

If it weren't his house, Gage would put *him* out.

"You didn't ask, Jeff."

Jeff. Jefferson. J.C… Gage preferred Prick.

"So Lara, where do you want this cake?" Gage interjected, wanting to end the homecoming atmosphere.

"I believe that's something you should ask me, Tomlinson." Prick was back in the saddle.

"Actually, Jeff, I was planning a certain set-up, so if you'll allow me my professional expertise, Gage and I will handle the presentation. You'll be pleased."

"Yes, well, we better be."

Gage had a feeling nothing would ever please this guy where Lara was concerned.

He followed her to the table, waiting until they were out of earshot before he spoke. "You were married to that?"

She laughed. "*That* is the perfect description. He is a piece of work, isn't he?"

"He's something all right. I can't believe you married him."

"He wasn't always like that. At least, not in the beginning. But he's definitely gotten worse as his bank account has grown. I've come to realize that Jeff's very insecure, so the amount of zeroes he commands gives him validation. Sad, really."

"You handled him well. He thought he was going to destroy you."

"You can set the cake here." Lara moved the box with the doves off the side of the table. "I refuse to give Jeff that power over me. I was devastated when I found out he'd cheated. Not with Alexandra by the way. In case you were wondering."

"I was only wondering what was going through his mind to cheat on you in the first place." He hefted the cake into the spot she'd indicated.

"If I knew that, I'd—"

"You'd what?"

She shrugged and started opening the cupcake boxes.

"I was going to say that I would've stopped it, but I realized that I couldn't. I'm not responsible for Jeff's happiness anymore than he's responsible for mine. That has to come from within you and that's what you share with your partner."

He didn't say anything to that as he thought it over. She wasn't making excuses, she wasn't putting it off on someone else. Her happiness was up to her. Just like his was up to him. Which meant that unless he made it happen, he was just as guilty of failing Lara as Prick.

They definitely needed to talk after this.

Chapter 35

All of the big wigs from Jeff's firm were there, including Weathers, and they all had a warm welcome for Lara.

Jeff hadn't realized what he'd done by hiring her, nor had Lara really considered it beyond the money he'd pay her, but his co-workers had liked her. She'd run into a few after the divorce and they'd all asked about her and seemed genuinely interested—and genuinely indignant on her behalf at Jeff's affair. Having them hang out at her dessert table, she realized that they did actually care about what she'd been going through—in a way they didn't care about Jeff. Or Alexandra.

Jeff was deluding himself if he thought this marriage was a stepping stone in his career. The disdain most of the women had for Jeff's fiancée was almost palpable. And Alexandra wasn't helping it with her aloof affectations.

Jeff would never learn.

"Would you all like me to get you a drink?" Gage asked her, Cara, and Jesse, his doo-rag replaced by one of the spare toque hats she kept in the van along with the extra chef coat, and the black pants he'd worn at Gina's party doubled as tuxedo pants.

If it weren't for the dark work boots, she'd never have known that, an hour ago, he'd been a sweaty mess in construction clothes, but a dip in Jeff's pool and the ad-libbed clothing made him the perfect employee.

Perfect being the operative word. He looked yummy in that outfit. But then, he looked yummy in any outfit.

Or *not* in any outfit…

"I'd love a gin and tonic," said Cara, "but I'm afraid it might loosen my tongue too much and I'd end up saying something to McMonster that I really want to."

Lara tried not to smile. She loved that Cara was so indignant on her behalf, but honestly, she'd come to realize, as Jeff had given her his digs and Alexandra had tried to look so superior, that she didn't care. She was happy with herself and anything Jeff could do or say not only wouldn't change it, but didn't affect it at all.

"Some ice water would be great. And Jeff can't complain about the expense."

"McMonster can complain about anything," Cara grumbled.

Gage flicked Cara's baker's hat. "Hey, don't let him ruin your night. He's not worth it."

Cara glanced at Lara then at Gage. "How can you be so blasé about this? I mean, after he and Lara…"

Gage shrugged. "He and Lara are no more and she's with me." He touched her back briefly. "One round of sparkling ice water coming up."

Cara fanned herself. "Okay, cuz, you totally lucked out in that department."

Yes, she had.

Gage circumvented the so-called happy couple. He'd seen people in the hospital happier than these two. Prick had his mouth so tight he looked like he was sucking lemons by the dozen, and Alexandra's smile was so brittle her face might crack.

These two were working the party way too hard.

He nodded at the bartender. "Four ice waters when you get the chance."

"Sure. No problem."

Gage stood off to the side, waiting for the guests go be served.

"So, young man, I trust you received the license you were asking about?" Lara's lawyer buddy strolled up to him and saluted him with his drink.

"I did. I have to thank you for interceding."

"No problem at all. Some folks are a little too prejudicial, you know what I mean? Take tonight, for instance. Half the people here are only here to size up the fiancée. McCullough made a big mistake letting Lara go and we all know it."

"She told me what you've done for her."

"I can't abide cheaters. There's no excuse for it. He deserves what's coming to him, and if that's Alexandra Prescott, the man better watch out." He chuckled. "Weathers Davis, by the way." He shook Gage's hand. "So tell me about this dance club of yours. How did you get involved in stripping?"

"You're a *stripper*?" Prick walked up at just the wrong moment.

Gage set the first glass of water on the bar, his fingers itching—just *itching*—to do some damage to that face.

Weathers took a too-tiny-to-be-real sip of his drink. "He owns a dance club, McCullough."

"A strip club, you mean, Mr. Davis."

Gage bit his lip at the fawning tone in Prick's voice. "That's another term for it, yes."

"Good God. I can't believe Lara went from me to a *stripper*." He chuckled. The ass actually chuckled.

Gage's fingers curled into a fist.

"I fail to see what's so funny, McCullough." Weathers took another non-sip of his drink. The man was a master at the put down and Gage just had to watch. "A viable business that will bring revenue to the town and revitalize part of the urban blight. A highly commendable effort, in my opinion. Matter of fact, I'm willing to invest in it if you're taking investors, Mr. Tomlinson."

Gage couldn't contain his surprise. "I'll… have to talk to my partner about that. We'll get back to you."

"Partner? You're gay?"

"Business partner." Gage didn't bother to hide his contempt. With Weathers on board, it gave him the legitimacy Prick would respect. Not that Gage gave a flying fuck for the guy's respect, but he did like the fact that the guy had to look at him through new eyes.

"Have you and your partner incorporated?" Weathers turned toward him, effectively cutting Prick out of the conversation. "It might be something to look into. Tax purposes."

"I do have some ideas I could run by you."

Weathers pulled a card from his pocket. "Give me a call. We'll set something up."

The bartender set out the rest of the water glasses. Gage tucked the card in the coat pocket and gathered them up. "Great talking to you. Thanks for your help with the license and I'll be in touch. If you'll excuse me, I have to get these back to the hard-working ladies at the dessert table. Make sure you try a piece of cake. Lara's amazing in the kitchen."

He left enough innuendo in that comment to get Prick thinking about where else she was amazing.

And got himself thinking. They hadn't done anything in the kitchen.

Yet.

It took ten minutes for the news of Gage's second job to make the rounds of the party—and Lara knew *exactly* where that information had come from. Jeff was walking around with his superior attitude on as if he were above every person at the party.

It started with coy looks from the married women. A couple of overt invitations from the single ones. The scowls from the husbands were the dead giveaway; Lara had become extremely familiar with those at Gina's party.

Then Alexandra had come to her table.

"Gage," she said in a way that made Lara's skin crawl. "I would consider it a personal favor to me if you'd give us a show tonight. We will, of course, make it worth your while."

Gage went dead still and Lara could feel the anger surge through him. "I don't dance."

"Nonsense. Of course you do. I've seen you."

Now Lara went dead still.

Gage glanced at her. "That was years ago. Back when we were starting out. I don't do it anymore."

"Oh I'm sure we can convince you. Everyone has his price." Alexandra's lips curved into a smile that made Lara's skin crawl.

"Not me."

Jeff, of course, showed up then. "Ah, come on, Tomlinson. Let's get a preview of this 'viable business that'll bring revenue to the town and revitalize urban blight.' You can't ask for better advertising than a rapt audience with money to invest."

There were undertones to Jeff's speech that Lara didn't understand, but she did understand that he was trying to embarrass Gage.

"You can come to the grand opening and see it then, McCullough." Gage hadn't moved a muscle. Well, except for his fingers. They were now curled into fists.

"No confidence in your product? How do you expect to sell it if you don't, well, sell it?" Jeff's grin was worse than Alexandra's. The two of them were perfect for each other.

"Fine. You want a sneak peek?" Gage ripped the hat off his head. "I'll give you a sneak peek."

He yanked his cell from his back pocket. "Lara, find the playlist and have him hook it up to the sound system. I need a few minutes to get prepared."

The playlist. How well she remembered the playlist.

Gage stormed off toward his truck while Cara stormed to her feet.

"You, McMonster, are the world's biggest prick. I can't believe you put him on the spot like that. You're going to pay double his normal rate for this stunt."

"Can it, Cara, or I'm kicking you out. And don't think I won't relish every minute of it. I wanted to do it every time you visited Lara."

"And I wanted to throw up on you every time I did, but apparently I was the only one who loved Lara enough not to dump all over her."

Lara tugged Cara's curls. "Please, don't engage him, Cara. Just let it go. He can't hurt me anymore."

"But what about what he's doing to Gage?"

Lara bit her lip and lowered her voice. "He thinks he's embarrassing Gage, but what do you think is going to happen once Gage starts dancing? Who's going to be embarrassed then?"

A smile spread across Cara's face. "Oooh, I like it."

She'd like it even more when Lara pulled off what she was about to pull off, too…

The electronic lead-in started to *Simply Irresistible* and all eyes turned toward Jeff's "terrace."

Gage had his back to the audience, arms outstretched, the chef coat still on, and one leg shaking just enough to make his buns move beneath it.

Just as before, the women were the first ones to move closer.

The downbeat hit and Gage spun around, ripping the coat open.

Nothing but skin and those black pants beneath it.

His hips gyrated, his muscles contracted, and Gage worked the crowd with his sexy look, each and every woman treated to his utmost concentration for the few seconds he made eye contact with her.

The catcalls started.

"Mother of God, he's hot." Cara fluttered her hands in front of her face. "I dunno, Lar. I think he's your payback for the shit you put up with from asshole over there." She nudged Lara. "Get a load of his face."

Lara didn't even glance in Jeff's direction. Not when she could be looking at Gage. "Do me a favor, Car? Stay here and man the table. I'll be back."

She didn't wait for Cara's agreement, but kept her eyes on Gage and walked—sauntered—through the crowd, the music moving through her as it had that other time he'd played this song.

Up on stage, his coat slithered down one arm. It was a thing of beauty the way his sculpted arm was revealed inch by sexy, mouth-watering inch. His pec flexed as he shrugged out of it, then he repeated the whole enticing slow-mo movement with the other side.

The women were now three deep at the steps.

Lara joined them.

Gage spun around again and rubbed the coat across his back, sliding it down lower… lower…

There, against his butt, and the women started cheering. Single, married, young, old, partner, intern, it didn't matter; they were all enjoying the show.

Gage worked their interest. He worked that coat, too. Lara would never look at a chef coat the same way again.

She unbuttoned hers. It was getting a little warm amid the crowd of aroused women. Especially since she was one of them.

He brushed the bunched-up coat over his abs, teasing his audience with that deliciousness that Lara had first-hand—and tongue—knowledge of.

She moved in time to the music, remembering shaking her booty at this point when she'd danced for him.

She did it again where she stood. Out of the corner of her eye, she saw Alexandra move closer. And she saw Jeff scowl. That only reinforced what she was about to do.

The music paused for the two heartbeats before the downbeat hit hard again. Gage paused, too, his hip poised to swivel down, and when the music started, it did, and oh was it a thing of beauty. His abs contracted, his pecs flexed, and his buns—oh God, his buns—shook with perfect rhythm.

And then he ripped off his pants.

He wore those tiny, tight, silky black shorts he'd had on before, and they hugged his thighs like her hands wanted to.

The women went wild.

The men looked like they wanted to be anywhere but here.

Lara wanted to be up there with Gage.

So she pushed through the crowd. She climbed the

stairs in rhythm with the music.

She unbuttoned the coat.

And when Gage turned around, she gave him the sexiest smile ever.

For the first time he could remember, Gage missed a step in his performance. But Christ, it was understandable. Lara was coming toward him *unbuttoning her coat*. With a swivel in her hips. And a look on her face he'd seen the night she'd danced for him.

Like she was doing now.

He licked his lips because his mouth had gone dry.

She licked hers just to drive him insane.

Then she shimmied the coat off for added insanity.

"What are you doing?" he whispered as she shimmied up beside him, her hips moving in time with his and much too close for these shorts to hide the effect.

"I'm dancing. What does it look like?"

He raised his hands over his head to please the crowd, knowing what it did to his stomach, but the truth of it was, this was rote. He was trying to wrap his brain around the fact that Lara—*his* Lara—was dancing in front of the crowd, and if she was doing what it looked like she was doing, she was stripping with him.

Her fingers unbuttoned the buttons on her shirt.

Gage's mouth went dry, and for the second time, he missed a step.

"Lara?"

"Dance, Gage. Just like you taught me." Her smile was wickedly sexy. "Jeff wanted a show? We're going to give him one."

And then Gage laughed. He couldn't help it. She was priceless.

He danced in front of her, working the crowd. Interesting that the men were now engaged, and for a moment—or six—a red flag flourished before him like a bull fight. He didn't want these men looking at her. She was his.

Then he recognized the hypocrisy and let himself enjoy the moment. She could dance all night for these guys, but she was going home with him.

He looked at Prick. The guy's expression was hysterical. His plan to embarrass Gage had utterly and completely backfired. Everyone in his office would definitely be talking about this party for years to come, but not for the reason Prick wanted.

He looked over his shoulder at Lara. Her short-sleeve button-down was un-tucked and she was working those buttons every bit as effectively as his guys did theirs. She'd paid attention at that bachelorette party. Either that or she was a natural.

He looked at the way her hips moved. Yeah, she was a natural.

Addicted to Love came on and he saw the tempo pick up in the crowd. Hips were gyrating, booties bumping, some minor grinding going on that would be worse if it were later in the evening after the alcohol had been flowing, but it was all good. Everyone was in a party mood. Everyone except Prick.

He was in a decidedly *un*party mood and looked like he'd like to cut off the music any second. But even he was smart enough to realize the mutiny he'd have, so he had to put up with it.

Gage danced over to Lara. "You're not really going to take it off, are you?"

She did a peek-a-boo of her shoulder with the shirt. "Why not? I've got pretty underwear on. No different from your shorts."

Except that he didn't care if anyone saw him in these shorts, but Lara's underwear should be for his eyes alone.

He smiled. "Go for it, babe."

She smiled back. "I intend to."

And she did. Lord, did she.

Gage gave up trying to hide his erection because he couldn't. The shorts were tight enough that he wasn't at full mast but anyone looking at him would know immediately that he was turned on. Which, ironically, only turned him on more. All those people were out there watching him and Lara do a dance that was as old as time. Seduction, desire, they were universal. And every single person out there wanted what he and Lara had.

She shimmied her shirt down her arms, and good God, her blue lace bra barely covered her nipples, pushing her breasts up with mouth-watering goodness. She hadn't turned around to the crowd yet, and he could feel the expectation humming with the music.

He stood behind her, his ass to the crowd—gave it a shake for good measure—and drew her shirt down her arms.

She turned slowly, her smile for him alone, and Gage wanted to kiss her. He didn't, because he'd never stop if he started, but he looked. Oh, yes, he definitely looked.

"Nice cupcakes," he said.

She threw back her head and laughed, her curls falling around her shoulders, and he'd never seen anything so beautiful in his life.

She put her right arm against his and danced her way around him, her beauty now on display for everyone to see.

Gage felt himself harden. Shit. Talk about unprofessional.

He danced behind her—not close enough to rub up against her. That was the border of public lewdness and he didn't want to give Prick any reason to throw them out. This was Lara's moment and he wanted her to revel in it.

She slipped her fingers beneath the waistband of her

pants.

Shit, he'd forgotten those would come off, too.

She wiggled and the pants moved lower.

She had a thong on.

Gage groaned. A thong. What happened to granny panties? Even boycuts? But a thong?

She was trying to kill him.

He looked at Prick. *He* wanted to kill him.

Gage hid his smile and worked his hips behind Lara.

The crowd had mingled again, the men with their women. With a lot more bumping and grinding going on.

Hmmm, maybe Lara was onto something. Integrated stripping. They could double the possible patrons if couples made it a date night. They might need a bigger venue.

Her pants slipped below her ass. Her sweet, perfect, round, temptingly tasty, *naked* ass.

He had to turn around. Keep his back to the crowd. He shook his ass, giving them that show because he couldn't give them the other one. The shorts had too much spandex in them.

Lara, however, got her own private show.

Her eyes widened, and she licked her lips. Which only made him harder. He jerked inside his shorts—so he wiggled his butt some more.

She slid her pants down and managed, somehow, to keep time with the music and slip them off one long, luscious, curvy leg at a time.

Then she stood and raised her arms, undulating them like a harem girl, but looking nothing at all like one in her skimpy scraps of sexy fabric that left nothing to anyone's imagination.

He heard the collective gasp of the crowd. What the two of them were doing was so far beyond stripping that it'd be illegal if they were touching.

Lara pivoted around slowly, her hips circling as she

gave everyone way too much of a show.

And she was loving every minute of it if the smile on her face was anything to go by.

God, he loved her. She was so in the moment, so utterly and perfectly there with him, as natural as breathing, and she took his breath away.

He didn't care what he had to do, but Lara had to be in his life. Forever.

The song ended and Lara was all ready to keep going when the next one started, but Gage was finished. He could only keep it together for so long—especially so publicly—and he needed to get her alone. Now.

He grabbed her hand—the only part of her he permitted himself to touch—and held it up. "Bow," he whispered, leading her down with him.

The crowd went insane. The catcalls were shrill, the cries of "encore" loud and boisterous—and tinged with more than a little frustration—but Gage ended the dance. Neighbors that hadn't been invited might end up calling the cops and the last thing either he or Lara needed was to get caught with their pants down.

Especially since he planned to be that way all night long. With her. In her bed.

He scooped up their clothes and led her into Jeff's house, locking the French doors behind them the minute they were inside.

Then he dragged her to the laundry room on the right, locked that door, and kissed her senseless.

"What on earth possessed you to do that?" he asked when they finally came up for air.

"You didn't like it?"

"Sweetheart, I liked it too much." He thrust out his hips. "I've been hard the entire time and everyone in the audience knew it."

She gave him that grin. "Good."

It *was* good. Just not appropriate. "Seriously, Lara, what made you do that?"

She stepped into her pants and pulled them up. A damn shame, in his book. "Jeff. He was such an ass, putting you on the spot like that, trying to embarrass you."

"He didn't embarrass me. I'm not embarrassed by what I do." And he wasn't. He realized that now. It *was* a legit business and one he was damn good at.

"I'm just so tired of him thinking he can call all the shots. That it's his way or the highway. So I decided to turn the tables on him. Most of the people here were upset at what he did to me. I wanted to show them I was okay. That it was Jeff's mistake, not mine, and I've moved on. And yeah, maybe I wanted him to know I wasn't who he thought I was, and that he had no say in how I live my life anymore. It was my choice, Gage. My choice. Do you know how freeing that was?" She shrugged into her shirt but left it unbuttoned and grasped his arms. "And I wanted to dance with you. I wanted all those women to know you were mine. They can look, but at the end of the day, you're going home with me."

"Forever?" he asked.

She stilled. "Forever? What… what do you mean?"

It was his turn to grip her arms. "I mean *forever,* Lara. I want to go home with you forever. I want you *in* my home forever. I want you to *be* my home forever."

He took hold of her shirt and started to button it from the top down. His fingers made short work of the first button, but the second—the one that was right over her heart—made him stop. "I love you. And I want to spend the rest of my life with you. Will you spend yours with me?" He slid the button home. "Will you marry me, Lara?"

He would never forget the look that came into her eyes at that moment. Never, in a million years, for as long as he lived, would he forget the love that filled her eyes.

Right before she threw her arms around him and hugged him harder than anyone ever had.

"Oh, Gage, I love you, too! Yes! Yes! I'd love to marry you!"

Then he didn't care who walked in on them. He kissed her and let himself get lost in the feeling.

But he had too much regard for her and their love to seal it with a quickie in her ex-husband's laundry room, so after a few minutes, he set her away from him with one last lingering kiss. "I know it'll be tough for a while. We're both so busy and the money… It'll be tight, Lara. I can't give you all that Jeff could—"

She cut him off with a finger to his lips. "I don't want what Jeff could give me. If you remember, I had it. And I walked away from it. Because the one thing he couldn't give me is what you can. And it's something I prize above everything: your heart. I don't care what we have to do to make it work. I'm not afraid of hard work. But if I have you to come home to, it'll be pure heaven."

He couldn't speak past the lump in his throat, but he tried. "And the dancing? You're okay with that?"

She arched an eyebrow and it was a sinfully sexy look on her. "I didn't just prove that?"

He wrapped his arms around her waist and pulled her against him. "What you proved, woman, is that you are the sexiest woman alive and I'm lucky to have you in my life."

"We're both lucky, Gage. We've found each other."

"And we're never letting go."

"Nope. We're not." She kissed him again, all tongue and heat, and he felt his resolve to make their first official time something memorable—and not a quickie in the laundry room.

"Come on, sweetheart, let's get back to the party, finish up, and get the hell out of here. I can't wait to get you alone."

"Um, about that."

He stopped. "About what?"

"Being alone. You have that big house you're paying upkeep on and I have my condo. What would you say if we were to sell my condo and put the money into, oh, I don't know, say, a night club? You know, one with *strippers*." She mimicked the Prick.

"You'd do that?"

"For partial ownership, sure."

"Ownership, huh?"

"Well, sure. A well-diversified portfolio is a good thing. And what I don't invest with you and Bryan, we could use for Connor's medical bills."

She humbled him. "Thank you so much, baby, but we're not touching your money for him. I'll make out okay. Don't worry about him."

"I will and I can, and if I want to help you, you aren't supposed to say no. Wouldn't you do the same for me?"

"Well, sure but—"

"It's no different."

"Hey, I have a better idea of what to do with your money."

She arched her eyebrow again, but this time it was skeptical, not sexy. "What could be better than helping your nephew?"

"Well, it'd be helping him, but it'd also be for us."

"What is it?"

"How would you feel about a honeymoon at a certain resort in Orlando, complete with castles and wishes and dreams? It's supposed to be the happiest place on earth."

"That might be their slogan, but the happiest place for me, Gage, is right here. In your arms."

The End

About the Author

Judi Fennell has had her nose in a book and her head in some celestial realm all her life, including those early years when her mom would exhort her to "get outside!" instead of watching *Bewitched* or *I Dream of Jeannie* on television. So she did—right into Dad's hammock with her Nancy Drew books.

These days she's more likely to have her nose in her laptop and her head (and the rest of her) at a favorite writing spot, but she's still reading either her latest manuscript or friends' books.

A PRISM Award and Golden Leaf Award winner, Judi is the author of the Mer series: *In Over Her Head, Wild Blue Under,* and *Catch of a Lifetime*; the Bottled Magic series: *I Dream of Genies, Genie Knows Best,* and *Magic Gone Wild;* the Once-Upon-A-Time Romance series featuring: *Beauty and The Best, If The Shoe Fits,* and *Fairest of Them All*; and the BeefCake, Inc. series, beginning with *Beefcake & Cupcakes.*

Made in the USA
Charleston, SC
21 February 2014